Blood Water Falls

A DCI Bone Scottish Crime Thriller

(Book 2)

T G Reid

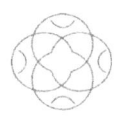

Glass Work Press

COPYRIGHT

Blood Water Falls

Published Worldwide by Glass Work Press.
This edition published in 2021.
ISBN: 9798767706020

Copyright © 2021 by TG Reid. The right of all named persons, to be identified as the author of this work, has been asserted in accordance with the Copyright, Design and Patents Act 1988. All rights reserved. No part of this book may be reproduced in any form or by any electronic or mechanical means, including information storage and retrieval systems, without written permission from the author, except for the use of brief quotations in a book review.

The story, all names, characters, and incidents portrayed in this book are fictitious. No identification with actual persons (living or deceased), places, buildings, and products is intended or should be inferred.

Editors: Emmy Ellis, Hanna Elizabeth
Cover: megjolly.co.uk, creativeedgestudios.co.uk
Typesetting: Emmy Ellis

© tgreid.com 2021

GLASS WORK PRESS

DEDICATION

To Nick and Mark (Obi Wan and Two) – with gratitude and love.

PROLOGUE

Richard Jones scrambled up the last few feet of Craigend Cap and onto the flat granite plate that perched precariously on the hill's summit. For a moment he stood in awe of the breathtaking vista before him; a CinemaScopic panorama of hills and glens, peeking above a thick carpet of whipped-cream mist that was stubbornly refusing to leave the valley.

When he'd set off the night before in the pitch-dark and the rain, he hadn't felt very optimistic of capturing anything worthwhile, but the forecast promised a glorious solstice day, so he'd persuaded his brain to forgo the seductive warmth of his bed, catch the last train to Carrbridge, and head for the hills.

He set up the tripod and snapped his large format camera into the clips on the top. With a quick readjustment of the tripod legs and a fiddle with the settings, he pressed the shutter button, and the camera took ten consecutive shots, capturing the spectacle before the sun rose too high and its beams ruined the image.

After another four or five shots, he carefully shifted the tripod over to the farthest edge of the outcrop, setting it down within a few centimetres of the sheer drop beyond. Reducing the height of the tripod, he dropped onto his haunches and squinted through the viewfinder, adjusting the angle and focus to capture the top of Braeburn Falls as the roar of bubbling, crimson-tinted water tumbled down the cliffside into the deep pool thirty metres below. At this time of year, the iron sediment in the river was at its highest, and the deep-red discolouration of the water gave the falls a strange and unique hue that attracted visitors from miles around.

He clicked some prep shots and checked the results. His heart raced. He knew immediately this was going to be very special. He glanced up at the ascending sunrise. A single ray flashed across the sky and hit the centre of the waterfall, the light exploding in all directions.

"Bingo!" Richard yelled with delight and pressed the shutter button again, capturing the fleeting, perfect moment before it vanished forever. Pulling the tripod back from the edge, he unclipped the camera and sat on a boulder and with shaking hands, he scrolled through his initial images until he landed on the money shot.

He held his palm over the screen and scrutinised the image. It was about as perfect as he could ever have hoped for. He let out another loud yell, his voice carrying across the valley and bouncing back moments later. Richard smiled, saved the collection of images to the SD, and packed away his gear.

Returning to the edge of the cliff, he checked the light conditions around the base of the waterfall. The rays had penetrated the deep, narrow gorge surrounding the waterfall and its pool. He picked up his bag and tripod, he clambered over the far side of the outcrop and rejoined the path down to the base of the falls.

At the bottom, he climbed over the stile and approached the falls. More sunlight bounced off the surface of the rippling pool as the waterfall struck the surface with a deafening roar. Up close, the crimson discolouration was even more dramatic and strange. He dropped his equipment, snatched his camera from his satchel and quickly snapped the spectacle.

He clambered over a few boulders and at the edge of the pool he peered into the dark waters. The pool was deep, possibly twelve to fourteen feet. Deep enough to tempt idiots to jump off the cliff, sometimes with tragic consequences. He glanced back up to the top of the waterfall and shook his head. *Idiots.*

He set up his tripod on a boulder-free patch and was about to start snapping again when he noticed a pink ring of foam gathered in the far corner of the pool. He unclipped his camera and went to investigate. The foam was more extensive than he'd first thought, covering almost a quarter of the pool. Approaching, he picked up a pungent chemical odour. He kneeled to examine the contaminant more closely. The foam was thick and appeared to be both above and below the surface. He snatched up a pebble and tossed it into the middle of the foam's mass. The foam consumed it, leaving a narrow hole that quickly closed.

"Fuck's sake," he muttered and began shooting. A loud splash had him turning. A second splash. Something hit the pool with force.

"Oh Jesus!" He glanced up to the top of the cliff.

A silhouetted figure stood on the edge. He checked the pool again, but no one was climbing out or floating unconscious, or worse, on the surface.

"Hoy, it's too dangerous!" he hollered up to the figure, but his voice was lost in the roar of the falls.

The figure disappeared. He scanned the pool again for idiots, took another couple of shots of the pollution and returned to his tripod. But the sun had shifted out of the gorge, and the promise of another decent photo had gone. With a sigh, he knelt to pack away his camera and to contemplate his long walk back to Kilwinnoch.

The roar of the falls silenced the crunch of boots on gravel approaching him at speed from behind and the muffled thud of a hammer striking the back of his skull. He fell forward, his face smashing onto the rocks and shattering his nose. Still alive, he scrambled forward and plunged into the pool. Half conscious, he thrashed his arms around in the water and kicked forward towards the torrent of water ahead.

Someone grabbed at his feet and calves, dragging him back. He kicked out and, reaching the falls, lunged through the wall of water. The waterfall struck the back of his head like a second hammer blow, and the force of it pushed him under.

Gurgling and choking, he reached out, and his hands connected with a narrow ledge protruding from the cliff wall behind the falls. He snatched at the slippery wet stone and pulled his head up and out of the water. He gasped and gurgled for air but swallowed more water as it pummelled his head from above. He kicked against the surface and finding a foothold, somehow managed to half haul himself up. But the waterfall continued to pound against his shoulders, and he slipped back into the water.

With one final, desperate push, he clambered up again, and on his stomach, he slithered along the ledge. As he reached the cliff wall, the weight of a body landed on top of him. A hand grabbed his sodden, blood- and water-drenched hair, and yanked his head back, twisting his neck so he could see his assailant's face. But before Richard could cry out for help or mercy, his attacker struck him again on the side of the head, this time, the weapon punching a hole through his skull and leaving the image of the assailant's sneering smile imprinted on Richard Jones's final memory.

ONE

"So, what you're saying is, you see dead people?" Constable Tam Windsor asked, chewing on the inside of his cheek.

"Well, I understand it's a manifestation of my subconscious and a symptom of PTSD," DCI Duncan Bone replied and instantly regretted that he'd started the conversation.

The support group sat in silence for a moment, staring at Bone. The central heating pipes in the counselling room hummed gently, adding to the tension.

"Is he here now?" DC Debs Mallory asked. She glanced around the room and over Bone's shoulder.

"He's not real, Debs, I'm just saying that—" Bone cut back.

"And he helps you solve your cases?" asked Constable Windsor.

The group members continued to stare, the semi-circle closing in around Bone.

"I know it sounds daft… oh jeez… I shouldn't have—"

"Can I just step in here?" Counsellor Brendan Nichols interrupted.

"Thank you." Bone sighed.

"As we've discussed in previous sessions, PTSD can affect our physical, emotional, and cognitive behaviour in all sorts of ways. Sometimes they may seem very strange to others."

"I didn't speak for four months," Community Officer Sandra Black said. "Not a single word. And no desire to either."

"Yes, that's very common," the counsellor replied. "The brain sometimes just needs peace and quiet and space to recover."

"Hardly, I've three kids and a husband with verbal diarrhoea. He was gutted when my voice finally came back," Officer Black said with a smirk.

"I used to see a giant chicken at the bottom of my bed," Detective Sandra Paterson said, shaking her head.

"What?" Constable Windsor sat back in surprise.

"Oh, aye, I'd wake up and it was right there, large as life, like that big rooster in those cartoons."

"Foghorn Leghorn," Officer Gail Braithwaite whispered and continued to stare at the floor.

"What was that?" Paterson asked.

"Ah said, Foghorn Leghorn!" Braithwaite boomed and added, "Ah said," with a smile.

"And how did you deal with that hallucination?" Counsellor Nichols asked.

"I used to talk to it. It made me feel calm," Paterson said. "My partner used to as well, once she'd got used to the idea of a big rooster in our bedroom."

"That's lovely and so supportive of your partner," the counsellor said.

"Did he ever speak to you?" Bone asked.

"What? Are you daft? It's a chicken." Paterson shrugged. "How?"

"Okay," Counsellor Nichols interrupted again. "It's interesting that this apparition made you feel calm. This tells us that it's your brain's way of helping you heal." He smiled reassuringly. "Just going back to your particular symptom, Duncan. Does this deceased suspect make you feel calm?"

Bone scanned the semi-circle again. Although all eyes were fixed on him, the faces around the group betrayed a spectrum of distracted thoughts.

"I wouldn't say—" he started.

"Is it the Peek-a-boo killer?" Windsor interrupted. "Is it him?"

Bone stared at Windsor as the constable continued to chew on his cheek; the horror of the serial killer case that had nearly cost Bone his life roared through his skull and punched at the scar left on his temple by the bomb.

"You don't have to talk about this if it's making you feel uncomfortable, Duncan," the counsellor said. "Remember, everyone, this is a safe space for us all."

"Could I just stop for now? Would that be okay?" Bone appealed.

"Of course."

"Sorry, mate, I didn't mean to…" Windsor pulled a face.

"One of the most challenging and often upsetting things about PTSD is that just when you think you're over it, it can return," Nichols continued. "Sometimes completely harmless moments or situations can trigger varying degrees of relapse. However, it's important to remember that as our brains heal, the fear and threat of its return slowly diminishes. We learn to find our best new ways to live."

Bone picked up his ancient canvas backpack and slipped his arms into his jacket.

"I'll see you," Bone said to the group.

Everyone in the semi-circle nodded back.

Counsellor Nichols stopped him at the door. "You know you can talk to me any time, Duncan. That's my job here."

"I'm fine, just need to get back to work."

"You did very well today. It's not easy facing the demons."

"They're not demons. I'm fine." Bone shrugged.

"Just keep talking, okay?" Nichols urged.

"I'm really okay."

"Well, we'll see you next month, or call me sooner if you need to."

"Sure." He gave the counsellor a reassuring smile and left.

Out in the car park, he let out a long sigh and marched across to his ancient, bottle-green Saab. He climbed inside, slotted a tape into the player, and the soft horn section of Billie Holiday's orchestra gently swelled and filled the car. He sat back for a moment and let his heart rate fall and the cogs in his head slow. Then Billie's warm and welcoming young voice soared above the wall of harmonious sound.

A sharp rap on the window by his head had him jolting upright, and he turned. Tam Windsor's flushed turnip face pressed up against the pane. Bone reluctantly hit the stop button and unwound the window.

"Hi, Duncan," Tam said. "I'm sorry if I upset you in there earlier."

"Not at all," Bone lied.

"You know, when I mentioned that evil bastard."

"It's okay. We're all dealing with all sorts of shit."

"I just wanted to say that I totally get it. There was this wee girl who was killed years ago. I wasn't even involved in the case, but it was nasty. Sometimes I hear her, you know, her screams. It's horrible."

"That's awful, mate," Bone said. "You should talk to Brendan."

"I do. It comes and goes, and it gets better." He stepped back from the car. "Anyhow, I totally get you don't want to talk about it. I shouldn't have been such a dick."

"Hey, that's what the session's for, isn't it?"

"What, being a dick?"

"Whatever it takes." Bon smiled.

Windsor glanced down at the car. "Nice wheels." He raised his eyebrows.

"Thanks," Bone replied.

"Where are the horses?"

"Horses?"

"To pull you out of the car park," Windsor joked.

"Classic car, this," Bone huffed.

"You just keep telling yourself that." He leaned back in. "You're coming back, right, I mean, next month?"

"I wouldn't miss it for the world."

"Good man." Windsor gave him a thumbs-up, the pain in his eyes lifting momentarily. "Well, safe journey," he snorted.

Bone started the engine.

Windsor applauded. "A modern-day miracle," he shouted over the cough of the engine.

With an unconvincing toot, Bone stuttered out of the car park and back out into the world.

TWO

DCI Bone rapped on DSU Roy Gallacher's door and entered.

"You wanted to see me, sir?" Bone approached Gallacher who was propped up at his desk, flicking through a copy of the morning's *Chronicle*.

"Good morning, Duncan. Sit," Gallacher said, gesturing to the empty chair opposite. "Sorry to drag you in at the weekend, but this can't wait."

"My social calendar isn't exactly busting at the seams," Bone joked. "What's going on?"

"Before we get to that, how are you?"

"I'm okay, thanks, sir."

"I mean up here." Gallacher tapped his temple.

"I'm doing fine. I was at a session this morning."

"And your injury? Not giving you any bother?"

"The odd headache, but all is calm."

"Good." Gallacher nodded. "And work?"

"Work saves me, sir," Bone said. "Though, it has been quiet of late, and sharing space with a bored Mullens is not good for anyone's mental well-being."

"Well, about that," Gallacher cut in. "Have you seen this?" He handed Bone the paper.

Bone sat and scanned the front page. "How many days is it now?"

"Four since he was last seen," Gallacher replied. "Head office have been on the phone."

"Have they now?" Bone rolled his eyes.

"They want us to help find this guy, hopefully alive."

"Isn't that Missing Persons' job?"

Gallacher leaned forward, careful not to disturb the perfectly placed array of stationery lined up in neat rows across the back of the desk. "Richard Jones is a highly respected local boy; head of the Geography Department at Kilwinnoch Academy and vocal campaigner and fundraiser for local charities and causes. In short, he's a highly respected and well-loved member of the community who everyone knows."

"So why bring in the Rural Crime Unit? Won't people jump to the conclusion that he must be dead if we're roped in?"

"Duncan, the guy is a local bloody hero. Head office is keen for this to be resolved as soon as possible. With our local knowledge and expertise, we're best placed to find him."

"Is there a possibility that he could have topped himself? I mean, teaching is a tough game, especially up there at Feral High."

"Possible, yes, and that would be a terrible tragedy. But head office needs closure before our friend and his plague-rat mates spin this into a police competence issue."

"McKinnon." Bone sighed.

"Our intrepid cockroach at our beloved local bum wipe, indeed."

Bone ran his finger down the scar on his temple. "I'm still not seeing why we should wade into this," he resisted.

"We are under direct orders from head office to take this on." Gallacher stopped. "Why are you pushing back on this? Are you sure you're match fit?"

"If that's what Edinburgh wants, then that's what Edinburgh gets." Bone ignored Gallacher's question. "So what do we know so far?"

"Not sure. You'd need to check in with the Missing Persons Team.

"Who's in charge then?"

"DI Irvine from the Carrbridge nick. His team is up at the Kilmorgan Stones, you know, just beyond Carrbridge reservoir. Apparently, the teacher went there every year to photograph the circle on the solstice."

"Was he a bit of a hippie, then?"

"No clue." Gallacher shrugged.

"Okay, I'll rally the troops and go speak to DI Irvine," Bone said.

"Good." Gallacher leaned back and flattened his heavily Brylcreemed barnet.

"And I can give Mullens something to do, which will save me the bother of murdering him."

"Keep me updated, okay?" Gallacher picked up the phone.

"Sir," Bone stood.

"Well, piss off then." Gallacher smiled.

THREE

In the incident room, DS Baxter looked up when Bone arrived.

"Morning, sir," she said with a smile.

"Morning, Sheila. Where's everyone?" Bone glanced round the empty office. "Did they all get the call?"

"As far as I'm aware, yes, sir." Baxter shrugged and carried on typing.

"I could murder a coffee," Bone peered over at the empty percolator.

"Oh, sorry, sir, I finished the leftovers from last night. I was just about to sort it," Baxter said.

"Don't worry, Sheila. I never expected there to be any. Just an impossible dream I have that one day I'll come to work and there will be piping-hot coffee waiting for me." Bone smirked.

"Mornin', arshooz," DS Mark Mullens mumbled, stumbling through the door.

"You're late," Bone said and resumed fumbling around in the cupboard in search of coffee filters.

"Aye, sorry, sir." Mullens slumped down at his desk.

"You're quiet. Too bloody quiet for my liking," Bone said. "Were you hoping for a lie-in?"

"It's not that," Mullens replied like a petulant five-year-old. "Sandra's put me on a diet." He sighed deeply.

"You, diet?" Bone's eyes widened in disbelief.

"I know," Mullens huffed. "She told me I was a fat bastard, and to be honest, it's hard to disagree." He stood and grabbed his stomach. "Look at this. Bloody monster truck tyres," he moaned.

"Well, you can't say we didn't warn you," Bone tutted.

"She's got me on this three-gallon of well-rotted silage-a-day diet," Mullens blew out his cheeks. "So be warned. I'm producing so much gas they should connect my arse up to the National Grid."

"And there we are." Bone sighed. "DS Mullens is back in the room. Thanks for that, Mark."

"You are very welcome. And I would suggest we keep all windows open for the foreseeable and keep Sheila away from her lighter."

"Where's Walker?" Bone glanced over at her empty desk, hastily changing the subject.

"Ooh, late!" Mullens exclaimed. "I beat the gingersnap in."

"Aye, wonders will never cease this morning, Mark," Bone joked.

"Sorry, sir." DI Walker appeared at the door. "Hospital appointment." She hung up her coat and attempted to restrain her errant red locks with a hairband.

"Morning, Rhona. Right, listen up, people."

"How come she doesn't get an earful?" Mullens complained.

"Because she's an impeccable officer and you're a slob," Bone shot back.

"Fair do's." Mullens shrugged. "But not for much longer." He patted his expansive gut again.

"Apologies for dragging you all in on Saturday. You've probably picked up the story about the missing geography teacher, Richard Jones."

"It's very worrying," Walker said, pouring herself a coffee.

"I know him," Mullens said.

"How?" Bone asked. "He's a teacher, you know, a civilized and educated person?"

"Ha bloody ha!" Mullens scoffed. "Jessie went out with him for a while a few years ago."

"Who's Jessie?" Bone asked.

"My other sister."

"How many sisters have you got?"

"Four, Jessie's the wee one."

"The youngest?"

"No, the only one under six foot. Five-ten, I think."

"Anyway, can we get to the point?" Bone sighed again.

"Oh aye, so Jessie did teacher training with him, but she dropped out. She couldn't hack it. Nice guy. I met him a few times. We got on, you might be surprised to hear, sir."

"Okay." Bone turned back to the team. "I've just spoken to the DSU, and head office would like us to investigate and try and find the guy as quickly as possible."

"Do they think he's dead, then?" Baxter asked.

"Not at all," Bone replied. "This is another of their damage limitation exercises. They want him found before the media decides to trash us."

"Again," Mullens jumped in.

"But surely if we're involved, the media will jump to the wrong conclusions?" Baxter continued.

"Not just the media, Richard Jones's family and residents of Kilwinnoch as well," Walker added.

"I know, and yes, we're also stepping on Missing Persons' toes. I did explain all of that to the DSU, but that's the order from on high."

Just then the incident room door opened, and the familiar bespeckled, youthful face of Harper appeared. "Good morning, everyone," he said with a warm smile.

"Will!" Bone exclaimed.

"The prodigal wean has returned!" Mullens added.

The team broke into spontaneous applause. Harper bowed modestly.

"I was expecting you back next week," Bone said.

"I'm bored out of my mind at home. I feel fine now."

"And you've had the all-clear from the doctor?"

"Yup. Raring to go." Harper rubbed his hands together.

"Well in that case, welcome back, DC Harper," Bone returned a smile.

Walker approached him and shook the lad's hand.

"What is it about you turning up just when we need you?" Bone said.

"Why, what's happening, sir?" Harper quizzed.

"Get yourself set up first."

Harper hung up his jacket and hobbled over to his desk by the window, adjacent to Mullens's chaotic mess.

"Are you sure you're okay?" Bone clocked Harper's limp.

"Oh, that's nothing do with what happened. I er…" He paused and shot Mullens a quick look. "I tripped over a shopping bag and sprained my ankle."

Mullens let out a loud guffaw. "So he survives the serial killer's apprentice but gets totalled by a Scotsave carry out." He laughed again, then grabbed his stomach. "Oh, mustn't do that," he moaned.

"Okay, so we've been tasked with finding the geography teacher, Richard Jones, alive, asap," Bone said, moving into the centre of the room.

"It's been four days, is that right?" Walker asked.

"Four since he was last seen," Bone replied.

"That's quite a while."

"Yes, there are serious concerns for his safety." Bone frowned.

"What do we know so far?" Baxter asked.

"The hundred-thousand-dollar question, and I know the very person to find out the answer."

"Okay, sir, will do," Baxter nodded.

"As much as you can, Baxter. His movements before his disappearance, family background, friends, enemies, any dodgy history. You know the score."

"Sir," Baxter replied and rummaged in her bag.

Bone checked his watch. "Already?"

"Addiction calls, sorry, sir." She removed a pack of cigarettes and a lighter from the outside pocket.

"Don't light that in here!" Mullens called over.

Baxter shook her head with disdain, threw her tweed jacket over her shoulders and sheepishly pushed past the DCI.

"Walker, can you go and speak to his partner?" Bone stopped. "He has a partner, right?"

"Divorced, or so I read. Lives alone in one of those new houses out on the Stirling Road."

"Those teeny wee shoeboxes the council call affordable homes?"

"Aye, those," Walker said. "I think the council are housing Lilliputians."

"And divorced dads with hefty alimony payments."

"Yup, and so they should." Walker frowned.

"What about parents, brothers, sisters?" Bone continued.

"No clue. Missing Persons will be on it, though. I could go and have a sniff around his house, if you like? I mean, it might be locked up but... er... you know." She winked.

"I know nothing, DI Walker." Bone winked. "Mullens, that means you come with me."

"Where to?" Mullens asked.

"To head off a row with Missing Persons and see what they've got on the case so far." He stopped. "And if you even mention or let out one single fart in my car, I will hit you with a hammer and dump you in a ditch, clear?"

Mullens pulled a face and adjusted the belt on his trousers.

"Anything you'd like me to do, sir?" Harper interrupted, his bespectacled head popping up from behind his screen.

"You just get yourself settled in for now," Bone replied. "And don't get assaulted by any carrier bags while we're out."

FOUR

The drive up to the Kilmorgan Stones took longer than Bone had anticipated, especially when his ancient bottle-green, Saab 96 suddenly decided upon age before beauty and refused to go into fourth gear.

"You really need to put this thing in a museum, sir," Mullens roared over the ear-splitting scream of the engine.

"This is my wee darling. I couldn't do such a thing. It would be like putting someone into palliative care," Bone roared back.

Mullens's eyes widened, and he turned to admire the view out of the window. The Campsies stretched out for miles above and beyond the narrow winding road. For once, it was a beautiful day, and the sun danced across the surface of the Carrbridge Reservoir, which opened up ahead of them.

"You forget sometimes how beautiful it is up here," Bone said.

"Aye, on the rare occasions you can see it," Mullens replied.

"Here we are." Bone nodded at the sign up ahead for the stones. He swung the car into the lane and headed towards a police van parked up on the brow of the hill.

He slowed and pulled the car onto the verge, and they both climbed out. An officer in a yellow vest approached them.

"DCI Bone and DS Mullens from RCU," Bone said, and they both flashed their lanyards. "We're looking for DI Irvine, head of the search team."

"They're all down there by the stream, on the far side of the stones," the PC pointed across the deep valley towards a line of police who were working their way slowly across a field.

"That's a belter of a view!" Mullens exclaimed, gazing down at the bowl-shaped glen, encircled by soft green hills and bathed in golden sunlight, with a near-perfect circle of standing stones in its centre.

"Which one's DI Irvine?" Bone asked.

"See that tall guy there, with the bald head and tache, leaning on one of the stones?" the PC replied.

Bone scanned the cluster of coppers again. "Got him, ta!"

The detectives set off down the track towards the search team.

"DI Irvine?" Bone asked as he approached.

Irvine straightened up, his lean figure stretching upwards like an extendable ladder.

"I'm DCI Bone, and this is DS Mullens, from the RCU at Kilwinnoch."

"RCU?" Irvine twisted the end of his moustache between his fingers. "So is he dead now?"

"Sorry, Detective, I assumed you would have been told. We've been assigned to the Jones case."

Irvine shook his head. "So, he is dead," he repeated impatiently.

"Not at all. We got the nod from my DSU this morning. Apparently, Edinburgh wants us to help you find him before it escalates."

"Why are we always the last to know?"

"Always the way." Bone smirked.

"It's a wonder they can find their way to work in the morning with their heads up their own arses," Irvine growled. "So, the Ivory Tower doesn't think we're capable of dealing with this, is that it?"

"It's all about face—the usual." Bone shrugged. "What the wigs want, the wigs get. There's no rhyme or reason."

"Well, I don't know what else you boys can do. Our whole team, plus the Fells Mountain Rescue Team, and over a dozen volunteers are all out looking for this guy. And we're not exactly novices."

"We do have local knowledge and members of our team have personal connections, so perhaps we can work together on this and get it done." Bone pushed back.

"Carrbridge is hardly Outer Mongolia. We're pretty familiar with these hills as well, you know." Irvine shook his head again. "Anyway, we're wasting time, and what's done is done. You're here now, so we might as well put you to good use. What do you know so far?"

"Only a very short brief from the DSU."

"He didn't show up for work Wednesday or Thursday, and then on Friday, the head teacher called it in. Being head of a department with classes to teach, going AWOL didn't exactly pass without notice. We've traced... sorry, hold on." Irvine cut off and marched over to the edge of the burn. "Downstream only!" he hollered at the line of police in the field. "Turn round!" He returned to Bone and Mullens. "Where was I?"

"You traced?" Bone said.

"Wednesday evening, he purchased a train ticket from Kilwinnoch to Carrbridge, and the platform CCTV at Kilwinnoch caught him boarding the last train just before midnight."

"To photograph the stones?"

"That's right. Every year, he'd come up here for some tree-hugging photographic competition."

"So are we talking serious hobby then?"

"I would think so aye. And it seems to be a bit of a thing in his department as well, apparently."

"How do you mean?"

"A colleague of his also enters the same competition each year, and for the last three years has won it."

"A bit of rivalry there then?" Bone asked.

"Looks like it."

"Who's this colleague then?"

"Eh, Brandon… something or other. I'll need to check—" Irvine's walkie-talkie crackled to life, and an incoherent voice rattled out a slur of words. "Hold on, sorry," Irvine grappled with the device attached to his belt. He pressed the button, and with a loud scream of feedback, the voice crackled again. "Tell them to press on," Irvine ordered, somehow able to understand the white noise coming out of the speaker. "The stones team are heading down towards you." He clicked the button and slotted the walkie-talkie back into his vest. "The second unit are working their way up the Braeburn from Kilwinnoch, in case he got lost on the way back down."

"So, the last time he was seen was Wednesday?"

"As far as we know, that is correct."

"Have you spoken to any of his relatives yet?"

"Mother and father both died of cancer when he was in his early twenties," Irvine confirmed.

"Jeez."

"That's a gene pool to die for," Mullens quipped.

"No siblings, and the ex-wife lives in Canada, so on his lonesome," Irvine added.

"Who are those people over there?" Bone asked, pointing to a small group huddled around a cluster of tents, on the far side of the glen.

"Sun-worshippers, druids, hippies, whatever the politically correct name is these days," Irvine said. "They're here for the solstice."

"Could we wander over for a wee word?" Bone asked.

"You can, but you won't get much out of them. Us lot aren't exactly at the top of their Christmas card list," the detective said. "I have to love you and leave you, I'm afraid," he added.

"Keep me posted," Bone said.

"Will do." And with a parting nod, the detective marched off down the bank towards the rest of his team.

"C'mon," Bone said.

He and Mullens headed over to the ragtag group huddled around a makeshift tent and smoking fire.

"Good morning," Bone said as he approached.

One of the group stood, a squat, middle-aged man with thick, grey, heavily matted dreads, a matching beard tied up in a tail dangling under his chin, and multiple facial piercings.

"I'm Duncan Bone, local detective, looking for…"

"We know," the man snapped back and dug his boot into the dirt, as though claiming territory.

"Sorry to intrude," Bone added, trying to avoid a confrontation.

"Come, sit with us," the old hippie gestured to the smoking fire where his friends were sat round.

"Okay," Bone replied in surprise.

The detectives followed him into the makeshift camp.

"What a beautiful place to set up for the solstice." Bone continued his charm offensive.

"We come every year. It is a very special place." The man stopped and turned. "For all of us," he spread his arms out, almost embracing the detective.

As the detectives approached, one of the group stood, flicked a very large roll-up into the flames, and disappeared into a homemade tent, which was made from an old tarpaulin and a few sawn branches tied together with twine.

"Sit down," the old hippie said.

Bone and Mullens awkwardly lowered themselves onto the remains of a dead tree trunk lying on its side by the fire. Mullens's huge bulk was in danger of toppling backwards at any moment. The group, three men and two women, scowled at the policemen. One of the guys spat on the ground.

"Hey, guys, everyone is welcome here, so chill," the old hippie admonished.

"When is a copper ever okay?" a young man with a purple mohawk growled back.

"The light is around us and within us. There is no place for negative energy. Welcome to you both," the old hippie continued to beam.

"They say that the ley lines run an exact line through the earth from Shetland to North Africa," Mullens said suddenly.

Bone glanced over at his colleague in surprise.

"You're familiar with our history?" the old hippie asked Mullens.

"Aye, I've always found the concept fascinating."

Bone tried to conceal a smirk.

"They run further, deeper, wider, and are more complex than any science or human brain could possibly conceive," the camp leader continued.

"You could well be right," Mullens agreed.

As the detectives approached, one of the group stood, flicked a very large roll-up into the flames, and disappeared into a homemade tent, which was made from an old tarpaulin and a few sawn branches tied together with twine.

"Sit down," the old hippie said.

Bone and Mullens awkwardly lowered themselves onto the remains of a dead tree trunk lying on its side by the fire. Mullens's huge bulk was in danger of toppling backwards at any moment. The group, three men and two women, scowled at the policemen. One of the guys spat on the ground.

"Hey, guys, everyone is welcome here, so chill," the old hippie admonished.

"When is a copper ever okay?" a young man with a purple mohawk growled back.

"The light is around us and within us. There is no place for negative energy. Welcome to you both," the old hippie continued to beam.

"They say that the ley lines run an exact line through the earth from Shetland to North Africa," Mullens said suddenly.

Bone glanced over at his colleague in surprise.

"You're familiar with our history?" the old hippie asked Mullens.

"Aye, I've always found the concept fascinating."

Bone tried to conceal a smirk.

"They run further, deeper, wider, and are more complex than any science or human brain could possibly conceive," the camp leader continued.

"You could well be right," Mullens agreed.

"So, you're here to look for the missing teacher?" the hippie asked.

"That's right." Bone nodded.

"We spoke to your colleague earlier and we saw nothing."

"Mr Jones. He taught me," a slight, pale-faced young girl with owl-like eyes, interrupted. "He was okay."

"He's well-loved in the town," Bone added. "So, you folks have been here a few days?"

"We got here on Wednesday," a grey-haired druid-hippie confirmed.

"And did any of you see Mr Jones or anyone else up here at the stones?"

They all shook their heads.

"It's been really quiet this year, for some reason. I think the weather was expected to be terrible, so maybe that put people off coming up," the camp leader said.

"And how did you get up here?" Bone asked.

The hippie looked at him suspiciously. "Why do you want to know that?"

"Just in case you spotted anyone on the way up. Don't worry, I really don't care where you set up your camp. It's always been my view that the countryside is for everyone," Bone reassured.

The head druid turned to his friends, but they all shook their heads again.

"Sorry, Detective, we don't know anything."

"Okay, no worries, but if you remember anything, no matter how small, something that you might think is insignificant, then ring me right away, okay?" Bone dug one of his cards out of his wallet and handed it over.

The leader stared at it for a moment, then handed it back. "We really don't have anything else to tell you."

The detectives stood.

"Thanks for your time, much appreciated."

Halfway back to the car, the pale-faced girl caught up with them.

"I didn't want to say anything back there, but I saw someone up on the ridge," she said between gasps, out of breath from her run over.

"When was that?" Bone asked.

"The Wednesday evening, the night before the solstice."

"Could you make out who it was? Was it Mr Jones?"

"The sun was going down behind them, so they were just shadows."

"They?" Bone interrupted.

"Aye, I think there were two, first one, then another."

"Are you sure?"

"Deffo," the girl nodded, her nose ring wriggling back and forth.

"So, was the second person with the first or following them?"

"I don't think they were together as it was a minute or so later, but who knows." She shrugged.

"Can you remember an exact time?"

"I don't follow your restrictive way of measuring time."

"Okay, so was it dusk?"

"The final rays of sunlight were behind them up there." She pointed again at the hill directly above the stones.

"Thank you," Bone said. "What's your name?"

"Firefly."

"No, I mean your birth name."

"Firefly is my birth name. I don't have any other names." She backed away.

"Okay, Firefly. Thank you very much. You have been extremely helpful. If we need to get in touch again, how can we reach you?"

"I don't know. We move and we rest with the sun and the moon."

"Fine, we'll find you if we need to. Perhaps don't move too far from the sun, for now." Bone smiled.

"I hope you find Mr Jones. He's one of us," Firefly frowned.

"He's a druid?"

"Oh no, well, maybe an honorary sun-worshipper. He understands the Earth's power and energy and movement of light. He fought beside us when we tried to stop the Cumberlang Bypass."

"He's an environmental activist?"

"I'd say more of a sympathiser, but he steps up when the need is there."

"Thanks again," Bone said. "And if you think of anything else, just give me a call, okay?" He produced his card from his suit.

She backed away again. "I can't be... I don't want to be involved." She glanced nervously at the camp then after another moment's pause, she returned.

"Two guys. That's interesting, innit?" Mullens said, peering up at the hill.

Very," Bone replied. "Let's go."

FIVE

On their way back to the station, Mullens's phone pinged. It was his wife. After a quick read, he stuffed the device back into his pocket. After a moment or two, he stopped his boss.

"Can I ask a favour, sir?" he asked sheepishly,

"Go on."

"Could you drop me at my old man's? I forgot I have to meet his new carer today."

"So you finally managed to persuade your dad?"

"More threats of violence and incarceration than persuasion, but yes. I just need to give the guy a quick once-over to make sure he's fit for my dad."

"That's a very tall order," Bone said.

"You're telling me. Even Mike Tyson would struggle to stay on his feet. It should only take me ten minutes. I'll hoof it back to the station."

"Okay, but ten minutes, and no stopovers at Dawson's Bakery," Bone ordered.

"Sandra has spies everywhere, and I'm very fond of my wedding tackle," Mullens joked. "Cheers, sir."

When Bone stopped Mullens at his dad's house, a flush-faced man in full NHS attire loitered outside the front door. Mullens approached him.

"Mr Turnpike, I'm DS..." He stopped himself. "Sorry, force of habit. I'm Mark Mullens, George's son."

They shook hands, and Mullens was impressed by the nurse's firm handshake.

"Good afternoon, Mr Mullens," the nurse said with confident authority. "I knocked on the door, and your father appeared, but then he... er..."

"Slammed it in your face?" Mullens butted in.

"Aye, he did." Turnpike nodded.

"Hopefully not a wee foretaste of things to come," Mullens said. "I assume the trust has filled you in on public enemy number one in there?"

"Oh yes, and believe me, I've heard and seen a lot worse than your father's track record. Don't worry, we'll be fine, I'm sure."

Mullens tried to conceal his sceptical expression. "Into the lion's den we go then." He unlocked the door.

"Da!" Mullens called. No reply. "Are you there, Da? It's me," Mullens tried again.

"Who's me?" a voice called out from the living room.

"Your son," Mullens called back with a tut and headed down the hall with the nurse in tow.

"Well, I know it's you, for Christ's sake. What I meant was, is it *just* you or…?" Mullen's dad looked up from his fusty armchair. "Who's this?"

"Da, this is Tim, your assigned care worker. Why didn't you let him in?"

"I didnae hear him," George snapped back and continued to fiddle with the TV remote.

"Your doctor has sent him over to help you. Remember we talked about you needing a wee bit of help around the house and the bathroom, things like that?" Mullens adopted his most tactful tone.

George glanced up again, frowned at the nurse, and increased the volume on the TV.

"Da, turn that off for a minute," Mullens said and, snatching the remote from his dad's grip, he switched it off.

"Hey, sir! I'm watching that. It's *Homes Under the Hammer*. I never miss it."

"You'll be under a bloody hammer in a minute. Just behave yourself for once, please," Mullens ordered his tact deserting him. "Sorry, Tim. As you can see, my da is…"

"Is what?" George interrupted.

"A stubborn old bastard."

"Charming," George balked.

Turnpike approached cautiously. "Good to meet you, Mr Mullens. I'm Tim." He held out his hand.

George stared at the nurse's extended arm and shrugged. "Get him out." He shuffled his weight from one side of his armchair to the other.

"Oh, come on, Da! We agreed on this yesterday. Don't bloody start," Mullens replied. Remember what we said will happen if you refuse help. Burngreen Home is still holding the room for you."

George's face dropped even further as he let out a long sigh.

"Good, right. Let's start again," Mullens continued. "Tim's going to be in…" He turned back to the nurse.

"I'll be here three times a day. In the morning to help you get up and get ready," Turnpike started.

"Ready for what?" Mullens's dad cut in.

"Just get you washed and dressed, make you a wee bit of breakfast and then set you up with whatever you like to do in the morning."

"I like to go to the casino and maybe hook up with some bunny girls," George growled.

"Da!" Mullens exclaimed.

"Haha, good one," Turnpike said. "Though, I'm not sure Campsie NHS Trust would approve."

George shook his head.

"Then I'm back at lunchtime, and again at dinner until we get you to bed," Turnpike continued.

"Will you wipe my arse and read me a wee story?" George interrupted again.

"For God's sake, Dad!" Mullens roared again.

"Aye, definitely the arse bit and anywhere else that needs a good scrub, and then a bedtime story, but only if you're good!" Turnpike attempted to lighten the mood.

But George just folded his arms in defiance.

"Right, then. Are we good, Da?" Mullens frowned at his father.

His dad shrugged and frowned back.

"Thanks, Tim. I'll be away now. Just give me a bell if you need anything, or a tactical arms unit." He lightly punched his dad's shoulder. "And you be good, you hear? You're on trial. One slip and it's the Burngreen for you."

George snorted angrily, then unfolded and refolded his arms.

As Mullens left, he squinted back at the pair of them. Turnpike had pushed up the sleeves of his blue shirt and was down on his haunches, talking, while his dad was staring at him with murder in his eyes.

"Oh, dear," Mullens muttered to himself and headed back to the station, via a route that avoided the high street and its many culinary temptations.

SIX

As Walker approached Richard Jones's shoebox of a house, the two officers perched on the wall by the door stood to attention. Walker flashed her lanyard.

"Mornin', ma'am," said the shorter of the two uniforms.

"All quiet?" Walker asked.

"Aye," the officer replied. "One of the neighbours was round asking after him, but apart from that, not a sausage."

"Is it okay for me to have a quick look?"

"I think the guy's landlord locked up after the Missing Persons Team left."

"Who's the landlord?"

"No clue. The young guy dressed like an estate agent."

"I'll just have a quick squint round the back," Walker replied.

"Okey dokey," the officer replied, his boredom getting the better of him.

His colleague glanced over at him and pulled a face.

Walker approached the front door and peered through the front window. Inside was dark and gloomy. She held her hand up to the pane, but she couldn't see beyond her own reflection. She went around the side of the house and up a narrow pathway between it and the next shoebox rammed as close as the developers could get away with.

The backyard was barely big enough to stick a second-class stamp, but well-organised, with the bins lined up in a neat row at the back gate and a single director-style chair positioned in the corner. Fishing a pair of gloves from her pocket, she pulled them on and tried the door, but it was locked tight.

She shifted over to the window and ran her hand along the frame. With a glance around the side of the house, she squeezed her fingers under the bottom pane and with two or three sharp jerks, swung it open. She hoisted herself up and through and dropped down onto the floor of a small galley kitchen. She shut the window, quickly unlocked and opened the back door, then scanned the room.

The kitchen was clean and tidy, with not a plate or cup in sight. She opened the compact fridge tucked in behind the hallway door. There were a few eggs, an opened packet of butter, and two bottles of untouched milk resting in the door shelf. She picked one out, peeled open the lid, and sniffed. The contents were still relatively fresh. She replaced the milk and shut the fridge door.

She spotted an A4 calendar hanging from the wall beneath a retro-style kitchen clock. *June* was written in bold capitals across the top of a dramatic image of a Scottish mountain. She took it off its hook. The dates of the month were set out in a square grid formation at the bottom of the page. Each date had a time scribbled in the top corner.

June 1st: *11:56 p.m.,* June 2nd: *12:32 a.m.,* June 3rd: *10:48 p.m.,* and so on all the way until June 14th, then they stopped. She ran her finger along the next row and paused on June 20th. There was a different note scribbled diagonally across that box and the one beside it. The pen scrawl was smudged, making it difficult to decipher. She turned the calendar sideways and then towards the window light. The scribble read *"Stones",* and there were no other entries beyond it.

She flicked the page back to May, which had another beautiful Highland scene displayed along the top. The dates grid had similar time references noted down in the top corners of each day. Aside from the times, there was nothing else. She turned another page. April was blank along with the rest of the year. She put the calendar back on its hook and ventured down the narrow hallway.

The living room was claustrophobically cramped, with a three-seater sofa dominating the room, one of the arms protruding into the doorway. A flat-screen TV was attached to the wall opposite with a coal-effect fireplace underneath. Aside from that, the room was austere and cold with magnolia paperless walls and a bare light bulb dangling from the ceiling. Walker spotted a small side table over by a window that was barely wide enough to fulfil its basic light-giving function. Negotiating around the sofa, she went for a look.

Photographs were scattered across the tabletop with more stacked up on a shelf underneath. She picked one out, a square twelve x twelve-inch image of a loch with low mist hanging just above the surface. It was stunning. She picked up another of a country road winding between two gigantic mountains covered in a blanket of deep-purple heather. The images suddenly made Walker feel nostalgic for her childhood home in Lewis. She set them down, retreated to the hall, and took the stairs to the first floor.

There was only one cramped bedroom with a single bed rammed up against the back wall, and Jones's clothes racked up in an open wardrobe, tucked in behind the door. Mounted on the wall opposite, an IKEA-style crimson cabinet ran across the width of the room and reached up to the ceiling, making the room feel even smaller.

Stretching, she slid one of the doors across, but it was locked by a combination padlock attached to the handle. She wiggled it for a moment, flicked at the row of numbers, then accepting defeat, she retreated to the landing. Pushing a second door open, she entered a narrow, white-tiled bathroom, with a three-quarter-sized bath, shower, and vanity unit tucked into the corner. She opened the unit and scanned the rows of men's toiletries squeezed into the space. Glancing up, she spotted a toilet bag hanging on the back of the door alongside a grey dressing gown.

Suddenly feeling as though she was intruding, she was about to leave when she noticed the top corner of the bath panel was sticking out. Kneeling, she gently pulled at the panel until the whole side popped out of its socket. Carefully bending the plastic back, she squinted under the bath. At the far side, behind the taps and pipework, there was a small black box about the size of a computer mouse tucked into the corner. She leaned in to reach it, but a voice calling out from downstairs stopped her.

"Shit!" She quickly stretched again, snatched it out. She popped the lid. But in her haste, she dropped it, and something fell out and skittered across the linoleum floor, disappearing behind the toilet bowl.

Boots thumped up the stairs.

"Fuck!" she muttered, and clambering to her feet, she dived for the door just as one of the PCs pushed at it.

"Do you mind!" She pushed back, and the door slammed shut.

"Oh, sorry, ma'am," the flustered officer said through the door.

Walker quickly fumbled behind the toilet bowl and retrieved the errant object. It was a USB stick. She dropped it back in its box, slid it back under the bath, and pressed the panel back on. She was about to leave when she turned back and flushed the cistern.

"Bloody hell, Constable. Do you often intrude on female officers on the loo?" Walker growled.

"So sorry, ma'am," the scarlet-faced PC repeated, his equally embarrassed colleague lingering behind. "I didn't know it was you."

"Who else did you think it was?"

"We thought you'd maybe headed back to the station or something."

"So did I sneak past you when you were on your phones, or maybe I teleported?"

"Again, I can only apologise, ma'am. We didn't mean to disturb you. It's just that we thought the landlord had locked it all up."

"Well, the back door was wide open. Not good. Whoever that letting agency is, they need to do one of our home security courses."

"I wouldn't wish that on my worst enemy, ma'am," the officer joked.

"Right, could you call in to the station and ask the desk sergeant to contact the agency and get this place secured again?"

"No problem, ma'am."

"Unbelievable." She rolled her eyes in mock disdain.

As she headed back to the car, she glanced back at the officers. One was on his radio and the other was back on his phone. She smiled, jumped in the pool car, and returned to the station.

SEVEN

Wee Boaby Ferguson, or Joaby as his so-called mates called him, attempted to clamber up the side of a boulder twice his diminutive size, but his soaking wet gutties slipped on the smooth granite surface and he slid back down.

"Wait for me, guys," Boaby called out. "I can't..." He tried again, but he couldn't find a hold. "Bastards!" he groaned.

A face appeared at the top of the boulder.

"What you doin' doon there, Joaby?" Caz, the gangly, flush-faced heart and soul of Boaby's gang of mates asked with a wide grin. "Hope you're no' pushin' another one oot?"

"I can't climb up. It's easy for you lot," Wee Boaby complained.

"Fuck's sake, here," Caz reached his arm down.

Boaby grabbed it, and Caz hauled him up the side with ease.

"Cheers, Caz," Boaby

"C'mon," Caz said.

Boaby raced after him.

"Here he comes, Joaby Shitemeister," shouted Fin Robertson, the self-appointed leader and head arsehole of the gang, when he saw the two boys approaching.

"Stop callin' me that," Boaby complained. "It wasn't my fault."

"Well, let's examine the evidence," Fin sneered, his pencil-thin excuse for a pre-teen moustache bobbing around above his lip. "Said Shitemeister shat himself in class. The last time I checked, we are responsible for our own arseholes, unless someone else is in charge of yours," Fin attempted to reel in the rest of the gang. "Like Mr Gunyon the history teacher, for example?"

The gang laughed.

"Give it a rest, Fin," Caz cut in.

"Aw, the big man doesn't like us teasin' lads," Fin sneered, exposing his yellowing teeth.

"Ah mean it, just fuckin' shut it. We've got ages to walk yet, and you're doin' my skull in," Caz continued.

"I'll do your skull in, if you're no' careful," Fin replied.

Caz shook his head. "Whenever you like, I'll be right here." He pushed past Fin and continuing upstream.

"You no' takin' your wee shitey-pants monkey with you?" Fin called out.

Caz stopped, turned, and marched back. "Let's go," he said, stooping over Fin and gently headbutting the top of his greasy mop.

Fin stepped back, smiled, and swaggered away with his closest ally, Fat Frankie McClusky, in tow. The remaining two boys, Sandy McRorie and John Banks, hung back, Sandy nervously squeezing at the acne peppered all over his face.

Caz sighed and, turning back to Wee Boaby, gave him the nod and carried on with the rest of the gang.

"Don't fall behind again, all right?" Caz barked at Boaby, who was still trying to keep up, his legs working twice as hard as Caz's lanky pins.

At the fork in the river, they all stopped.

"How much farther now?" Fat Frankie puffed, now stripped to the waist.

"Haud yer wheesht, fat boy," Fin retorted and carried on, taking the left-hand fork.

"It's this way," Caz shouted after them.

"Fuck it is!" Fin roared and marched on.

"That goes up to the Carrbridge Reservoir, the falls are up over that ridge," Caz insisted.

Fin stopped and gave Caz the finger. Fat Frankie stood between the two boys, unsure of which way to go.

"What's it to be, Frankie, a ten-minute walk with us, or a two-hour hike to nowhere with your great leader?"

"Frankie, c'mon!" Fin hollered, now almost lost in the trees.

"I'm goin' with Caz!" Frankie shouted back.

Fin rewarded him with another two-fingered salute and disappeared into the woods.

"Is it okay just lettin' him go off on his own like that?" Boaby asked.

"What do you care?" Caz replied and set off again, sensing a successful coup d'état.

Boaby and the rest of his new gang followed.

When they reached a steep bank leading up over the first of three waterfalls, they jumped at a rustling in some nearby bushes. Out of nowhere, a figure lunged at the group. The boys scattered, and Sandy fell to the ground.

"Boo!" Fin bellowed, running towards them, arms waving. He stopped and broke into an uncontrollable fit of laughter.

"Jesus, Fin," Caz said.

"Your faces. Sandy, I thought you'd done a Wee Boaby."

"So I was right, then?" Caz asked.

"I couldn't get past. Some bastard farmer's put up a ten-foot security fence that wasn't there before."

"Aye, right." Caz grimaced and set off up the slope with Frankie behind.

As they passed the second waterfall, Sandy hopped across a couple of rocks to get a closer look at the pool. But as his foot landed on the second, he slipped and tumbled sideways into the water with an almighty splash. The gang erupted in laughter as Sandy let out a loud yell as the freezing water penetrated his clothes and sent his testicles northward. Arms flailing, he splashed and spluttered towards the edge of the pool as though he was under attack from a great white shark and clambered out.

"Freezin' in there!" Sandy winced, teeth already clacking.

There were more roars of laughter and the gang caught up with Caz.

When they finally reached the falls, Caz stopped by the pool and looked up.

"Check that out, man," he said, staring at blood-red torrent haemorrhaging over the side of the cliff.

"That's weird," Fin said. "What is it?"

"It's iron," Caz replied. "That's why it's called Blood Water Falls, you dipshit."

"All right." Fin glanced up. "So who's up for jumpin'?"

"I don't know, Fin. That's really high." Sandy cowered.

"Oh, come on, don't crap out now. You're already wringin'."

Sandy pulled a face.

"What about you, bawsack?" Fin asked, turning to Caz. "Are you going to bottle it, too?"

Caz shook his head and headed off up the cliffside to the top.

Fin turned to the rest of the gang. "Any other pussies?"

Wee Boaby hung back by the pool.

"Joaby, you comin'?"

Boaby shook his head.

"What the fuck are you here for if you're no' goin' to jump?"

"It's too high for me, Fin," Boaby explained.

"Fuck's sake!" Fin rubbed his nose. "I suppose it's just as well. You'd probably just shite yourself all the way down and we'd have to swim in it." He shrugged. "C'mon, Sandy."

His reluctant mate shuffled over to join him on the track.

At the top, the jumpers gathered on the outcrop, and they stripped down to their boxers.

"Is that a pirate flag on your pants, Frankie?" Fin guffawed.

"Ma maw bought me them," a flush-faced Frankie replied.

Caz inched closer to the edge. "See that big rock there near the edge of the pool?" He pointed over the side.

The rest of the shivering gang joined him.

"You need to land between that and that big flat boulder there on the right, see it?"

Fin peered over, his arms crossed, clutching his chest. His eyes widened when he saw the drop.

"That's the deepest bit of the pool. If you miss it, you're deid," Caz grinned. "Ladies first, Fin?"

"Piss off," Fin snarled.

"I'll go," Frankie said, stepping up to the edge.

"Hold on," Caz grabbed his arm. "You need to be a bit farther this way."

Frankie readjusted his position.

"Tuck your legs in, but not too high or you'll lose your front teeth," Caz instructed.

"I know. I've done it before," Frankie returned.

"When?" Fin asked in surprise.

"My big brother brought me up last year. He showed me." He turned, raised his arms, and in a single bounce disappeared into the roaring abyss.

Caz rushed to the edge and peered down. Frankie was swimming about at the bottom. He looked up and waved.

"You next?" Caz asked Fin, who was looking increasingly worried. "You're shittin' bricks."

"No, I'm no'," Fin grumped and pushed past Caz.

"If you jump from there, it's curtains," Caz said.

Fin crooked a painful smile. He stepped back. "Show me, then."

Caz sidled up and shifted this way and that. "See you in hell, sucker!" he cried and leapt.

Fin shuffled to the edge and watched Caz dive-bomb into the centre of the pool. The boys at the bottom cheered and applauded his perfect descent and entry. Caz resurfaced and let out a loud yelp, then he waved at Fin to jump.

Fin continued to stare down, his face white with fear. The gang waved him on from the side. He took a deep breath, pinched his nose between his thumb and forefinger, and jumped. On his way down, he forgot to tuck his legs in and he hit the water with such force, the loud smack bounced off the sides of the gorge. He disappeared into the deep. After what seemed like hours, he finally re-emerged with a violent splash and a scream.

Caz swam over to him. "Are you okay?"

"My guts!" Fin hollered.

"That was some bellyflop," Caz said.

"Aw, fuck!" Fin laughed. "But fuckin' brilliant!" He splashed his arms around. "Fuckin' brilliant!" he roared up at the sky. "Let's go again," he said to Caz, who swam towards the falls. "Where are you goin'?"

When Caz reached the wall of water, he ducked under and disappeared.

"What the fuck's he doin'?" Fin said, swimming over for a look.

When he reached the waterfall, he peered into the frothing pink torrent. Caz was on the other side, pointing down and gesturing for him to join him. Fin held his nose again, dived under, and pushed through the falls to the other side. He popped up, gasping for air. Caz was scrambling up onto a narrow plinth of rock that jutted out of a high, soaking-wet wall of smooth black granite.

"This is amazing," Fin cried out over the deafening roar and clambered up to join the other boy.

Caz grabbed his shoulder and pointed to the far side of the platform.

A man leaned against the wall. He was naked, his arms outstretched. His head and neck rested at an odd angle.

"What the fuck?" Fin mouthed.

They sidled along the ridge using their arms to stop them from slipping back into the pool. As they approached, the plinth widened. They slowed and then stopped about six feet from the figure.

The man's eyes were wide open, staring into the water. His legs were slightly buckled as though he was about to topple over. Caz looked back at Fin and drew his finger across his throat. Fin's eyes widened, and he leapt off the ridge, back into the pool.

Caz inched closer. The man's chest was smeared in an inky crimson substance that emanated from a wide gash in his temple. Two metal spikes had been driven through his outstretched palms, pinning his limp, lifeless body to the wall and preventing him from falling off. Up close, Caz had a better view of the man's contorted, broken features.

"Oh Jesus!" he cried out in horror when the penny dropped that he was staring into the cold, dead eyes of his geography teacher. He jumped off the ledge and swam through the waterfall. He emerged on the other side, shocked and spluttering, and swam out of the pool.

Fin stood by a rock, shivering and shaking his head.

"What's goin' on?" Wee Boaby asked when he saw Caz's expression.

"Mr Jones is in there," Caz stuttered, finally.

"Who?" Sandy asked.

"What?" It was Frankie's turn to be confused.

"You mean Jiz-face Jones, our geography teacher?" Sandy's baby-blue eyes were wide with disbelief and confusion.

"He's deid," Caz returned.

"Deid? Jiz the Jones?" Sandy persisted.

"Fuck's sake, Sandy. Mr Jones the geography teacher is in there with his head mashed in, and he's nailed to the fuckin' cliff!"

"Aye, righto!" Frankie said, shaking his head.

"We need to phone the polis," Caz ignored him. "Where's your phone, Fin?" he shouted over the din of the falls, which now seemed to be roaring even louder.

Fin shook violently, oblivious to Caz's request.

"Fin!" Caz repeated.

"I've got mine," Wee Boaby said, fishing his mobile out of his shorts.

"Hold on," Frankie interjected. "You two are pullin' our chains, right?"

"Ring, Boaby," Caz repeated.

"What number do I dial?" Boaby asked.

"For God's sake, nine-nine-nine."

Fin rushed over to Boaby and snatched the phone from him.

"What you doin'?" Caz exclaimed.

"We can't ring the cops," Fin said, his voice still shaking.

"We have to," Caz replied.

"No!" Fin yelled and fiddled with the back. "My da'll kill me if he finds out I've been skivin'."

"We have to ring, Fin. C'mon," Caz tried to appeal.

Fin held the phone aloft. Caz lunged at him, and they fell to the ground, fists and feet flying. After a few mutual blows to the head and ribs, Caz finally forced Fin's arms down and twisted his wrist until he dropped the handset. He grabbed it, jumped up, and hit the emergency button. Fin scrambled to his feet and ran at Caz, but Frankie stuck his leg out, and Fin tumbled forward, his head and shoulders landing in the pool.

"Police, please," Caz said when the call connected.

Fin crawled out of the pool, slumped down on the ground, and wiped the water from his eyes.

"Hullo, aye. We've found a dead body," Caz continued, now shivering.

Fin got to his feet and joined the rest of the gang around the phone.

"We're up at Braeburn Falls. Aye, that's right, Blood Water Falls."

After a moment, Caz nodded. "Oh aye, deid as a dodo."

EIGHT

When Bone arrived back at Kilwinnoch's station, Sergeant Brody jumped up and stuck his head through the reception hatch.

"Gallacher wants to see you," Brody said and flinched.

"With some good news, I hope?" Bone asked.

The desk sergeant shrugged. "His face wasn't in any hurry to smile."

"Oh dear," Bone groaned.

"He's gone down to the canteen," Brody added.

"I'll head back to the incident room," Mullens said, "before bawheid here mentions canteens again." He marched off.

"He's on a diet and unbearable," Bone offered by way of explanation.

"More unbearable than normal, then?" Brody joked and returned to his papers.

The canteen was deserted, with only a couple of PCs at a table by the door, hunched over their bacon baps. Gallacher was at the till when Bone intercepted him.

"If you're paying, I'll have an Americano, sir," Bone smiled. "Unless the moths have eaten all your money."

The young lad behind the counter tried to conceal a grin.

Gallacher spun round. "Duncan!"

But Bone could see from his boss's expression that he was in no mood for jokes.

"Let's sit down." Gallacher carried his coffee over to a table at the back of the canteen. "A body has been found up at Braeburn Falls." He fixed his eyes on Bone.

"Jones?" Bone asked.

"With no formal identification, we can't say for sure, but I think it's safe to say it probably is." Gallacher shook his head.

"Who found him?"

"A group of wee lads who decided to skip school and go for a swim. The search team came across them on their way back down. A day they're never going to forget, tragically."

"Oh dear," Bone replied.

"Oh dear indeed. SOCO are on their way up there now, and a second unit has been dispatched to Jones's property. We have to keep this under wraps for now, at least until the body is identified. The town is going to go ballistic. The press, especially that weasel McKinnon, must not hear of this until we're ready to tell them. Okay?"

"Absolutely. Though with officers all over a beauty spot and Jones's house, that's going to be impossible, and once that cockroach is on this, he'll whip the town into a torch-wielding, crazy mob… and as usual, guess who'll get the blame?"

"RCU."

"And me in particular. It'll be like I killed the guy myself." Bone shook his head.

"So, what do you have so far?"

"With all due respect sir, you only assigned the case to us a couple of hours ago. We're working on it, and now if it's a murder investigation, we'll have full authority."

"You need to work fast here, Duncan," Gallacher stirred a spoonful of sugar into his coffee.

"We always work fast. That should be our bloody motto."

"Though, I don't want you to be under too much pressure. You're not that long back and you've been through so much already." Gallacher eyeballed him.

"I'm okay. As I said before, work is what makes me tick."

Gallacher continued to stir the cup. The spoon rattling the side loudly. "I'm serious. Any sign of stress and I'll pull you."

"If you followed that philosophy you'd have to pull most of the force," Bone joked.

"I mean it. We can't mess up here. This geography teacher is a local hero, for Christ's sake, and I've already—"

"Don't tell me," Bone cut in. "You've had your old chum Chief Superintendent Laverty on the blower."

"Don't be a smartarse, Duncan," Gallacher snapped back.

The two PCs glanced over, and Gallacher leaned across the table.

"Head office has all ears and eyes on us yet again, and we need to nail this before it escalates any further," he said quietly.

"We're on it. We'll get it done. I get the message." Bone nodded.

Gallacher paused. "We've been friends a long time, Duncan.

"Govan seems like an eternity ago now.

It's recent enough to remember the promising, but cocky smart-arse young recruit I knew from his first day on the job that he was going to make his way."

"Kind of you to say, I think."

"What I'm saying is, don't let that smart-arse idiot call the shots. He made the wrong choices for you back in Govan and he'll do it again, but this time you can't play the young and naïve card. And there will be no way back. You hear what I'm saying?"

Bone was about to respond but changed his mind.

Gallacher sat back. "Right, that's all for now. Meeting over."

"Sir," Bone got up, and left.

NINE

"Okay, listen up, team," Bone said sharply, scanning the incident room. "Wait—where's DS Baxter?"

"Where do you think?" Harper said, approaching Bone.

"Okay, I'll—"

The incident room door opened.

"Sorry, sir," Baxter interrupted and sheepishly tucked her tobacco, papers, and lighter into her handbag.

"I've just been speaking—"

The door flew open again, and Mullens stumbled in.

Bone checked his watch. "Twenty minutes. Well done, Detective."

"I'm a new man," Mullens grinned.

"So, now that we're all present, may I proceed?"

"Sir," the team replied in unison.

"Right, a body has been found up at Braeburn Falls," Bone continued.

"Oh Jesus," Mullens muttered.

"Although we don't have a formal ID, I think it's pretty safe to assume that it's the body of the missing teacher, Richard Jones."

"Are we talking murder, suicide, or misadventure?" Walker asked.

"At this stage, we just don't know. The site team is on their way up there now. Not easy considering the location."

"Blood Water Falls, that's pretty bloody ironic," Mullens cut in. "This is going to upset quite a few people round here."

"That's why we have to work fast and sort this before the hysteria starts."

"And that turd-face McKinnon starts stoking the fire," Mullens added.

"Correct, DS Mullens. We need to keep this locked down for as long as we possibly can."

"But the minute the site team lands on the falls, the hyenas will be all over it," Walker said.

"Until we have a positive ID on the body, technically this is still a missing persons case, and we'll play that card as long as we can to buy us time." Bone turned back to the team. "So no blabbering about this, okay?"

"Sir," the team replied.

"Mullens?" Bone repeated.

"Of course, sir," Mullens said, chewing at his nails.

"SOC teams are heading up there now and to Jones's house," Bone resumed. "How did you get on over there, Rhona?"

"Well, would you believe it? Jones's letting agency had left the back door wide open."

"Unbelievable." Bone smirked.

"His place is tiny, I mean stupid-small, and pretty austere."

"Turn up anything?"

"Something a bit odd. There was a calendar on the wall, and every day for the last month and a half, he'd scribbled down a time, and all of the entries were around midnight."

"Reminder to put the cat out?" Mullens joked.

"Anything else?" Bone asked.

"In his bedroom, there was this huge wall cupboard, totally out of scale for the size of the room, and it had quite a heavy-duty combination lock on it."

"Don't tell me, it just fell off when you brushed past it?" Bone sniggered.

"No, sorry. No chance. Bolt cutters required for that one."

"Right, so we'll need to—"

"Sorry just one more thing," Walker interrupted. "The last room I checked was the bathroom."

"And?"

"All his toiletries were there, including his toilet bag, so it doesn't look like he'd planned any kind of long trip. But as I was leaving, I noticed that the bath panel was loose and when I checked behind it, I spotted a small box tucked behind the pipes, like it was hidden."

"What was in it?"

"A USB."

"Did you bring it back?"

"Sir, of course not. Without a warrant that would make anything on it inadmissible."

Bone pointed at her. "Good, just testing you."

Walker rolled her eyes. "Anyway, the uniforms interrupted me, so I put it back and left."

"Right. Baxter, can you alert the SOC team at Jones's property to check the bath and bring in the calendar?" Bone ordered.

"Sir," Baxter replied.

"And what have you uncovered so far?" he added and leaned against the nearest desk.

"I've been working through Jones's life leading up to his disappearance," Baxter replied. "He was a member of, and involved with, a number of local charities, environmental organisations, and pressure groups."

"So, quite political, then."

"Indeed, everything from the Kilwinnoch branch of the environmental pressure group, ECO NOW, to the local Ramblers. I rang and spoke to various committee members, and they all had nothing but praise for him. He was also involved in quite a forthright campaign to clean up the river and he volunteered at the local food bank once a month."

"How do you mean, forthright?"

"Last year, he wrote a series of open letters to the *Chronicle*, accusing Grinlay's—you know, the pie maker—of dumping chemical and animal waste in the river."

Mullens suddenly wailed like he'd just been harpooned. "For God's sake, Sheila. Why did you mention *them*? Are you deliberately trying to torture me?" He rubbed his stomach and moaned.

"So, not everyone thought of him as a local hero, then?" Bone pressed on, ignoring him.

"For many, yes, but for those with vested interests, absolutely not. He was a thorn in their side. Grinlay's actually began litigation proceedings against both him and ECO NOW, but strangely, they pulled the lawsuit."

"Why?"

"No clue." Baxter shrugged.

"Okay, keep digging." Bone turned to his young colleague. "Will, can you see what you can find in the way of CCTV footage? Train stations between Kilwinnoch and Carrbridge, or anywhere else between here and the falls. Mullens, get yourself—" He stopped. "Mullens, what the hell are you doing?"

Mullens was hovering behind Harper, staring at his Tupperware sandwich box, perched on the edge of his desk. Harper spun round.

"Bloody hell, Mark," Harper complained.

"Just admiring your lunch, buddy," Mullens said through gritted teeth.

"Back off."

"Mullens!" Bone shouted.

"Sir?" Mullens turned his hunger-crazed gaze back to Bone.

"Get yourself up to Kilwinnoch Academy and quiz Jones's work colleagues about his disappearance."

"Aw, sir, can't DS Harper no' go, or Rhona? Rhona knows the head."

"I've only met her once." Walker shrugged.

"What's the problem, Mullens?" Bone asked impatiently.

"It's just that, well, I was a bit of a heid-the-baw at school and…"

"You're still scared of your teachers, aren't you?" Walker joked.

"No. Well, aye. Maybe just a bit."

"For God's sake, Mullens. Go *now*," Bone ordered.

Muttering, Mullens snatched up his jacket.

"Oh, and Mark," Bone caught him at the door "Don't let on we've found him, eh?"

Mullens nodded and left.

"Right, Walker, let's go."

"Where, sir?"

"Blood Water Falls," Bone replied. "I hope you've brought your walking boots."

TEN

Bone drove up into the Campsies as far as the Monklands' farm, perched on the upper slopes of Meikle Hill. He swung the Saab into the yard and pulled up next to a few SOC vehicles parked alongside an imposing, steel-structured hay barn, rammed full of neatly stacked bales.

"This is as close to the falls as we can get," Bone said and climbed out of the Saab. "The Monklands aren't exactly the friendliest of folks, but the son has agreed to let us through the perimeter fence they erected to keep visitors from using the shortcut."

"That's illegal, isn't it?" Walker asked. "Isn't it a right of way?"

"It's been going on for years. The council wins and forces old Monkland to tear down the fence. He puts up another one. And round and round it goes. I think even the National Environment Agency got involved at one point."

"Has it ever got out of hand?"

"Oh, yes," Bone replied. "And you'll see why shortly."

Walker scanned the farm, taking in the row of pristine tractors and various attachments parked by an equally immaculate milking shed. Behind them, a whitewashed three-storey farmhouse, complete with doorstep granite pillars and window boxes overflowing with colourful flowers.

"This is impressive," she said. "I thought farmers were hard up these days?"

"They have eight hundred acres of some of the most fertile land in Scotland, and they host shooting and other country events."

"Where the toffs come and splash the cash."

"And slaughter most of the wildlife, aye, that." Bone glanced over at two men the size of Hereford cattle charging towards them. "Brace yourself," he warned.

"You can't just park up in our yard like this," the older of the two men hollered as he approached.

"Mr. Monkland, DCI Bone, and this is—"

"I don't care if you're Inspector bloody Taggart. I never agreed to this," Monkland senior barked again, the buttons on his checked shirt straining with his rage.

"Dad, it was me," the flustered young man cut in. "I told that policeman who was here earlier it would be okay to park up. They're looking for that teacher who's gone missing."

"What bloody teacher, and what's it got to do with us?" The elderly farmer tucked his shirt into his belt as though preparing himself for a fistfight.

"Claire's old geography teacher, I told you before. God's sake." The son pulled a face. "Sorry, Officers," he nodded apologetically.

"No bother," Bone replied. "Thank you for agreeing to let us use the shortcut to the falls."

"If this is some sly way of takin' doon the fence then I'll be on to my solicitor," the old man warned.

"Not at all. We're not interested in any of that. We just need to find the teacher."

"Of course," the son said. He turned to his father. "Why don't you go back inside, Dad? I'll sort this."

"I'm not happy about this at all. In my eyes, you're trespassing, and I have every right to go back and get my bloody gun," Monkland senior growled.

"I hope you have a licence for that, Mr Monkland." Walker jumped in.

Bone shot her a look of disapproval.

"Who's she?" Monkland senior stabbed his work-fattened index finger at her.

"This is my colleague, Detective Inspector Walker."

"Okay, Miss Whoever You Are, my family have farmed this land for four hundred years. You honestly think in that time we wouldn't understand basic laws of the countryside?" He sneered at her, his ruddy cheeks puckering under the pressure. "And if you wreck my fence, I'll sue." He tugged at the brim of his tweed cap and marched off towards the farmhouse.

"Sorry about him," the other man said when his dad was out of earshot. "My old man is very protective of his property."

"You don't say." Walker winced.

"You have different views?" Bone probed.

"Well, it's not the nineteenth century anymore. We need to move with the times. But he's the boss." The young farmer shrugged.

"Mr Jones is a member of the Kilwinnoch Ramblers. Has your dad had any run-ins with them over the erection of the fence?" Bone continued.

"To be honest, he probably has, but my dad has run-ins with just about everyone these days. Ever since my mum died, he's not really been coping very well. But it's all hot air and grief."

"Well, we thank you for your help, er…" Bone said.

"John Monkland. That's John junior."

"Okay, John, if you could show us where to go?" Bone asked.

"Of course, but be warned, it's a bit muddy down in the lower field."

Walker glanced down at her pristine Italian brogues and sighed.

When the detectives finally arrived at Braeburn Falls, the SOC team were already there with a cordon around the perimeter. Three or four police divers emerged and then disappeared into the dark pool engulfing the site. Bone spotted Chief Forensic Pathologist, Andrew Cash, in his trademark 'man-in-black' romper suit, kneeling next to a pile of

"The body is behind the waterfall. The divers are beginning the recovery process now. The body is naked, arms outstretched, with its hands pinned to the cliff face…" He glanced up. "In other words, crucified."

"So definitely a murder, then?" Walker interjected.

"Or some weird misadventure gone wrong, but yes, I'd say so," Cash said. "You can see here, look." He held up the tablet he was holding and turned up the sound. "The divers are wearing body and head cams and live-streaming the recovery."

Bone studied the shaking images, the hiss of the waterfall screaming out of the tablet's tiny speakers. One of the head cams caught a flash of a section of the torso, and the camera panned down the arm to the wrist and hand. The palm was open, and the black outline of a climbing piton was just visible.

"Let me switch to cam two for a wider shot," Cash said and tapped the screen.

The image switched, and the screen filled with a full-length shot of the body slumped, arms outstretched, and head sideways at an odd angle. Every few seconds the image disappeared under a foggy mist as the diver moved in and out of the waterfall directly behind him. A gloved hand appeared and wiped the lens. Cash flicked back to the first cam, and a close-up of the victim's face filled the screen.

"That's definitely Jones," Bone said.

"What's that protruding from his mouth?" Walker pointed at the screen.

equipment and oxygen tanks. He stood when he saw the detectives approach.

"Of all the places to get yourself killed, it would have to be up here," Cash complained. "It's taken us two hours to manhandle all our gear up here, with zero access for any kind of vehicle backup. Total nightmare."

"We saw your vans parked up in the Monklands' farmyard," Bone replied. "You can't get a helicopter up here then?"

"A helicopter? With all these cuts?" Cash scoffed. "And don't get me started on that miserable old bastard. He gave us such a hard time. If it hadn't been for his son, we would have had to hump the gear upstream all the way from the town."

"A lovely man." Bone smirked.

"Anyhow, I would say it's a joy to see you again, but…"

"Indeed, we have to stop meeting like this You know DI Walker?"

"Yes, of course. She's the sensible one in the RCU," Cash greeted the detective who returned a wry smile. "So, the body was discovered at approximately eleven-ten this morning, by a group of young men who had skipped school to come for a swim. They were picked up by the search team who were working their way up the river, and the rest is history, as they say."

"Where's the victim?" Bone asked, scanning the scene.

Cash picked up a set of headphones with a mic attached and plugged them in. "Excuse me a second. Bill, can you hear me?" The headphones crackled. "Okay, can you gently open the victim's mouth and see what that is sticking out? Did you get that?"

A wetsuit-gloved hand appeared in the shot and pulled carefully at Jones's lower jaw. A second hand slowly inserted two fingers into the mouth and widened the orifice. The detectives leaned in closer to the screen. There was something in there, but they couldn't make it out through the relentless stream of water pouring down the lens. The headphones hissed again, and Cash looked up.

"Our diver says it appears to be some sort of plastic is tied around the tongue."

"Jesus," Bone said.

"In more ways than one," Cash replied. "The next stage is to gather as much forensic detail as we can, though to be honest, anything that was there would have been washed away a thousand times over by that bloody waterfall. Then we'll get the body back to the mortuary for a deep dive, so to speak."

"What's all that foam over there?"

"At first I thought it was summer algae, but that weird, creamy yellow colour suggests something a little bit more man-made and chemical. We'll take samples and have them analysed for contamination."

"The water is so red this year," Walker added.

"Yes, just to add a little more drama to our gruesome job. It really does shake your faith in humanity when a community loses one of its good guys." Cash sighed.

"You knew Richard Jones?"

"He taught my daughter. She practically worshipped the guy during her schooling, and he was the reason she went on to study Environmental Science. He's a local hero."

"Tragic," Walker said.

"Sometimes I think that the war with evil has been lost and we are at the mercy of very dark forces indeed," Cash's brows dropped into a deep frown.

"Okay, Andrew, thank you very much. And you'll let us know as soon as you have any more?" Bone interjected, recognising Cash's signature dark turn.

"Milton was right, our paradise was lost before it was found." Cash bemoaned.

"We'll leave you to it then," Bone said and left Cash, staring at the ground in brooding contemplation.

"Let's get back. This place is giving me the creeps," Bone said and he and Walker headed up the path.

ELEVEN

As Mullens drove through the gates of Kilwinnoch Academy, memories of his troubled school days flooded in, and his heart sank deeper into his chest. A couple of kids stepped out in front of the pool car, and he slammed on the brakes. The two boys turned and in unison gave him the finger. Mullens smiled.

"Not a lot changed here, then," he muttered and carried on. He pulled into one of the visitor parking bays and climbed out.

Two more kids approached him.

"Are you the paedo catcher?" one sneered.

The other sniggered.

"No, I'm your worst nightmare, beat it!" Mullens growled.

But the kids just laughed.

"Dweeb," the first one snarled.

"Mr Thomson and Mr Hutchens!" a voice bellowed across the playground.

Mullens turned. Mrs Haywood, the head, stood at the top of the entrance steps, scowling at the two boys.

"Get to your classes, now! Or would you prefer my office?" she barked.

The boys shrugged and huffed, then retreated around the side of the school building.

"Sorry about that," Mrs Haywood said.

"DS Mullens. He flashed his lanyard.

"Yes, I've been expecting you. I'm Mrs Haywood, the head. Come on in."

Mullens followed her through the front door into the oak-panelled foyer, barely changed since he was at school. He shuddered.

Mrs Haywood unlocked her office door. "I have it on good authority that you studied here."

"Aye, that's right, but I don't think I did much studying," Mullens replied.

She ushered Mullens into her office. "Take a seat."

Mullens scanned the room. Aside from a few plants and some soft furnishings, the head's office was pretty much exactly how he remembered it. In his third and fourth years, he must have spent more time in there than in the classroom. He dropped down onto the chair opposite the desk and immediately felt as though he was in trouble.

"It's such a terrible thing. We are all so worried for Richard. Do you have any more news?" Mrs Haywood asked.

"Nothing yet, I'm afraid."

"Oh dear. You can't help but fear the worst." He lips tightened.

"Could you fill me in on Mr Jones's movements leading up to his disappearance?" Mullens asked, moving things along.

"Yes, of course. Although, I already spoke with one of your colleagues earlier this week."

"The smallest of things can often lead to a breakthrough." Mullens removed a notebook from his suit pocket.

"Indeed. Well, he was at work on the Wednesday," the head continued.

"The twentieth of June, is that correct?"

"Yes."

"How was he that day?"

"I didn't actually see him. I mean, I saw him in our morning briefing. We have a ten-minute all-staff catch-up every day. He was at the back, as usual, head down, probably on his phone. But aside from that, I didn't speak to him."

"And" —Mullens's stomach let out a loud, lingering rumble, like an approaching thunderstorm— "he taught as usual all day, that day?" he pressed on trying to ignore his hunger pangs.

"Yes, that's right."

"So, when did you first learn he was missing?"

"Thursday during the briefing. I noticed he wasn't there, assumed he was late."

"Was he often late?"

"Rarely, so it did register with me. Then about ten minutes into lessons, his colleague, Mr Morton, came and told me Richard wasn't in class."

"What did you do?"

"Aside from arranging cover, nothing. To be honest, I was so busy, once I knew his classes were covered, it went out of my head."

"And all of the other teachers in his department were in as usual?"

"Yes, of course. I mean, one out is bad enough, but to have a second from the same department would be catastrophic."

"Then what about the Friday?"

"Well, it really wasn't like him to not call in sick, so I asked Margaret to ring his home and find out what was going on."

"Margaret?" Mullens interrupted.

"Margaret Wilson, our school secretary. But she couldn't get a hold of him."

"What did you do next?"

"About an hour later, I phoned him this time, but again, no reply."

"Did this worry you at all at this point?" Mullens asked.

"Well, yes. It really wasn't like him. Even when he was going through a very complicated divorce, he never let his emotional turmoil affect his work. He's one of our star teachers, well-loved by all the pupils, even some of the more challenging ones."

"So what happened next?"

"Well, during the lunch hour, Mr Morton went over to his house to check everything was okay. Richard wasn't there, and his milk deliveries were still on the doorstep."

"Friday the twenty-second?"

"Yes, and then I believe Dawn—that's Dawn Chalmers, another of Richard's colleagues in the Geography Department—called Richard's ex-wife, but she hadn't heard from him in weeks. That's when I rang the police."

"Does this ex-wife live in Kilwinnoch?"

"No, she emigrated to Canada shortly after their separation."

"Okay, that's good. Thank you. Could I now have…?" Mullens's gut growled loudly again, ending in a high-pitched whistle, like an over-boiling kettle. "I'm so sorry, Miss…er, Mrs Haywood. My wife has put me on a diet, and to be honest, I don't think it's agreeing with me." He pulled a face.

"It'll be worth it in the end, Detective." Mrs Haywood glanced down at his hefty bulk squeezed into the chair. "I find Cup a Soups take the edge off the urge to comfort binge."

"Liquidised sawdust." Mullens grimaced.

The head smiled and checked her watch. "The break is just about—" A loud bell sounded outside the office, interrupting her. "Right now. I'll take you down to the Geography Department's staffroom."

They both stood.

"Asparagus is tolerable," the head said and led Mullens out.

As they went deeper into the school, classroom doors simultaneously flew open, and a tsunami of pupils rushed out, shouting, screaming, laughing, and punching each other. The head ploughed on through, the kids jumping out of her way, like Moses parting the Red Sea. Mullens followed in her wake.

At the end of the corridor, they took the stairs. The first floor seemed even noisier and more frenetic. A memory flashed through Mullens's head of a screaming boy, dangling upside down outside one of the windows and Mullens holding on to his ankles, laughing and playfully threatening to drop him.

"Mark Mullens!" a voice bellowed above the din.

Mullens spun around, expecting a thump round the ear. At the far end of the corridor, he spotted a grey-haired man in a dishevelled suit. Mullens smiled nervously and waved.

"Mr Gunyon, how are you?" Mullens approached his childhood nemesis. "I didn't recognise you without your gown."

"Sadly, no longer standard issue, Mark," Mr Gunyon replied. "I must say, you've filled out. I don't think I'd be able to reach that ear of yours anymore," he quipped.

"Sorry about all the grief I gave you," Mullens said, almost ending with a 'sir'.

"Well, you've turned out all right in the end, so we must have done something right. So what are you now?"

"Detective Sergeant." Mullens resisted adding a 'sir' to the end.

"And to think you once nearly set fire to the school," Gunyon joked.

The head glanced over at Mullens in surprise.

"So, Mr Gunyon was your history teacher, Detective Mullens?"

"Yes, taught me a few lessons, that's for sure," Mullens joked nervously.

A wry smile cracked across Gunyon's face.

Just then a boy ran past, clipping the history teacher's side on the way past.

"Walk, you imbecile!" Gunyon roared, sending another shiver down Mullens's spine.

The kid instantly slowed and cowered into the wall as though to protect himself from further verbal blows.

"And tuck your shirt in!" Gunyon added.

The boy grabbed at his shirttails and almost fell over as he frantically rammed them into his trousers.

"We're three days away from the end of term, so the demob madness has landed," the head said. "This way, Detective." She carried on down the corridor.

"Good to see you, Mark," Mr Gunyon said.

"Likewise, I think," Mullens winked.

Before he could follow her, the history teacher grabbed his arm. "You should talk to some of these wee feral toerags. You turned yourself around and you might just save a few from Borstal or worse."

Mullens winced. "Oh, I don't know if these walls could take much more of me."

"Think about it. You're an inspiration," Gunyon added with a hint of a sentimental tear in his eye.

"Och, away with you," Mullens replied, feeling moved by his old teacher's belated affection.

He extended his hand, and they shook briskly.

"See you later, Gorgon heid."

"Insolent boy!" Gunyon barked back.

"Richard's colleagues should all be in here," the head said when Mullens caught up with her.

She opened a door marked *Staffroom*, and they stepped inside. It was cluttered with books and papers lying scattered and piled up on a large table in the centre.

At the back, two teachers sat on a couple of tatty old armchairs, clutching steaming mugs. One of the pair, a late-middle-aged, mop-haired, thin-as-a-rake woman in a woollen cardigan tried to balance a teetering custard slice between her fingers. When she saw the head and Mullens come in, the end of the cake dropped from her hand and landed in her lap. Mullens's eyes fixed on the remains of the slice, still dangling from the teacher's fingers, too close for comfort. The second teacher, a fit-looking man sporting an Edwardian-style beard and rolled-up sleeves, sat upright and put his mug down. By the back wall, a younger teacher was on his knees, rummaging in an adjacent fridge.

"Good afternoon, everyone," the head said.

All conversation stopped, and the teachers turned.

"Sorry to interrupt your break. This is DS Mullens from Kilwinnoch Police Station. He's here to ask you a few questions about Richard." She went over to the table. "Who's marking is this?" She scowled at the chaos before her.

"Sorry, that's mine." The young teacher dashed over from the fridge and bundled up the array of books and papers. "I was just in the middle of it," he added.

"You need to stay organised, Mr Morton. We've talked about this many times."

"Sorry," the teacher replied, his face flushed with embarrassment.

"Could we bring a few chairs over for the detective, please?" the head instructed.

The teachers put down their drinks and snacks and shuffled over.

"Afternoon, folks. I won't keep you too long," Mullens assured them.

"You have…" The head checked her watch. "Seven minutes before the next bell, Detective."

"Okay, so I believe an officer from the station may have already interviewed you, but as we proceed with our investigation, we need to be sure we've turned over every stone."

"We're all so worried, Detective," the middle-aged teacher said.

Mullens spotted a tiny dollop of cream clinging to the corner of her mouth.

"We are working day and night on this. Rest assured, we'll find him one way or another," he said and then instantly wished the ground would open up for him to jump in.

"What do you mean?" asked the ruddy-faced teacher, clicking his neck loudly.

Mullens noticed he leaned to one side, his left shoulder down.

"The search is intense and ongoing," Mullens replied. "Could I just take your names for my notes?" He glanced over at the older teacher. "You must be —"

"Mark Mullens," the older teacher interrupted. "I remember you. You were that wee troublemaker in 1F."

Mullens studied her alarmed expression. "Miss Chalmers! I thought I recognised the name." He feared where this was heading.

"You're the one who put the kipper in my handbag," she said with a stern stare.

The others joined in.

"And superglued my hand to the classroom door handle." she continued.

Mullens raised his hands in submission. "Miss Chalmers, I can't begin to apologise for my behaviour."

"The fire crew that released me thought it was hilarious," she added.

Mullens was about to apologise again when the old teacher giggled.

"Don't worry," she said, "it's all in the past. But please call me Dawn."

"Aye, of course…Miss… er, Dawn. So you must have worked with Mr Jones a good wee while then?"

"Ooft. Must be seven or possibly even eight years. He is such a lovely, lovely man." Her smile tumbled, and her eyes welled up.

"And when did you last see Mr Jones?"

She hesitated for a moment. "Same as everyone else, I would think," she said, finally. "Last Wednesday."

"And how was he when you saw him?"

"He seemed fine to me. Just his usual positive, happy, energetic self. In the morning break, I asked him about his divorce and how that was going, but he just rolled his eyes. He didn't like talking about his private life much."

Mullens turned to the ruddy-faced teacher. "And you?"

"Brandon Kinross," the man said. He twisted his head again until the bone let out another loud *crack*. "I've worked with Richard for six years, and to be honest, I don't really remember when I last saw him." He cracked his neck again. "Me and Richard have very different perspectives on life, so we don't really mix in the staffroom much. He was a great guy, though, don't get me wrong." A frown tugged at his eyebrows.

"So, did you have a lot of disagreements, then?" Mullens probed.

"Well..." The teacher laughed. "We're both very forthright in our views, put it that way, and neither of us likes to lose arguments. I mean, aside from our world views that are poles apart, I think we're actually quite alike."

"Like squabbling siblings?" Mullens asked.

"Not quite, but close to that I suppose, yes."

"I hear you're both keen photographers, is that right?"

"Yes, that's a passion we both share."

"And does that rivalry extend to your photographic skills?"

"Oh yes, but don't get me wrong, it's all friendly, and we keep each other on our toes, push each other's capabilities."

"And does Mr Jones get annoyed when you win competitions you've both entered?"

"Furious," Kinross attempted to joke. "But all light-hearted stuff."

"You have two minutes left, Detective," the head interrupted.

Mullens quickly scanned through his notes. "So you must be Oliver Morton," he asked the young teacher, who still seemed to be reeling from his reprimand from the head.

"Yes, that's right, though call me Oli," the teacher replied. "Only my mother still calls me Oliver, usually when she's telling me off about something."

"So how long have you worked with Richard?"

"Three years, or four, if you count my teacher training. I was assigned to Richard's class for my placement. He was an amazing tutor. This was my second placement, and I'd had an awful time on the first. I was on the brink of giving up, but he gave me the confidence and will to carry on."

"Would you say you're friends with Richard?"

"Oh yes, most definitely."

"And it was you who alerted the head about his disappearance?"

"That's right. It just wasn't like him to not turn up for work like that. If he was going to be off sick, he'd always call in. He'd never want to let anyone down, especially the kids."

"Where did you do your first placement?"

"At Spring Park High."

"Tough gig." Mullens grimaced.

The bell suddenly sounded.

"I'm afraid that's the end of the break." The head jumped in. "You're going to have to let the teachers get back to their classes, Detective."

"Okay, no worries. But if you think of anything, no matter how small or seemingly irrelevant, give the station a call and ask for me, Detective Mullens."

The teachers nodded and, picking up bags and books and various teaching apparatus, they filed out of the staffroom.

"Thanks, Mrs Haywood. You and your team have been very helpful." Mullens followed the head out.

"We're all desperate to find Richard, Detective," the head said. "And I'll keep my eyes and ears open here for any more information that might help your search."

"Thanks again."

"I'll take you back to the front door," she added.

"Aye, that would be great. Before I land myself in detention or worse," he joked.

Out in the fresh air, Mullens sighed with relief to be free of the walls once more and climbed back into his car. He was about to reverse out when he spotted

Miss Chalmers running down the entrance steps towards the car. She ran over and rapped on the driver's window.

"Could I have a word?" She glanced nervously back at the school building.

"Aye, sure, shall we go back in or…?" Mullens started.

"No, no, in private," she replied.

Mullens leaned over and opened the passenger door. She got in and sat for a moment, staring ahead.

"What can I do for you, Miss… er, Dawn?" Mullens prompted.

"Sorry, this is quite difficult." She sniffed.

"Just take your time, it's okay."

"I just couldn't sit there and say nothing. It wouldn't be right," she started chewing at her lower lip.

"About what?"

"The dinner party," she said finally.

"The what?" Mullens quizzed.

"It was one of the last times we all saw Richard outside of work. He invited us all round to his to celebrate the end of the year. We take turns, and it was his this year."

"You mean the Geography Department?"

"Yes, the three of us and, of course, Richard, who was the host."

"So what happened?"

"It all started so well. Richard had made some canapés that had gone horribly wrong. He might be a local hero round here, but he's a terrible cook. So we were all having a laugh about that."

"And then?"

"We all got so drunk. It's been a really tough year, tough kids, you know?"

"Oh aye, I do know." Mullens smirked.

"I think we were just so relieved to make it out alive…" She stopped. "Oh, I didn't mean…"

"That's okay, go on," Mullens pressed.

"We were having a nice time, but then things went downhill when Oli brought up that stupid photo competition that Richard and Bran enter every year."

"You call him Bran?" Mullens interrupted, and his gut let out a loud rumble. "Excuse me, carry on."

"To be honest with you, Oli is a bit of a shit-stirrer, for want of a better expression."

Mullens glanced over, surprised by the swear word coming out of his former teacher's mouth.

"Anyhow, as predicted, an argument ensued, as it always does. And Bran, well, he's not much better. He's so competitive, he won't leave anything alone until he's won."

"So what happened during this argument?"

"Ach, men!" she exclaimed. "They ended up outside. I couldn't believe it. I tried to calm things down, but they were so drunk it was pointless. Next thing, they're both rolling about on the front lawn, trying to knock lumps out of each other. But honestly, I've seen five-year-olds with better fighting skills than those two."

"And what were you and Mr Morton doing while all this was going on?

"I was screaming like a fishwife for them to stop." She paused. "I'm so embarrassed."

"Listen, I superglued your hand to the classroom door, so I win on that front," Mullens reassured her. "And what about Mr Morton?"

"He was jumping about like a madman, goading them on. If I'm honest he was behaving like a nasty little child." She dropped her head into her hands. "It was just so awful, I mean, even the neighbours came out, and in the end, Richard was so upset, he just told everyone to go, and then we left."

"And that was the end of it, or did the argument continue the next day?"

"Richard and Bran never mentioned it again, and they seemed to be on speaking terms the next day, at least professionally anyway. It was only Oli who kept going on about it. In the end, I told him just to leave it." She took another deep breath. "I know Richard thinks very highly of him, but I just don't like him and I never have."

"And has anything else happened since?"

"Only that Oli and Bran tried to talk me into not saying anything to you about that night."

"Did they say why? I mean, that's what you call withholding evidence."

"I really don't know, and I was so worried about it for that very reason."

"Thanks, Dawn," Mullens said.

"I don't want to get anyone into any kind of trouble," she added. "But I wasn't going to let them pressure me into not saying anything."

"Well, you did the right thing."

She opened the door. "I hope Richard is okay."

"We do, too," Mullens replied.

She climbed out slammed the door.

Mullens quickly backed out of the car park and headed down the drive to the front entrance and freedom.

TWELVE

Back at his flat, Bone dropped his bag in the hallway and picked up a pile of mail scattered beneath the letterbox. As he quickly rifled through, a memory-flash of the Peek-a-boo horror flicked across his mind. In the kitchen, he dropped the bills and junk ads on the modest kitchen table tucked in by the window and opened a cupboard. Aside from a tin of condensed milk and a packet of Ritz crackers, it was bare. He shook his head.

"Why?" he muttered. He couldn't even remember buying the condensed milk. Maybe it had always been there and he'd inherited it from a previous tenant.

Glancing over at the fridge, he spotted his son's art decorating the door. The drawing at the top showed a police car with a Picasso-like three-armed Bone standing next to it, clutching what looked like a large lollipop but was probably a rifle. Next to Bone, Michael had drawn his mum with her hands aloft, either in celebration or surrender.

He searched his jacket pocket for his phone and opened his contacts. His finger hovered over Alice's number. One of the conditions of his fortnightly access was that he wouldn't hassle his ex-wife in between. But two weeks often felt like half a lifetime, and the pain of separation from both of them was unbearable at times. He was about to press the button when his phone screamed to life.

"Jesus!" he cried out in surprise, and he answered. "DS Baxter, good evening."

"Sorry to disturb you after work, sir," Baxter replied. "It's just that I hoped to catch you before the end of the day,"

"Aye, it took us longer than expected up at the falls."

"How did it go up there?" she asked.

"It's definitely Jones."

"Well, that's just bloody terrible."

"Tragic," Bone replied. "What did you need to speak to me about?"

"Oh, yes. I've been doing a bit of digging and discovered that there's an osprey nest about three miles north of the falls."

"And?"

"There's a team from the Bird Sanctuary Association up there guarding the nest, the exact location is strictly under wraps. I spoke to the team leader to check if they'd seen anyone in the area around the time Jones went missing. They told me that they'd reported seeing two men too close for comfort to the nest."

"Two men?"

"That's what they said."

"And did you check with the coppers who attended?"

"Of course," Baxter confirmed. "The BSA team leader reported that their intelligence sources—"

"The Bird Sanctuary Association uses intelligence sources?" Bone said in surprise.

"It threw me, too, for a moment, but apparently there's a lucrative black market in rare bird eggs, kidnapping and all sorts. Stuffed and mounted birds of prey are all the rage with the Russian Mafia, apparently."

"What did the Sanctuary say?"

"So their sources told them that two notorious rare bird egg thieves were in the area."

"Do they have names?"

"They do. The Springsteen brothers."

"Seriously?"

"David and Robert Springsteen. They are not local."

"New Jersey?" Bone joked.

"Not quite. Newcastle. The officer who attended said he warned the team to be very careful as the brothers have a history of violence, and police records confirm a long, sorry story."

"Okay. I'll go and speak to the BSA team in the morning. Thanks for your hard work today."

"No problem. Have a good evening, sir." Baxter hung up.

Bone rubbed his forefinger up and down the scar running the length of his temple and into his hairline. Retreating to the living room, he headed over to his old Dansette record player resting on top of a Sixties-style, fake mahogany side unit. Kneeling, he opened the smoked-glass door and flicked through a rack of LPs lined up inside. He picked one out and examined the front.

Herb Albert's *A Taste of Honey* was written in psychedelic font across the top and beneath, a semi-naked girl emerged from a giant cream cake, with dollops of cream strategically placed to cover her modesty. Bone shook his head, pushed the album back into the collection, and tried again.

This time his finger stopped at *G for Dexter Gordon* and plucked out the LP. The cover image was a moody deep-blue-and-crimson shot of the jazz saxophonist standing under a streetlamp. His sax rested in one arm while he held a cigarette in the other, thin trail of smoke snaking towards the night sky. The image instantly relaxed Bone. He removed the record, popped it on the Dansette's turntable, and set the needle down.

With a crackle and a gentle hiss, the soft, melodious tone of the sax wafted into the living room. Bone slumped down in an armchair and let out a long, weary sigh. The last three or four months had been very quiet at work with only a couple of investigations that had turned out to be false starts. He was feeling a little out of form and short of pace, but he'd get there. He always did.

He closed his eyes and let the music pass into and through him. A faint whisper jolted him from the edge of sleep. He opened his eyes. The creature, his PTSD hallucinatory companion for the last three years since his injury, was within a hair's breadth of his face. He sat back in shock. The monster's disfigured, rotting skull twisted closer to him.

"Loser," the creature hissed. A sneer stretched across an exposed jaw bone, revealing a gaping hole in the creature's cheek.

Bone threw a punch, but the apparition seemed to swerve and bend to avoid contact with his fist.

"Loser," it repeated.

Bone jumped out of his chair and swung again. "Fuck off!" he hollered, his arms flying left and right.

The creature retreated to the farthest corner of the room.

"You're the fucking loser. You died. I live." Bone picked up a book resting on the table by his chair and lobbed it with force at the ghost.

The book passed straight through the creature's black coat, clattering off the wall and dropping to the floor. With a final sneer, the Peek-a-boo apparition flicked a black hood over its head, melted into the wall, and disappeared.

"Jesus," Bone puffed, his heart pounding. He stumbled through to the bathroom and splashed cold water on his face and ran his wrists under the tap until his pulse slowed back to normal. He glanced in the mirror. The fear was still visible in his eyes.

Will I ever be free of this monster?

His head pounded, the plate in his skull pressing against his temple. He pushed the ball of his hand against the front of his head. Searching the cabinet, he snatched at a bottle of painkillers—a new lot, recently prescribed by his GP—popped a couple, and gulped down mouthfuls of water straight from the tap. He staggered through to the bedroom, dropped onto the bed, and after a few minutes of tossing and turning, snakes alive in his limbs, he finally plunged into a deep, drug-induced sleep.

THIRTEEN

The next morning, the press clustered at the bottom of the station steps. Bone sighed as he pulled up outside. His head still pounded from the night before, and a barrage of questions was the last thing he needed.

He climbed out, and was instantly besieged by film crews, photographers flashing their cameras in his face, and manic reporters clutching oversized mics. He spotted McKinnon trying to force his way through the mob.

"Is it true a body was found at Blood Water Falls?"

Bone recognised that voice—McKinnon.

"Is it Richard Jones?"

"No comment." Sighing, Bone quickly leapt up the steps and through the double doors. The proverbial cat was definitely out of the bag.

"Mornin', sir," Brody said. "I take it you've met the welcoming party?"

Bone moaned and rubbed his head.

"Bloody hell, what were you on last night? That looks like some hangover you're nursing," Brody added.

"I wish. Migraine." Bone grimaced.

"I've got some ibuprofen somewhere in here." The desk sergeant rummaged in a cabinet beneath his desk.

"No, you're all right. I'm loaded with pain relief. If I take any more, this job will become bearable," Bone replied and headed through the security door to the incident room.

The whole team had assembled and waited for his arrival.

"Oh, dear God, you look even worse than I feel this morning, sir." Mullens jumped in first. "Are you sure you shouldn't be down in the morgue?"

"Funny. How's the diet going?"

"Fine, easy-peasy lemon squeezy." Mullens shook his head. "Oh, now there's a thought. A big fuck-off slice of lemon drizzle cake." He attempted to lick his cracked lips. "Oh, dear God, this is fucking torture. I'd rather jet wash my bowels with Listerine than suffer this torment any longer."

"You're looking better for it, though," Harper said with one of his eternally optimistic smiles.

Mullens frowned at him. "Is that supposed to be funny? The two week I spent in Tenerife with dysentery was more fun than this."

Bone went over to the coffee percolator. As expected, it was completely drained of all caffeine. "Buggeration," he muttered.

"I'll go and get some more, sir," Harper offered.

"Oh God, please don't send hop-along. By the time he gets back, we'll be comatose," Mullens said.

"Okay, everyone, listen up," Bone interrupted. "So yesterday, the SOC team found the naked body of Richard Jones, nailed the to the wall behind the falls.

"When you say nailed?" Baxter asked.

"His arms outstretched in a crucifix position with two metal spikes driven through his hands."

"Jesus." Baxter winced.

"Indeed," Bone said. "There were clear head injuries, but also something rammed into his mouth."

"I don't suppose we know the cause of death yet?" Harper asked.

"We're waiting for SOC to come back with more and for the man in black to cut him open." Bone leaned back on the desk behind him, his head gently spinning. "So we'll need to act quickly now before the hyenas get wind of this. Where are we up to so far?"

"I've made a start on the incident board, sir," Baxter said.

Bone glanced over at the wall, and Richard Jones's talking head glared back at him.

"I found out something very interesting up at the school," Mullens cut in.

"Hold on, Mark." Bone stopped him. "Sheila continue."

Mullens huffed.

"Right, so, I spoke to you last night, sir, about the Springsteen brothers." Baxter continued.

"The who?" Mullens interrupted again.

"David and Robert Springsteen are two of the UK's most infamous bird of prey thieves."

"Are they Scottish? I mean, where were they born?" Mullens asked.

Bone raised his hand. "Don't even bother, Mullens. It's too obvious."

"There's an osprey nest approximately three miles from the murder site," Baxter carried on. "The nest is in a secret location and being guarded twenty-four-seven by the…" She stopped, reached back across her desk, and picked up her notepad. "The Campsie Fells Bird Sanctuary. They reported that the Springsteen brothers were spotted by a member of their team in Kilwinnoch High Street, four days before Jones was reported missing."

"When Mullens and I interviewed some local travellers up at the Kilmorgan Stones, one of the girls said they saw two men on the hillside on Wednesday night, solstice eve, though she wasn't sure if they were together or one was following the other," Bone added. "Anything else?"

"Well, I did a bit of digging around the victim's private life, and it would appear he had quite a few enemies. He was an active environmental campaigner and a member of Ramblers."

"Right, that's it. I'm not paid enough to be messing with the Ramblers. They are totally mental," Mullens said, half seriously.

"Pretty fearless folks, and spot-on when it comes to keeping megalomaniac landowners and big business in its place." Walker said.

"Jones had been involved in a couple of campaigns. One to open up the public path between Castle Bank and Braeburn Falls." Baxter resumed.

"The path that runs straight through the Monklands' farm?" Bone asked.

"That's correct, yes. And the Ramblers have reported a number of altercations between themselves and the Monkland family, or the father, that is."

"No surprises there," Bone smirked.

"However." Baxter raised her hand. "Before we all get overexcited about a significant lead here, I checked up on the Monklands' movements around the time of the victim's disappearance,"

"And?" Bone asked impatiently.

"The date coincides with the Highland Show in Perth, and the Monklands had two prize bulls up for medals, and they won. So they have an alibi as tight as a drill sergeant's drum."

"Drill sergeants don't have drums," Mullens interjected. "Can I speak now, sir?"

"Just hold up a minute, Detective," Bone insisted. "No way one of them could have slipped out and…?"

"Very tenuous indeed, and highly improbable, sorry."

"So what was the second campaign Jones was involved in?"

"That was to do with the rising levels of pollution present in the river. Jones was also involved in a campaign to expose alleged waste disposal issues at Grinlay's Pie Factory, about eight miles upstream."

"There you go again, Baxter. I've warned you once already about mentioning food, and I'm not afraid to use pepper spray if necessary," Mullens complained.

"I wish you'd just go and get something to eat, Mark," Baxter grumbled back. "You're driving me nuts."

"Anything else?" Bone tried to keep them on topic.

"He was in communication with our local MP about this issue." She waved for Bone to approach her desk. "He wrote an open letter that was published in our beloved local rag."

Baxter sat back down at her desk and tapped at her keyboard. The screen flashed on, and a screenshot of Jones's letter appeared, commanding top spot on the *Chronicle's* letters page. Alongside the correspondence were two pictures, the first the same teacher personnel shot of Jones in his shirt and tie, dressed for battle, and the second an image of a muddy riverbank with two dead trout lying side by side.

Bone ran his finger up and down the scar on his temple. "Okay, thanks." He turned to Will. "Any more on Jones's movements the day he disappeared?"

"For God's sake..." Mullens whined again.

"Just wait a second, Mullens. I won't tell you again!" Bone snapped.

Mullens folded his arms like the errant schoolboy he used to be.

"I ran checks on all CCTV footage out of Kilwinnoch station on the twentieth of June," Harper replied. "And also all footage between here and Carrbridge."

"Bloody hell, that's good going, Will," Walker said.

"Well, I'm using a facial recognition kit which speeds things up."

"Found anything yet?" Bone asked.

"Confirmation that Jones boarded the last train to Carrbridge at ten twenty-nine p.m. on June twentieth. But then the software picked him up getting off at the next stop shortly after departure at Cromer."

"You mean that godforsaken excuse for a station in the middle of nowhere?"

"That's the one, yes."

"And did he catch a train back to Kilwinnoch?"

"Too late, the last one back to Glasgow Queen Street had already gone through. Footage caught him leaving the station, so he must have legged it back and then possibly carried on up to Braeburn Falls."

"And what time did he leave Cromer?"

"The CCTV footage records indicate ten forty-one, twelve minutes after departure from Kilwinnoch."

"And no one else got on or off?"

"One moment, sir," Harper said and returned to his desk.

Bone joined him.

"The app picked up footage of a second passenger getting off the train." Harper fiddled with his keyboard, and his screen came to life. "I've copied this extract from the hours of footage to show you, but I warn you, it's quite short and the quality is pretty poor." He pressed play, and a grainy black-and-white image of Cromer Train Station appeared.

Bones stared at the screen for a few seconds. "Is this actually moving?"

"Wait," Harper said.

The grey roof of a train appeared at the bottom of the screen. It pulled into the station, and moments later a figure descended onto the platform, walked towards the camera, turned towards the station building, and disappeared off-screen.

"So the app has confirmed that this is Jones." Harper tapped the screen.

A few moments later, a second figure appeared, from a carriage at the opposite end of the platform and walked up the platform. The figure appeared to be wearing an anorak with the hood up.

"Unfortunately, this passenger has their back to the camera."

The figure paused, then followed Jones through the exit and out of the station.

"And there's no other footage?" Bone asked.

"No, that's it."

"Bugger," Bone cursed.

"It could be perfectly innocent. Maybe a farmer returning from the pub," Harper added.

"Indeed, or it could be something more sinister. I mean, would a farmer bother with a hood?"

"I'll keep digging around for more footage and see if I can get an ID on this character."

"Good work, Will." Bone smiled at his young colleague.

"Sir," Harper replied.

"And has the SOC team recovered the USB that Walker found behind the bath?"

"Yes, along with Jones's laptop." Harper confirmed.

"But no phone?"

"No sign of it. I was just about to go down to digital forensics and give them a hand." Harper smiled.

"Yes, please. Might shave a few weeks off our investigation," Bone joked. "Baxter, I hope you're clocking all this to put on the board?" He turned. "Baxter?"

"She's gone for her morning hit, sir," Mullens said. "Or should I say, her third hit of the morning."

"Says, Holier Than Thou Calorie Counter in the Smug Corner," Walker countered.

Bone turned to Mullens. "Right, Mark. Your turn now. Spit it out."

"Finally." Mullens sighed. "So I was up at my old school interviewing Jones's colleagues, and there wasn't much to report. Aside from Jones, nobody else was AWOL the day after he went missing. They all seemed pretty shaken up and worried, including me. Jesus, it was bloody terrifying going back in there. It was a sharp reminder of the bloody toe rag I was when…"

"Mullens," Bone cut him off.

"Sorry, but then on my way out, my old teacher, Miss Chalmers, accosted me in the car park and told me that there had been a fight between Jones and one of the other teachers at his house during their end-of-term bash."

"What sort of fight, physical?" Bone asked.

"I think so, aye. The other teacher involved was another photographer, Brandon Kinross. Miss Chalmers said that a third teacher, a younger one, was stirring it and made things worse."

"That's pretty significant. Why the hell didn't you say something earlier?" Bone winked.

"Funny, haha!" Mullens threw his arms up.

"So we'll need to reinterview the teachers, probably better in their own homes and separately," Bone said.

"You don't want to bring them in?" Walker asked.

"At this stage, no. We're running a delicate balance here, and these people have reputations. If the press got wind of us sniffing around, they'd have a field day."

"Fair point," Walker agreed.

"First things first," Bone continued, "Mullens, get yourself up to Cromer station and speak to staff up there."

"It's in the middle of bloody nowhere, sir," Mullens complained. "There's never anyone around."

"Well, just check, okay?" Bone was losing patience with him. "Then on your way back, swing past Grinlay's and see what Mr Grinlay has to say for himself—"

"Are you actually trying to do me in?" Mullens exclaimed in disbelief.

"It did cross my mind, yes." Bone nodded enthusiastically.

"Aw, sir, please don't send me there. Send Baxter. She hates pies."

Bone tutted.

"Sir, I'll do anything, anything at all. But not that."

"Great song," Harper said, his smile widening.

"You go, Will, please?" Mullens begged. "I'm not sure I'll be able to control my primal urges."

"Nothing new there then," Harper joked.

"No, DS Mullens. I want you to go, end of," Bone ordered.

Mullens returned to his desk, muttering.

"Will, keep digging around in the footage and maybe check nearby farms and rail staff. See if they have anything more for us on this mysterious stalker."

"Should we put out an appeal for witnesses?" Harper asked. "Quite a few early commuters got on at Kilwinnoch. They might have clocked something."

"Let's give ourselves the morning for a head start on the vultures. We'll see where we are and then deal with the teachers, clear?"

"Sir," the team replied, with Mullens's quiet acknowledgement following behind.

"And when Baxter gets back, tell her to keep digging into Jones's backstory."

Harper nodded and returned to his desk.

"Walker, you're with me," Bone said.

"Where are we going?"

"To see a man about a bird," Bone said, adding, "of an endangered variety."

On the way out, Walker caught Bone's arm. "Are you okay?" she asked quietly. "You don't look too good."

"Aw, thanks, you say the nicest things to me." Bone forced a smile. "I need a cup of coffee, to be honest."

"And something to eat," Walker replied. "I thought you were going to keel over in there. When's the last time you ate anything?"

"Aside from half a can of condensed milk this morning? Not sure. But I'm fine."

"Right, that's it. I'm driving, no arguments. Breakfast, my shout."

Bone shrugged, too weak to argue, and followed Walker out the back door of the station to the row of pool cars parked up at the rear of the staff car park.

FOURTEEN

The tumbledown café on the banks of Braeburn Loch was busier than the detectives expected, possibly due to a sudden improvement in the weather.

"Out or in?" Walker asked, approaching the ramshackle hut, the inviting smell of bacon wafting out through open windows.

"A little bit of vitamin D would be good," Bone replied. "Over there, look." He pointed to a vacant bench down by the side of the water.

They sat, and moments later, a young woman bedecked in Goth apparel appeared from the shack and approached them.

"What can I get you?" she asked, her thick, black mascara and pale face giving her the appearance of a monochrome starlet from the silent era.

"Good band, that." Walker pointed at the girl's *Mission* T-shirt.

"You know them?" the girl asked, the piercing in her tongue whistling gently as she spoke.

"I used to be a huge fan," Walker enthused.

Bone glanced up in surprise.

"Amazing live," she added.

"Wow. I wish I was old enough to have seen them live in their heyday," the girl said with a smile.

Walker rolled her eyes.

"Where's Craig?" Bone asked.

"He's on holiday. I'm his sister, Jane."

"Nice to meet you, Jane." Walker smiled.

"Where's he gone, Morocco?" Bone joked.

"No, the US, California."

"Ah, that figures. Is he there to pick up some cultivation tips?" Bone pointed at the roof of the shack.

"Sorry?" The girl looked befuddled.

"Ignore him," Walker cut in. "I'll have an Americano, black, no sugar, and one of your fab Danish pastries, please."

Bone who scanned the menu attached to the surface of the table.

"What would you like?" the waitress pressed.

Bone huffed and puffed, then finally he decided. "Just a black coffee, please."

"Oh no, you don't." Walker shook her head. "Eat something."

"Do as your wife says," the girl giggled.

"Oh, he's not my partner. Well, not that kind of partner anyway. We're police colleagues."

"Oh, right. Sorry, it's just you seemed kind of domestic, ken?" the waitress's giggle escalated.

"Ha!" Walker guffawed.

"Okay, I'll have a square sausage breakfast bap, please, and a black coffee." Bone conceded.

"Good choice," the waitress said and returned to the shack.

Bone sat back and took in the view of the reservoir. After a moment, Walker broke the silence.

"So, what's going on with you?" she asked.

"What do you mean?" Bone replied, feigning innocence.

"Oh, come on, you're not eating, probably not sleeping, you look like death without a pulse, and you almost collapsed in the incident room about ten minutes ago. Is your PTSD bad again?"

"Not a lot gets past you. I'm just a little…"

"What?"

"Tired, you know?"

"Tell me." She gently probed.

"I'm finding this whole access thing with Michael a bit tough. Two weeks feels like a bloody lifetime."

"So, it's not Alice you're missing, then?" Walker asked with a wry smile.

"No, of course not." Bone retorted. "Well, it's hard to just stop a relationship dead in its tracks. Sometimes it feels like I've got the bends. That probably sounds daft."

"You've suffered a life-changing injury followed by a life-changing separation. You'd have to be made of granite to come through that without a psychological scratch, never mind the physical damage."

Bone sighed. "I'm just tired of wallowing in my own self-bloody-pity."

The waitress reappeared from the hut carrying a tray of coffees and the Danish. Bone sat back and sighed again.

"Lorne on its way," she said and about-turned.

"Anyway, I'm doing okay and I'll just plough on like I always do. There's no need to worry about me." Bone took a sip from his mug. "Wow, that's good."

"Maybe you should tell Alice how you feel and try to change your visiting rights?"

"Ah, man, I've tried, and she just digs in. Then it gets ugly. It's not worth it." He took another sip. "Anyhow, enough about my pity party, what about you?"

"What about me?" Walker asked.

"You know what I'm talking about."

"Oh yes, that. Well, we finally got the papers through and are now officially on the adoption list."

"What? Oh my God! You've just let me rant on and you're sitting on this fantastic news, Rhona. Congratulations!" He leaned over the table and gave her a slightly awkward hug. "You both must be over the moon. It's taken a while."

"Maddie thought it was never going to happen, but she's so chuffed. We both are."

"So how long will you have to wait?"

"How long is a piece of string? Dunno. It's all a waiting game, and when it's a baby it can take longer."

"You've just made my bloody day, cheers," Bone raised his mug.

Walker clacked hers against the side and they both enjoyed their drinks for a moment.

"So what are your thoughts on this case so far?" Walker asked, finally.

They were interrupted again by the waitress, who dropped Bone's breakfast bap down in front of him.

"Enjoy," she said.

Bone gazed down at the teetering tower of Lorne sausages topped with two fried eggs and a thick river of butter oozing out of the sides.

"Can you imagine what Mullens would make of this?" Bone chuffed.

"He'd actually behead you to get to it."

"I don't even know where to start." He reached around the construction then retreated again.

"Oh, shut up and just shove it into your cakehole," Walker ordered. "It could be a case of wrong place, wrong time for the poor sod," she continued, referring to the case.

Bone held up his hands while he munched his way through a mouthful of the bun.

"Possibly," he mumbled finally and wiped the grease from his mouth.

"Here," Walker said, handing him a napkin.

"But it looks like he was a bit of a troublemaker and has ruffled a few dangerous feathers." He took another bite, his hunger now in full command of his actions.

"Troublemaker for some, hero for others," Walker added.

"This whole local hero thing bothers me."

"Why?" Walker raised her pastry and took a modest bite.

"For one thing, we'll have the whole town all over us, waiting for us to mess up. But this hero-worshipping thing. You just have to consider the mad-as-a-March-hare Tennyson and her obsession with Peek-a-boo to know where that can go."

"Well, yes." Walker nodded.

"I'm afraid to say it." He glanced round, checking that they were out of earshot. "Jones's death could turn out to be a total bloody nightmare for us."

"I think it's already heading that way," Walker replied. "But hey, when is it not a bloody nightmare? That's why we love our jobs, right?" She held up her mug.

"Aye, right, cheers!"

Bone clattered his mug against hers again, and they both laughed.

"Right, let's get up to the bird sanctuary and see what nightmares await us up there." Bone pushed his half-finished bap to the edge of the table.

"Please don't tell me you're done?"

"Stuffed. There's enough there to feed the entire Scottish rugby team."

Walker shook her head "Never mind our jobs, you're the bloody nightmare."

"Tell me about it," Bone agreed and pushed a tenner under the plate.

"Hey, I said it was my shout."

"Consider it a thanks for the chat. You get the next one."

Walker frowned and they headed back to the pool car.

FIFTEEN

The Campsie Fells Bird Sanctuary was located deep into the hills, about two miles north of Carrbridge Point. Walker pulled the car into the modest gravel car park and stopped in front of a large, dome-shaped wooden lodge.

"Looks like something out of *The Hobbit*," Bone commented as they stepped out.

A man in a wax jacket, knee-length walking shorts, and boots appeared on the terrace that encircled the structure. He jumped down the log steps to greet them.

"Inspector Bone?" he said.

"Yes, and this is DI Walker," Bone replied.

Walker nodded.

"I've been expecting you. I'm Don Roxburgh, the sanctuary director." He extended his hand to shake Bone's hand vigorously. "We are all deeply concerned for Richard. He's been a huge champion for us and a lovely man." He paused. "Sorry, come inside."

The detectives followed Roxburgh back up the steps and into the lodge. The interior opened up into an open-plan space that seemed even bigger than the outside structure. The craftsmanship of the internal skeleton was on full display, with huge oak beams extending up from various points on the floor to form the dome shape.

In the centre was a round wood-fired stove with a steel chimney reaching up through a hole in the middle of the dome. Around the outside of the room were posters of wild birds and animals, and display cabinets filled with information and more images of local wildlife. But the most impressive part of the building was a curved bay window that stretched from the floor to the ceiling with a jaw-dropping vista across Carrbridge Point.

Walker went over for a look.

"That's quite a view," she said, staring open-mouthed at the rolling hilltops peeking out above low-lying clouds.

"Yes, it never fails to impress," Roxburgh said. "Have you never visited us before?"

"This is a first for me," Walker replied.

"I should bring my son here. He would love this," Bone added.

"Yes, we do children's talks and wee tours in our Land Rover and trailer. They are very popular." Roxburgh Leaned over the carved oak reception desk behind him, picked up a leaflet and handed it to Bone.

"Thanks," Bone scanned the brochure.

"Carol Banks, our events manager, is in charge of the tours. Her email's on the back."

"I'll sort something out," Bone said and pushed the leaflet into his pocket.

"So shall we go to my office?" Roxburgh offered.

The detectives followed the director through a door at the rear of the dome, into a narrow wooden corridor. This opened out into a second hut with a small desk pushed against a wall at the back, almost overwhelmed by an ancient desktop computer and monitor, and framed by two beige metal filing cabinets.

"Excuse the mess," Roxburgh said. He removed a pile of magazines from a chair and moved it over to his desk. "Could you grab that chair by the door?" He gestured to Walker. "Just drop that file box on the floor. I'll sort it later."

The two detectives squeezed in next to the director's desk. Roxburgh sat and fired up his computer.

"I just wanted to show you some footage we caught on one of the many CCTV cameras we have dotted around the nest." He stopped and glanced up at the duo. "I'm sure you're up to speed with our osprey watch?"

"Yes, and you have reason to believe that there may be thieves operating in the area?" Bone confirmed.

"The Springsteens are not just any old thieves. They are notorious experts in the highly specialist trade of birds of prey, alive or dead, their eggs, and even their chicks." He frowned. "We've been worried for some time that the pair might have discovered the osprey nest. Their eggs can fetch thousands. So we tightened our security, employed more people, and added a few more cameras. These men are seriously nasty, and their clients are even nastier. So it is a worry, to say the least."

"So, this footage?" Bone asked.

"Yes, hold on a sec," the director tapped at his keyboard. He stopped and stared at the monitor for a moment. "Oh, come on." He puffed. "Sorry about this. I'm in serious need of an upgrade." He continued again and then, grabbing the monitor, turned it slightly to allow Bone and Walker to see the screen. "Okay, so this was last Wednesday."

"Twentieth of June?"

"Correct, about ten forty-three p.m. We have a night camera positioned just off Carrbridge Road, about a mile from the osprey site." He hit the play button.

The grainy image showed a narrow lane with steep banks on either side. It was raining, which blurred the image slightly. Bone leaned in and peered at the screen. A car appeared from behind the camera and stopped about ten feet ahead. Two men emerged. One walked round to the boot and, opening it up, removed what appeared to be a rucksack and a long, thin object. The second man joined him. They turned to each other for a moment, and then together, walked back towards the camera. They were both wearing knee-length coats with the collars turned up and flat caps pulled down, obscuring their faces.

"Just about here." The director stabbed at the pause button.

The shaky image caught one of the men glancing up towards the camera, his pale face and pupils glowing brightly in the infrared lens.

"So you think these men are the Springsteens?" Bone squinted at the blurred image again. "It's quite difficult to ID this man."

"Sadly, this face is all too familiar to us. We've been plagued by these characters for years. This is definitely the Springsteens."

"Could we have a copy of the recording?" Walker asked. "Our digital forensics team might be able to clean this up."

"Sure, no problem."

"And do you have any more sightings on video?" Bone continued.

"Unfortunately not . But they are definitely sniffing around. At this stage, we're not sure if they know the exact location of the osprey nest. Even MI5 doesn't know that." His eyes widened.

"So is it far from here? Could we see it?" Bone asked.

"Are you serious?" Roxburgh looked up in surprise.

"Yes, the location may be important in our ongoing investigation."

"Maintaining secrecy is an ongoing war, Inspector Bone. We cannot allow any possibility of the location being leaked. It would probably spell an end to not only the nest and the eggs but would have a huge impact on the entire species and the osprey population in Scotland."

"I thought breeding programmes had been pretty successful?" Walker interrupted.

"You're familiar with bird populations?" the director asked.

"I'm from Lewis and I understand that the Highland osprey's population is on the rise."

"You're from Lewis? I'm from Harris, originally. Hello, neighbour."

"Small world," Walker replied with a smile.

"Though, I moved to Inverness when I was eight, so barely an islander."

"Could we see the nest and its location?" Bone continued.

"Well, if it's going to help find Richard, then yes. But we can't have police swarming all over the area."

"We'll keep it under wraps.," Bone assured. "This is strictly investigation purposes only."

"Okay, let me grab the keys for the Land Rover and I'll drive you over."

"How far is it from here?"

"Fifteen minutes? Just south of our lane, near the Braeburn River."

Bone glanced over at Walker.

"This way," the director said.

They picked their way out of the office, back through the main lodge, and out into the car park.

"Where is everyone?" Walker asked.

"Combination of holidays and osprey watch. We're so paranoid, I've instructed the whole team to join the vigil." The director opened the door on a mud-splattered, canvas-topped, sixties Land Rover.

"This is a nice vehicle," Bone nodded his approval.

Walker shot him a look of total disbelief.

"The boneshaker—you like it?"

"I love it."

"You may not be saying that by the time we get to the nest," the director added, the white of his teeth gleaming through his beard. "I'm afraid one of you will have to climb in the back."

Bone invited Walker to sit up front, and she accepted without argument. The director dropped the hatch on the rear of the Land Rover and helped Bone scramble into the back. Squeezing past a roll of wire fencing and posts, Bone sat on a narrow wooden bench running along the side.

"Right, hold on to your innards. There may be a spot of turbulence shortly." He started up the Land Rover, and with a loud roar and a plume of black smoke, they set off out of the gate and up the lane.

As the ancient vehicle bounced, rattled, and roared down lanes and farm tracks, Bone thumped violently up and down on the hard bench, every blow pummelling his privates like a sledgehammer smashing walnuts. At last, the Land Rover came to an abrupt stop, and Roxburgh climbed out. Bone stumbled to the hatch, and Roxburgh helped him down. He spotted Bone's pale face.

"You okay, Detective?"

"I feel as though I've lost a couple of things in there."

"Ah yes, you'll be singing soprano for the rest of the day," Roxburgh joked. "Right, let me take you down to the hide. This way."

The detectives followed Roxburgh over a stile and across a field by a stream. They cut through a thicket of trees and crossed the stream by a fallen log. Then up the other side of the bank, the Braeburn River appeared ahead. Roxburgh approached a hillock protruding from the side of the slope and, ducking down, rattled on a door tucked into the corner. It opened, and another hairy man stuck his head around.

"We have visitors from Kilwinnoch Police Station," Roxburgh whispered.

The man opened the door wider, and they stepped inside.

The hide was dark and gloomy inside, and it took Bone a moment or two for his eyes to adjust. The construction was similar to that of the lodge, but considerably less finished. Along the front wall, there was a narrow open window running the length of the hide. Three people were propped up on stools, gazing through wide-lensed binoculars resting on tripods attached to the windowsill.

Roxburgh gestured to the first man. "Inspector Bone, this is Fergus McAllister. Fergus is in charge of the hide and coordinating the osprey watch."

"How do," Fergus grunted quietly.

"And this is Detective Walker," Roxburgh added. "They're investigating the disappearance of the geography teacher. I told them about our unwelcome visitors, and so they wanted a quick look at the nest."

"No bother. Would you like to see our wee weans?" Fergus asked them.

McAllister gestured them over to the window. One of the other watchers, a young woman in a khaki shirt, stepped down from her stool.

"Hi," she smiled and shifted out the way.

"This is Doctor Meg Moorcroft," McAllister said. "Meg is our resident behavioural psychologist."

"For the animals, I assume?" Bone said.

"You'd be surprised how similar we are to most living beings," Meg said.

"Except Mullens," Walker added.

"Sorry?" Moorcroft asked.

"So, was it you who spotted the two bird thieves?" Bone continued.

"No, that was Matty." She turned to the watcher at the far end. "Hey, Matt?"

The man spun round, smiled, and jumped down from the platform.

"Matty is probably the world's top expert on ospreys, but please don't tell him I said that." Moorcroft grinned.

"Sorry, I was caught up in a little bit of drama there," Matty said, his thick Liverpool accent rolling around the hide. "I thought the mum was about to push an egg out of the nest. I'm Dr Matt Duckworth, chief ornithologist."

"Oh God, please don't tell me she did," Meg asked expectantly.

"No, she was just trying to turn one and got the measurements wrong." He approached the detectives, rubbing the top of his closely shaved head.

"I do that with IKEA furniture," Walker joked again.

Bone shot her a look. She glanced down at Matt's T-shirt, which was slightly obscured by his black leather waistcoat.

"You like *Runrig*?" she nodded at the ban's logo printed across his chest.

"Oh yes, great band. And you?"

"Love them. I've seen them countless times. Fabulous live."

"Oh, here we go again," Bone moaned.

"Ignore him, he has no taste," Walker said.

"Excuse me, sir. Billie Holliday, Miles Davis, and John Coltrane? I mean, really?" Walker scoffed.

"Come have a look," Meg said, breaking up the banter.

She stepped back up onto the platform, and the detectives followed. Bone leaned into Meg's binoculars.

"It's easier if you sit down," Meg said.

Bone slowly lowered his bruised coccyx onto the stool and peered through the viewfinder. A close-up of the osprey nest appeared, as though right in front of his face. He pulled back to locate it in the trees, but it was too far away to spot.

"See those three trees there clumped together in a line?" Meg said. "The nest is on the top of the one just to the right."

Bone squinted at the view across the treetops but couldn't see it.

"Got it," Walker cut in.

Matt gestured to his plot. "You can have a look through that one if you like," he told Walker.

She climbed up to join Bone, and they both squinted through their respective binoculars.

"Bloody hell, they are beautiful, aren't they?" Bone said, watching the mother, perched precariously on her nest of carefully woven branches, teetering on the very top of the tree, tending to her clutch. Out of nowhere, the dad swooped down and landed alongside the mum, and with some jostling, they both settled in together. The male stretched his wings.

"Incredible, aren't they?" Meg said. "And they are so loving and caring for each other and their chicks, when they finally hatch."

"I can't believe anyone would want to do anything to harm them. It's horrific," Walker adjusted the lens.

"Mindlessness and money, a very dangerous combination," Roxburgh rubbed his forehead. I need a coffee."

"So if I were to walk across the hills from here to the Kilmorgan stones, how long would it take me?" Bone asked.

Roxburgh gave Bone a once over. "Are we talking you, or an experienced hillwalker?" He joked. "It's not actually as far as you might think, especially after driving up here on all those windy roads. The Sanctuary and the Stones are both close to the Craigend Ridge. You can see the top of it just over there." He pointed to the steep rise just beyond the nest. "The ridge runs nearly the entire width of the Campsies stretching from the edge of the Ochils, all the way down to the Braeburn and the outskirts of Kilwinnoch."

"So you walk along the ridge?" Bone quizzed.

"Exactly. You'd need to know what you're doing mind, as parts of it are a bit treacherous. But for an experienced walker with some decent weather, the walk could be done from the Stones to here in about two to three hours."

"And then on to Kilwinnoch?"

"About another couple, but you'd have to negotiate the river and the Braeburn Falls."

Suddenly, the walkie-talkie attached to Roxburgh's belt screamed to life. "Sorry, excuse me a minute." He snatched it up and fumbled with the volume. "Bloody hell," he exclaimed. "Turn yourself down."

"Yes?" he whispered through the mouthpiece and then held the walkie-talkie to his ear. "Okay, five minutes," he said and slotted the device back onto his belt.

Roxburgh marched to the door. "That was Stephen and Max over on Comrie Hill. They've spotted two men crossing a field and heading our way."

"Shall I come with you?" Matt asked.

"No, you stay here in case we miss them. Detectives, could you assist me?"

"Of course," Bone replied. "Does it involve the nutcracker?"

"Yes, 'fraid so. But the team's only five minutes away."

Roxburgh and the detectives retraced their footsteps back to the Land Rover. With a groan and an adjustment of his belt, Bone climbed into the rear, and the director reversed at breakneck speed down the track and, to Bone's relief, onto the smooth tarmacked lane.

About two miles deeper into the hills, Roxburgh pulled off the lane and parked by a far gate. A man in a khaki bomber jacket came running over the field and jumped the stile in one swift move.

"We spotted them on the far side of the next field. Two guys clambering over a fence," the man gasped, trying to catch his breath.

"Let's go," Roxburgh said.

Together they clambered over the stile and ran along the side of the field. When they reached the other side, they took a second stile and ran down a steep slope towards the river.

"There's Max and the others," the security man said, pointing down at three figures making their way along the riverbank.

Approaching, one of the men whistled and gestured towards the woods running down to the river's edge. Roxburgh veered right and headed straight for the trees. When they got to the woods, Roxburgh's walkie-talkie hissed again.

"Where?" he asked through laboured breaths.

"The far side of the trees," the voice rasped through the tiny speaker.

Pulling at the fence wire, Roxburgh scrambled under and gestured for the others to follow him. "You come with me, Inspector Bone. Max, you go around the perimeter with Detective Walker and we'll try to head them off."

"At the pass," the security guard added with a smile and jumped straight over the fence.

Walker started to follow, but then, before she raised her leg, she changed her mind and scrambled under, and they disappeared into the trees.

"Come on," Roxburgh hold the fence up for Bone to duck through.

They raced into the heart of the woods, weaving through narrow gaps between the overgrowth. Pushing deeper, the canopy above them closed in and the light started to fail. Suddenly, Roxburgh stopped.

"Did you hear that?" he whispered.

Bone turned to listen, but only the swish and creak of the trees blowing and bending in the breeze could be heard.

"There again," Roxburgh repeated.

This time, a loud crack sounded somewhere just ahead of them. Roxburgh knelt, and Bone followed. He gestured with his fingers to his eyes and then ahead. Bone peered into the gloom but couldn't see a thing. Roxburgh crept forward, gesturing for Bone to be as quiet as possible.

Roxburgh stopped again, and after a few moments continued on. Bone moved forward but stepped on a twig, and the snap shattered the silence. Roxburgh glared.

A figure emerged from behind one of the trees and dived into the darkness. Roxburgh and Bone gave chase. Within a few strides, the trees had almost entirely enclosed them, and while Roxburgh seemed to run through them, Bone smashed into branches and careened off tree trunks, the tangle of trees ripping his suit jacket and scratching his face. The figure up ahead attempted to cut through a gap to their right. Roxburgh raced on, with Bone struggling to keep up.

"Come here, you bastard," Roxburgh hollered as he closed in.

But as he got within a few feet of grabbing distance, the figure suddenly spun round and punched him square on the chin. Roxburgh crumpled to the ground, out cold. Scrambling over a fallen trunk, Bone hollered after Roxburgh's assailant.

"Police, stop!"

But he knew it was pointless, and the figure ran off into the darkness again. He ran over to Roxburgh who was coming to.

"I'm okay, go!" he said and pressed his palm against his ruddy chin.

Bone set off in pursuit. Stumbling through the trees, he regained a visual of the figure, who moved towards the light at the far edge of the copse. Bone cut to the left, hoping for a shortcut. He reached the perimeter fence and open space. The sudden rush of light dazzled him for a second. He rubbed at his eyes and scanned the fence and edge of the woods, but there was no sign of the attacker.

Out of nowhere, the man came running at him. Bone turned in time to avoid the same fate as Roxburgh and, ducking around a swinging arm, he rugby-tackled the man to the ground. The assailant's face was covered by a black, full-head balaclava, with only the eyes and mouth visible.

The man fought back, punching Bone in the ribs. Winded, Bone fell sideways, and the man laid a second punch. He was now on top of Bone, his arm around his neck, twisting his head. Bone swung his fists up but couldn't make contact. The man tightened his grip, squeezing the air from Bone's windpipe. Bone now choked for breath, and his limbs were losing their strength. He tried to speak, to plead for him to stop, but the words were trapped in his gullet. Then, remembering his police training from way back, he stopped resisting, let his body fall completely limp, and feigned unconsciousness.

After a moment, the man relaxed his grip, and Bone seized his chance. He rammed his head back with such force he split the man's nose, and blood sprayed out across his balaclava. Bone threw a punch backwards and connected with his assailant's cheek. The man fell sideways. Bone slid out from under him, jumped up, and punched him again on the same cheek. The man slumped to the ground, moaning. Grabbing the man's arms, Bone forced him over onto his front and, reaching for his cuffs, snapped them on the man's wrists with force. Just then, the security guard and Walker appeared, running by the perimeter fence.

"Just in time, not." Bone slumped down onto the ground, clutching his neck.

"Are you okay, sir?" Walker asked.

"I've had better days out," Bone groaned.

"Looks like he gave you a nasty gash there." the guard said, wincing at a deep cut on Bone's cheek.

"That wasn't him, that was those bloody trees," Bone complained and dabbed at the bleeding wound with his palm.

Walker kneeled over the moaning man splayed out on the ground. "Who have we here, then?" She whipped the balaclava off, and the man sneered up at them.

"That's one of the Springsteens," the security guard said. "I'd recognise that wee rat's face anywhere." He went over to Springsteen. "Where's your brother then?" He nudged him with his boot.

"That's enough," Walker intervened.

The guard stepped back.

"These two have been giving us the run-around for weeks," the guard snarled.

"Well, we'll be dealing with this one for now, okay?" She turned back to the whining captive. "What's your name?"

"No comment," the man mumbled.

"You're only making it worse for yourself. I'll ask you again. What's your name?"

"I want a solicitor," he gurgled through a mouthful of blood.

"Oh yes, you're definitely going to need one of those. Let's see what we have, trespassing, resisting arrest, assault—"

"I didn't know you were coppers. I thought you were heavies."

"Oh yes, and I look like a nightclub bouncer, don't I?" Bone interjected. "In my ripped-to-shreds expensive suit." He pulled at a flap of fabric dangling from his jacket sleeve. "And we did shout loud and clear that we were police officers."

"I didn't hear you," Springsteen protested.

"You do not have to say anything..." Walker continued.

"I want my solicitor," he interrupted again.

"But, it may harm your defence if you do not..."

"Fuck you."

"So sweet. A credit to the community," the guard snarled.

"I'll call in a wagon," Walker said once she was done reciting the police caution.

"Yes, let's get this sorry excuse for a human being back to the station." Bone clambered to his feet and leaned over Springsteen, who had now managed to squirm onto his side. "Where's your brother, then, Mr Springsteen?"

"Haven't seen him in months," Springsteen snapped.

"Oh, he talks," Walker jumped in. "Keep that up and you'll reduce that sentence down to... What do you reckon, sir?"

"Eight years?"

"Och, I'd say more like ten," Walker grinned.

"Fuck you," Springsteen howled.

"No, I think you're the one who is fucked, Mr Springsteen," Bone replied.

With the help of the security guard, they hauled Springsteen to his feet. Just then, Roxburgh staggered out of the woods, still clutching his jaw.

"You okay?" Bone asked.

"I'll live. Glad you caught the scumbag," Roxburgh put his finger in his mouth to check his teeth.

"That was quite a left hook you landed there, Mr Springsteen," Bone said. "Very impressive."

"Lucky punch," Roxburgh huffed. "There would have been no second chance."

"I quite believe it," Bone tried to conceal his lie. "Right, let's get you back to the station. I can't wait to properly introduce myself to you, Mr Springsteen."

The captive tried to shake free, but Bone and the guard tightened their grip and pushed him towards the road.

SIXTEEN

Even before he caught his first glimpse of the famous Grinlay's wee boy with the giant pie logo peeking up above the tree line at Carrbridge Cross, Mullens's stomach was doing somersaults.

"Just not fair. This is worse than fucking waterboarding," he moaned as the imposing brick factory walls emerged up ahead.

He pulled up to the gate, and the security guard approached.

"Meat to see Mullens," Mullens stuttered. "Sorry, DS Mullens from Kilwinnoch station, here to see your boss."

He held up his lanyard at the vacant guard, who stared for a moment at Mullens's ID, back at the detective, then at the ID again.

"Believe it or not, that was eight years ago. If anything, I think I look younger," Mullens said sarcastically and shook his head.

"Huh?" the guard grunted.

"So, front cover of *Vogue* material? What do you reckon?"

"Naw, yer awright," the guard replied, unsure of what was going on.

The guard returned to his booth, flicked the button on the barrier, and Mullens drove through. On his way past the guard he blew him a kiss, and the guard waved back, oblivious to Mullens teasing.

He drove into the car park adjacent to the factory and turned into one of the visitor bays. He climbed out. The smell of cooking pastry and minced meat hit his nostrils, and he let out a loud groan. Spotting an employee in full factory floor overalls and hairnet, he approached.

"Excuse me, where can I find Mr Grinlay's office?" Mullens asked, noticing the hairnet was almost busting at the seams with voluminous amounts of hair.

The man looked Mullens up and down for a second. "Through the front door and then ask the receptionist to call the lift." He pointed up to the top of a central brick tower with a massive clock in its centre and a moving part version of the company logo teetering on the very top, the wee boy raising and lowering the giant pie to his mouth, in sync with the second hand of the clock below.

"Cheers," Mullens said, and on his way he spotted a gleaming Triumph motorcycle, with a Scottish flag adorning the tank, parked at the bottom of the steps. "Whose bike?" he called back.

"The boss's."

"So he's pretty young then?"

"He's nearly seventy." the man shrugged and disappeared into a side building.

Mullens carried on up the steps and into the main building. Inside was a vast reception atrium with two Art Deco chandeliers stretching down from an expansive ceiling high above Mullens's head. The walls were panelled from top to bottom in dark mahogany, and the tiled floor sported the company logo made out of tiny mosaic squares.

The smell of cooked meats and baking dough was now almost overpowering, and Mullens felt faint. He approached a vast reception desk, made of the same mahogany panelling, and the diminutive receptionist almost lost completely behind it.

"Detective Mullens from Kilw—" Mullens began.

"Yes, Detective," the receptionist interrupted. "Mr Grinlay is expecting you." She stood, but it barely made any difference to her height. She emerged from behind the desk. "The front lift is out of order, so I'll take you through to the rear."

Mullens followed, careful not to fall over her.

"This way," she said and took him into what appeared to be some kind of changing room. "Please put these on." She handed him a pristine white coat and hairnet.

"Wait a minute. You're not taking me through the factory, are you?" Mullens asked, his eyes wide with panic.

"I'm afraid the rear lift is the only way up to Mr Grinlay's office." She nodded at a row of white wellington boots. "And put those on when you're ready. They're laid out by size."

Mullens reluctantly pushed an arm into the coat. By the second arm, the receptionist had already transformed him into a full-blown factory worker. Hurrying, he grappled with the hairnet. It pinged out of his grip and landed at the receptionist's wellies-clad feet.

"Start with the front and work your way back," she said.

Mullens tried again and just about managed to squeeze the top of his giant head into the contraption. "Will that do?"

She sighed, nodded, and led him through a second door onto the factory floor.

In contrast to the post-Victorian austere elegance of the reception, the factory was an ultra-modern, steel-and-glass arena, with gleaming silver hi-tech machines and conveyor belts carrying row upon row of Grinlay's products in all directions.

The smell was now in near-full possession of Mullens senses. He followed a line of meat pies disappearing into a vast, gaping mouth of metal, emerging on the other side, ready packed and labelled. He wiped a dribble of saliva from the corner of his mouth.

"Follow me," the receptionist said over the low hum of the machines.

The factory floor was strangely absent of workers, robotic arms and metal grabbers replacing human paycheques.

They walked across the football-pitch-sized factory floor, following a precisely marked pathway. Mullens's eyes diverted to a line of bridies that dropped down by his side and seemed to jiggle around as though laughing at him.

"Oh my God!" he exclaimed, no longer able to control his delirium.

The receptionist turned back. "Are you okay?"

"It's all these pies. They're driving me bananas."

"Ah, try working here. You'll soon go off them." She said and carried on.

When they finally reached the other side of the factory floor, Mullens turned and waved a fond farewell at Grinlay's freshly baked temptations.

Out in the corridor, the receptionist fished a set of keys out of her overall pocket, approached a lift, and pushed the key in the call button panel. A light flashed on, and within a few seconds, the lift door opened.

"Mr Grinlay is number one," she said.

"I'm sure he is round here," Mullens muttered, his mind still on sinking his teeth through thick layers of pastry.

"No, number one button. Press that, and the lift will take you straight into his office."

"Ah, okay." He glanced down at his attire. "Can I take this off now?"

"No, you'll need it when you leave."

"You mean I have to walk the bridie mile again?" Mullens winced and rubbed his stomach.

"'Fraid so," she said, and with a quick nod, she about-turned and left him.

Mullens shuffled into the lift and hit the button. Moments later, the door opened into a vast penthouse office suite. A second receptionist sat straight in front of him.

"I'm—" Mullens started again.

"Go right in," the young man said, nodding towards a door on the other side of the room.

Mullens carried on, his wellies squeaking loudly as he walked. He knocked on the door and went in.

Grinlay's office was a spectacularly huge glass-and-steel box perched on the very top of the factory tower. Mr Grinlay, who was on the phone when Mullens entered, hung up and came over to greet the detective.

"Detective Mullens?" Grinlay asked with a rough, growling voice.

Mullens was surprised by how tall he was, and despite his age and face that looked like it had done ten years in the ring with Tyson, he seemed pretty nimble and youthful on his feet.

"Yes, correct." Mullens glanced over Grinlay's Clydesdale-sized shoulders at the panoramic view across the Braeburn Valley. "I wouldn't mind coming to work every day with that view and those smells."

"Aye, it's a sheer joy… Well, most of the time anyway," Grinlay rasped and rubbed his flattened broken nose briskly.

"It's an honour to meet you, Mr Grinlay. Your family's pies and bridies have been a huge part of my dietary world for my whole life," Mullens half-joked.

"Yes, we have been around for quite some time. I like to think we're like family to our local community," Grinlay smiled proudly.

"I was admiring your Triumph Bonneville parked up outside."

"Ah yes, my wee toy. My wife's birthday present to me a couple of years ago. I promised her I wouldn't actually ride the bloody thing, but who could resist that beauty?"

"Indeed."

"So what can I do for you, Detective?" He gestured for Mullens to sit on one of the strange glass chairs adjacent to his expansive glass desk.

"We are investigating the death of a local teacher who you might know. Richard Jones?"

"Death?" Grinlay interrupted.

"Yes, sorry to say, his body was found yesterday afternoon at the Braeburn Falls, not too far from your factory here. Is that the Braeburn running through your site?"

"That's terrible," Grinlay replied, ignoring Mullens's question. "So what happened? Was it suicide?"

"Why would you say that?" Mullens probed.

"Oh, I don't know. He was a very intense, serious sort of guy. He was involved in all sorts of campaigns." Grinlay rolled his eyes.

"So, you knew him?"

"Well, it's no secret that he spearheaded a campaign that unfairly targeted our factory as responsible for the river pollution."

"So you were not exactly best mates?"

"He has... sorry... had a right to his views. But him and his..." Grinlay paused to select an appropriate word. "...fellow campaigners had no proof that the source of the pollution was coming from here. I ordered a full review of our waste disposal strategy. I called in local and national environmental health officers and paid for it all out of my own pocket."

"So what was your position?" Mullens pressed.

"The pollution was coming from farm waste run-off. The evidence was irrefutable, but Richard Jones refused to accept it."

Mullens reached beneath his coverall and searched for his notepad. As he flicked through it, Grinlay tapped his desk unconsciously with his forefinger.

"I believe that on the fifth of May this year," Mullens continued, "police were called to the premises following reports of an altercation between the deceased and a number of your employees."

"Mr Jones was trespassing. He'd somehow bypassed our front gate and got into the compound. His sidekick had a megaphone and was ranting and raving, most of it libellous. I asked my security to politely ask him to leave."

"That's not what the police report said," Mullens replied.

"Well, things got a little out of hand when Mr Jones took a swing."

"The report states that your men were heavy-handed, and Jones was the worse for wear."

"He was very physical with my men," Grinlay retorted. "They were using reasonable force to restrain him while we waited for the police to arrive."

"You used to play for the national rugby team, didn't you?" Mullens continued.

Grinlay looked up in surprise. "Yes, that's right. Many moons ago. Only four caps, mind you. When I broke my femur, that was that." He sighed. "I played for Lothian Lions for six years, though. Happy days. Still miss the lads and the buzz."

"You still look young for your age." Mullens charmed.

Grinlay chuckled. "I'll take that though it's amazing what a bit of money and a personal trainer can do for you."

"So I bet you could hold your own in a scrap," Mullens landed his gut punch.

"Well, there are things you don't forget…" Grinlay stopped. "Hold on, I see where this is going."

"It's not going anywhere, Mr Grinlay. I'm just wondering how handy you are with your fists." Mullens carried on.

"I wasn't involved in the incident with Jones. I was up here the whole time, and I have plenty of witnesses to prove it, including the police officers in attendance," Grinlay growled, his bulk seeming to swell under his tight, checked shirt.

"I'm not sure why you're being so defensive, Mr Grinlay. It was a simple question."

"You lot never ask simple questions."

"Oh, you would be surprised," Mullens shot the boss another wry smile.

"Look, I only met Mr Jones once at a council meeting. We had an exchange of views, verbal only, no fists involved, and that was that. He turned up here throwing his weight around and was clearly in the wrong. My men had every right to remove him from our private property." Grinlay was becoming more and more agitated.

"Why did you drop the lawsuit against him?" Mullens kept up the pressure.

"Here we go." Grinlay tutted. "I thought you'd bring that up," "He'd made some unfounded and slanderous allegations in a series of letters to the paper. I decided enough was enough."

"So why drop it?"

"Following legal advice, I decided that it wasn't in anyone's interests to pursue."

"Was that because he was right, and you thought if the courts started digging, then the truth would come out?"

"Of course not!" Grinlay snapped back. "I just thought that the reputation of the family name was on the line and pursuing a local, and for some reason, well-loved teacher was not a good look." He shook his head. "I'm telling you, Detective, if you continue with this line of questioning I'm going to have to curtail this conversation and consult with my solicitor."

"This is all part of our investigation, Mr Grinlay," Mullens said and attempted to clamber out of the glass contraption squashing his legs together. "You've been very helpful, thank you."

"Have I?" Grinlay said in surprise. "So, am I on your suspect board now then? Mr Evil Business Tycoon Murders Local Hero, is that your angle?" he spat out, his rage building by the second.

"As I said, no stone unturned, Mr Grinlay. Thanks for your time."

Mullens went over to the door, and Grinlay followed.

"You know, I actually admired the teacher. He had focus and conviction, and passion for his cause coming out of his ears. I would have employed someone like that in a shot," Grinlay said. "I hope you get to the bottom of this, Detective."

"So do I, Mr Grinlay," Mullens replied, and when the lift door opened, he shuffled inside.

On his way back through the factory, he held his breath and kept his head down to avoid eye contact with his meat-filled tormentors. When he reached the changing room, he quickly clambered out of his protective gear and returned to the reception area. On his way past the desk, he nodded at the receptionist.

"Oh, Detective?" she called to him before he disappeared through the door.

He turned back.

"Aye?"

The receptionist disappeared under her desk, and moments later re-emerged clutching a large cardboard box. "Compliments of Grinlay's. She handed him the box.

The bottom and sides were warm and the soft, savoury smell of freshly baked shortcrust wafted out from the corners. Mullens almost sank to his knees in religious rapture, then he remembered his pledge.

"I'm really sorry but..." he started, but the aroma was tearing his senses and his willpower to pieces.

"What?" the receptionist asked. "We like to give all visitors a wee treat when they leave."

Mullens stared at the box for a moment longer. "Please thank your boss for me. That's very kind," he said sheepishly. He could already hear his wife roaring expletives at him. He blocked the thought and headed back to his car.

As he drove back across the bridge and out of the compound, he glanced down at the box, like a serial killer eyeing up the remains of a recent kill.

Three miles later, he pulled into a secluded lay-by, turned off the engine, and checked no one was around. With a loud rumble of his gut, he ripped open the box and stared open-mouthed at the three bridies lined up in a neat row.

"Oh please, God, help me for I know not what I do!" The sweet smell of meat and warm pastry flooded his nostrils again. Plucking one out, he held it up to his nose for a moment, prolonging the torture.

His phone rang, and he nearly dropped the lot in his lap. It was Sandra, his wife.

"Fuck!" he muttered and answered. "Sandra, darlin'."

"You're eating, aren't you?" she said, her voice crackling with accusation.

"No, of course not." He scanned the interior of the car for a hidden camera.

"You can't kid me. I know when you're lying," Sandra's cross-examination continued.

"I'm telling you, Sandra, darling. I've been really good and resisted, but it's been absolutely horrendous. I'd rather read one of your Jackie Collins than have to suffer this any longer. He eyed up the bridie box again.

"Well, you need to stick with it, Mark. I don't want you keelin' over and leaving me with your shite widow's pension."

"Charming," Mullens replied. "I promise, darlin', I am still on the slurry. Two glasses at lunch and looking forward to the rindless pork chop with boiled spinach for dinner."

"Right, see you tonight, and be good."

"I will, darlin'," he prayed he'd got away with it. He held his breath.

"And stop callin' me darlin'. Any more of that and I'll think you're in the curry house in town." She hung up.

"Fuuuuckkkk!" he roared. He tossed the bridie back in its box, slammed the car into gear, and accelerated at speed out of the lay-by.

On his way back to the station, he detoured and stopped off at his dad's house to relinquish all temptation.

Clutching the box and breathing through his mouth to avoid the wafts of slowly stewed meat, he was about to knock when his dad bellowed, "You useless idiot! Where do they find these tumshy heids?" he roared.

"Oh shite," Mullens said.

Leaning over, he peered through the living room window, but to his surprise, George sat on his armchair in front of the TV with *Tipping Point* blaring out. He waved his arms around at the screen while supping on a bowl of soup. Tim, the young carer, sat next to him, attempting to ensure the soup bowl didn't fly off the portable table and spray its contents across the room.

Mullens smiled and knocked on the door. Moments later, the carer opened it.

"Hello, Tim, sorry to disturb you both," Mullens said.

"Come in," Tim said. "We're watching *Tipping Point*, and your dad's having some lunch."

"No bother. I just wanted to give you both these. He thrust the box into Tim's arms and as far away from his nose as possible.

"What's—?" Tim began.

"Bridies, compliments of Grinlay's. My da's favourite," Mullens replied, adding, "and mine," with a look of total dejection.

"Are you sure you don't want to come in?"

"No, you two carry on. It looks like he's settling down a bit."

"Fingers crossed. It was a challenging morning." Tim grinned. "But hopefully, I think we might have turned a corner."

"Good man, well thanks, and enjoy."

He returned to his car, and although it could never quite compensate for giving up his box of bridies, he felt relieved that at long last, his dad might finally be coming round to the fact that he needed professional support.

SEVENTEEN

Back at the station, Bone instructed the desk sergeant to take Springsteen down to a holding cell, and the two detectives returned to the incident room.

When they entered, Baxter approached. "Sir, I have some more information on this altercation at Jones's house."

"Go on."

"Police records confirm that officers attended Jones's property on the twelfth of June," she continued. "At eleven thirty-three p.m., one of Jones's neighbours called the station to report a fight taking place in the front garden."

"Miss Chalmers didn't tell me the police were called," Mullens interrupted.

"However, when the police arrived all was quiet, and when they made enquiries at Jones's property, Mr Jones denied any altercation and said he was enjoying an evening with friends."

"They must have got wind that coppers were coming and legged it back into the house," Mullens added.

"The officer who filed the report does say, though, that Richard Jones was sporting a shiner and appeared flustered. But no charges were brought, and the incident was logged and put to bed."

"Good work, keep digging," Bone said to Baxter.

"You know, the more I think about that guy Brandon whatshisface—" Mullens chipped in.

"Kinross?" Bone asked.

"Aye, him. He's a bit of a fitness nut. You know, three hundred press-ups before his bowl of desiccated rabbit poo and strained goat mucus for his five a.m. breakfast." He ran his hand across his stomach. "God, I'd even eat that now."

"Keep going," Bone insisted.

"He was nervous, and looked very uncomfortable when I asked him how he got on with Jones. Maybe that has something to do with the fight. It's not great is it, scrapping with your workmate then days later he's dead?"

"Indeed," Bone replied.

"And then there's Oli Morton, the shit-stirrer as Miss Chalmers described him, though he seemed genuinely upset and worried."

"They were very good mates. It would be odd if he wasn't."

"Aye, I know, but something doesn't quite add up about the pair of them."

"Okay, so a few home visits tonight," Bone said. "But first, I need you both to come with me down to the interview room."

"Who have you brought in?" Mullens asked.

"One of the bird-poaching brothers."

"The Springsteens?"

"Correct, and the wee bastard tried to throttle me. So he's in deep doodoo."

"Shall I save the *Born to Run* gag for later?"

"Don't even go there, please."

Bone let Springsteen sweat it out in a cell for a bit longer before two uniforms moved him into one of the interview rooms. They bundled him in, and he slumped down on a hardback chair opposite Bone and Walker. Mullens stood alert by the back wall, staring down at the suspect. Bone nodded for the two uniforms who'd brought him in to leave.

"I want my solicitor," Springsteen said, scanning the detectives' faces.

Out of his coat and balaclava, he seemed a great deal smaller and leaner, but clearly knew how to throw a punch or two, so was not to be trusted. Bone noticed a scar running across Springsteen's throat, with the stitch marks still visible.

Bone placed Springsteen's driving licence down on the table in front of him. "Good morning, Mr Springsteen, or may I call you Robert?"

Springsteen grimaced and folded his arms.

"Would you care for a tea or coffee, or a glass of water before we start our tête-à-tête?"

"I don't want coffee. I want my solicitor," Springsteen grumbled.

"Yes, I believe Mr…"

"Cranston," Springsteen interjected.

"Yes, Mr Cranston is on his way up from Edinburgh. Quite a fancy law firm, Cranston and Wall. You must have a few bob to afford him."

"No comment."

There was a knock at the door, and the desk sergeant appeared.

"Sorry to interrupt, sir, can I have a word?" he said.

Bone got up and joined the desk sergeant in the corridor.

"What's up?" Bone asked once the door clicked closed behind him.

"Your suspect's solicitor firm called to say that they have declined to represent Robert Springsteen."

"Did they say why?" Bone asked.

"Nope, sorry. Just that the solicitor would not be attending."

"Right, okay. Well, that's interesting. Thanks." Bone returned to the interview room. "I'm afraid I have some bad news, Mr Springsteen," he said as he entered the room. "Mr Cranston will not be joining us this afternoon."

"What?"

"The firm has declined to represent you."

"But that's not right. They can't do that!" Springsteen jumped up.

Mullens lunged forward and grabbed Springsteen's arm.

"Sit down, Mr Springsteen, or I will give Detective Mullens here the nod to fully restrain you, and believe me you wouldn't wish that on your own enemies." Bone exclaimed.

Mullens snarled at their captured prey.

After a few huffs and shoves, Springsteen dropped back down onto his chair. Mullens remained directly behind him.

"It looks like your paymaster has abandoned you," Bone said. "You've become something of a liability, what with all these charges racking up."

"The bastards can't do this to me," Springsteen spat.

"I think they already have. And who exactly are 'these bastards' you speak of?"

"No comment," Springsteen said, shaking his head.

"DI Walker, perhaps you could read out the charges to remind our friend what he's facing," Bone carried on.

"I'm telling you, I didn't know you were coppers," Springsteen interrupted before Walker could start reading out the list. "I thought it was that bloody farmer's heavy squad."

"What farmer?" Bone asked.

"Last week I had a run-in with this farmer and his two sons. The old guy threatened me with his shotgun and told me to get off his land."

"What were you doing on his land?" Walker asked.

"I love hillwalking. The Campsies are one of my favourite places to go."

"I bet they are," Walker added.

"So, you're up here just rambling around, taking in the scenery?" Bone asked.

"Aye, and these bastards start chasing me across a field. He even sent his Labrador after me. I just managed to jump the fence before it got me."

"So, you know nothing about any birds of prey that might be just coincidentally in the vicinity of your rambling route?"

"What birds of prey?"

"Oh, come on, Robert," Bone tapped the desk in frustration.

"Okay, okay, I admit it doesn't look good."

"It looks decidedly shite from where I'm sitting," Bone said. "You assaulted a police officer. I would even go so far as to describe it as attempted murder. You are in the very deepest of shit, Robert."

"I know, but like I said, I thought you were employees of that bloody farmer. I was defending myself."

"In a balaclava?" Walker added. "I don't remember that being Ramblers association regulation kit."

Springsteen glanced across at her. "I genuinely thought—"

"You'd lamp a copper, correct?" Bone persisted.

"No, I was in fear for my life." Springsteen glanced over his shoulder at Mullens still looming ominously behind him.

"Where were you on the twentieth and twenty-first of June?" Walker asked, opening up a file in front of her.

"What?"

"Simple question. It wasn't that long ago."

"I was… wait. I was out walking. Yes, that's right."

"For two days on the trot?"

"I have a lightweight two-man tent that I just pitch where I fancy."

"You say two-man, was your brother with you, then?" Bone asked.

"My brother, why would he be with me?"

"Oh, I don't know, perhaps to steal some rare birds and their eggs."

Springsteen's knee bouncing up and down erratically. "I told you, those days are over for me, and I haven't seen my brother for months. He was the one who got me into all that crap in the first place."

"You're lying," Walker said.

"What?"

"You and your brother were spotted near the Kilmorgan Stones on the night of the twentieth of June."

"Well, that wasn't me or my brother as I was nowhere near there, and God knows where he is."

"Have you heard about the disappearance of the local teacher, Richard Jones?"

"Eh, aye. I read about it in the paper," Springsteen replied.

"He's dead. We found his body this morning up at the Braeburn Falls."

"That's terrible. How did he die? Did he top himself?"

"Why would you say that?" Walker asked.

"I dunno. It's a tough job, teaching. A lot of pressure. Maybe it all got too much for the poor guy."

"Or maybe he happened to stumble into you two on your way to the osprey nest and he became an inconvenient witness." Bone said, turning the screws a little tighter.

"What? You think I bumped off the teacher now? Oh, come on. This is a joke!" Springsteen groaned. "We had nothing to do with whatever happened to him."

"We?" Walker cut in.

"What?"

"You said 'we'."

"I meant me," Springsteen explained.

"Oh dear, a schoolboy error and so soon." Bone grinned.

"I'm not saying any more. I still have a right to a solicitor."

Bone sat back and, turning to the recorder, said, "Interview paused at three twenty-three p.m.," and hit the stop button. He leaned over the table to within a foot of Springsteen's face.

"This is off the record. We know what you and your brother were doing up there, we have witnesses who will testify against you. I'm willing to drop the assault charges if you come clean and be straight with us."

Springsteen shrugged. "I didn't kill the teacher. That's just mental."

"Officer, take Mr Springsteen back to his cell," Bone said.

Mullens pulled Springsteen to his feet and shoved him into the arms of the waiting uniform.

"We're not done with you yet, not by a long mile." Bone added.

Springsteen sneered back at him, and the officer pushed him out of the room, Springsteen's bellows echoing all the way up the corridor and into the stairwell.

Mullens slammed the door. "What a total ball sack."

"What do you think?" Walker asked.

"I think he and his brother are up to their necks in all sorts, and quite capable of snuffing the teacher," Bone replied.

"I can hear a 'but' in there."

"But I don't think he killed him. He looked genuinely surprised."

"So, what next then?" Mullens said.

"We try and find his brother then play the bargaining chip again. They could be sitting on relevant information and may be willing to spill now that their Svengali has bailed on them."

"So, who is the Svengali?" Walker wondered.

"Some oligarch maybe, or a fence that specialises in endangered animal trade? I'll get Baxter on it."

"And the Sanctuary may know more about them, too," Mullens added.

"Yup. What time is it?" Bone asked.

"Twenty-five past three, you just recorded it?"

"God, yes, I must be tired. Time to head home," Bone said through a yawn.

"I might call in on Morton on my way and get more information on what went on at Jones's house that night," Walker said.

"Okay, but don't work too late. You have important family matters to attend to," Bone said with a weary smile. "You too, Mark. Bugger off."

Mullens yawned and stretched his arms until his fingers touched the ceiling.

"Hasta mañana, sir," Walker said.

The two detectives left Bone alone in the interview room. Returning to the desk, he picked up his phone and notes and was about to leave when a hooded figure appeared in the corner adjacent to the door.

Bone sighed. "What do you want?"

The apparition raised its arm, and a charred hand emerged from the darkness, the bone in the index finger visible through puckered, split skin. The finger pointed directly at him.

"It's rude to point." Bone scoffed.

The figure shifted forward towards him slowly and stopped. Now Bone could see the outline of the creature's charred face and cheek, buried inside the hood.

"Loser," the creature whispered.

"Is that the best you can do?" Bone shrugged and moved towards his hallucination.

The creature held firm, but then when Bone was within four or five feet, it rushed forward and straight through Bone's chest, its ice-cold invasion sending an explosive shiver the length of Bone's spine. Bone staggered backwards, almost toppling over the desk behind him. Spinning round, he scanned the back of the room, but the apparition had vanished.

"Arsehole," he muttered, rubbing at the scar on his temple that was now throbbing with pain. He retrieved his things from the floor and headed for the rear car park and the reassuring safety of his old Saab.

EIGHTEEN

As Walker drove into Balcastle Avenue, she slowed down to clock the numbers on the well-maintained row of ex-council semis.

"Forty-seven, forty-nine, fifty-one, bingo," she muttered and stopped the car.

She pushed the low, iron gate and approached Oliver Morton's front door and rang the bell. A woman with bone-white, tightly permed hair peered around the gap.

"Yes?" she asked nervously.

"Sorry to disturb you," Walker started.

"Not today, thank you," the woman said and shut the door.

Walker rapped on the door again. No reply.

"It's the police," she called out.

The lock clacked again, and the door finally swung open.

"What's happened?" she asked anxiously.

"Sorry to alarm you. I'm Detective Walker from Kilwinnoch Police Station."

She lifted her lanyard, and the woman scrutinised it for a second or two.

"We're making enquiries into the disappearance of the local teacher, Richard Jones, and we'd like to speak to Mr Morton. We believe this is his home address, is that correct?"

"Oh, yes, of course. I'm Carol Morton, Oliver is my son. He works with Mr Jones. The papers are saying you've found Richard's body up at Blood Water Falls. Is that true?"

"Our investigation is ongoing, but you may have to prepare for the worst."

"It's absolutely devastating. Oliver is just beside himself with worry."

"Is Mr Morton in?" Walker asked, redirecting the conversation.

"Yes, he's..." She glanced back into the house. "Come away in, please."

Walker followed Mrs Morton into a neat, tidy, and quaintly old-fashioned hallway.

"Oliver and Richard were very good friends as well as colleagues." Mrs Morton continued.

"Yes, we know. We're hoping your son can give us a few more insights into our investigation."

"He was a very kind soul, Richard," Mrs Morton said. She stopped at the bottom of the stairs. "Oliver!" she called up. There was no reply. "Oli," she tried again. Still nothing. "He can't hear me. He's probably in the loft again. Just go right up to the top of the stairs and you'll see the ladder. If you don't mind, my knees are giving me bother today."

"Thanks, Mrs Morton. I'll find him," Walker said and started up the stairs.

On the landing, a loft hatch was open with a wide wooden stepladder filling most of the floor space. Walker started to climb. The loft was larger than she expected, the expansive roof space high enough to stand up in. But there was no Velux or dormer, so the loft was gloomy, and there was a strong smell of solvent or paint. She spotted Oliver at the far end, leaning over a long table that stretched across the width of the loft. The back of his head was illuminated by an overhead lamp, not unlike one of Cash's examination lights. Walker clambered up and approached him.

"Mr Morton," Walker asked quietly.

The young teacher spun round in his chair in surprise. There was something strapped around his head.

"I'm Detective Walker from Kilwinnoch station." She glanced down at the table in front of him. It was covered in a multitude of tiny metal figures.

Morton looked up at Walker through a set of thick-lensed craft glasses that magnified his eyes to twice their size.

"God, I nearly jumped out of my skin there," Morton said, removing his glasses.

"Sorry to disturb you," Walker said. "We're investigating the disappearance of your colleague,

Richard Jones, and we'd like to ask you a few more questions." She moved closer to the table.

"Oh yes, er… of course. I spoke to your colleague at work. So have you found Richard? Is he dead?"

"As I told your mother, our investigations are ongoing, but the situation is pretty bleak, to be honest," Walker replied.

Morton shook his head. "It's just so desperately heart-breaking."

Walker glanced down at Morton's hands. He held one of the tiny toys in one and a matchstick-thin paintbrush in the other. The figure appeared to be some kind of soldier. Walker looked back at the table again. There were literally hundreds of similar soldiers lined up in rows and in groups, along with die-cast horses and carriages, some with covers and some with guns. At the back, there was what appeared to be a miniature field hospital complete with rows of tents. The tiny army almost completely overwhelmed the tabletop, and they continued on either side, reaching almost as far back as the loft hatch. Walker felt like she'd stumbled into a scene from *Gulliver's Travels*.

"This is an incredible collection you have here," she said. "Are they antique toys?"

"Not toys, not anymore. They are highly collectable works of art, in my view."

"I was just thinking this must be worth a bob or two."

"Some of the rarer individual pieces can fetch thousands at auction," Morton replied. He glanced back at Walker. "I suppose you probably think it's all a bit geeky and strange, and my colleagues do take the piss, but this is a lifetime passion for me. This is my sanctuary. To be honest, I'm kind of hiding up here as it's just too much to take in." He placed the soldier carefully back down on the table and settled the brush in a jar of clear liquid.

Walker kneeled by the bench. "So is this the battle of Waterloo?"

Morton looked up in surprise. "Well done, yes. I'm impressed."

"My little brother was into all this as well, but he was into the plastic variety."

"Ah yes, we don't talk about those up here," Morton said and smiled.

"Is that The Duke of Wellington over there?" She pointed at a figure on a horse brandishing a sword.

"Yes, he's not quite restored yet. I finally tracked him down on eBay last month. I've been searching for him for years."

"Shame there's no cone on his or the horse's head though?" she joked.

"You know I did think about that but my pedant brain got the better of me."

"So what did he set you back?" Walker asked with genuine interest.

"I'm too embarrassed to tell you, but put it this way, in two or three years I'll have probably doubled my investment."

"So what are those over there?" She nodded at a group of soldiers clustered together on their own on a separate table.

Morton smiled. "Ah yes, the Trojan Horse. So, during battle, the top brass would often send a battalion off to create a distraction and lull the enemy into thinking it was an advance. The enemy would respond, leaving them open and vulnerable to an ambush from the main army. Classic manoeuvre. The French were masters."

"It's a strange hobby for a geography teacher," Walker cut in.

"I did a joint honours degree in geography and history. They are interdependent in so many ways."

"So you and Mr Jones have been colleagues for four years, is that correct?" Walker returned to the job in hand.

"Sorry for going on. That's me running away again." Morton grimaced. "Yes, we were good friends. He was my tutor and mentor when I did my teacher training, and I think he championed me getting the job in his department."

"So Kilwinnoch is your first teaching post?"

"Yes. I learnt so much from Richard. He was such a brilliant teacher and boss," Morton said, biting down on his lower lip.

"Did you see each other socially much?"

"Not a huge amount. We saw each other every day, so probably didn't feel the need for a lot more. But I suppose once or twice a term, we'd go for drinks or round for meals. He maintained a very tight department. Everybody adored him."

"Tell me about the night of Richard's party," Walker continued.

Morton looked up in surprise. "What party?"

"The party where the police were called, that party."

"The police, when? No, really?" He stumbled over his words.

"Neighbours reported an altercation on Richard Jones's front lawn."

"Oh, honestly, that was of nothing."

"Is that why you decided not to mention it to my colleague when he spoke to you at the school?"

"It was such a trivial, stupid thing I just thought, well, we all thought that it wasn't worth mentioning. But now, of course, I wish it had never happened."

"So, what did happen?" Walker pressed.

"Oh, it's all a bit foggy as we were all… well, drunk really, and that's another reason not to say as we are all deeply embarrassed about it."

"You know it's a criminal offence to withhold information from the police?" Walker persisted.

"Yes, and it was a complete mistake on our part, and I am truly sorry. I suppose we just thought he'd return from one of his magical mystery tours with some more of his stunning photos."

"Okay, so what went on then?"

"The demon drink is the culprit here, sadly," Morton said. "We don't usually get so pissed but we'd just finished a long, hard marking stint and we were all up for letting our hair down. Unfortunately, it went a little too far."

"How did it start?"

"I think somebody mentioned something about Richard's photographs being better than Bran's. They were just mucking around, but it seemed to spark another row between the two of them."

"So they row a lot?"

"Like, all the time. You name it, they'll disagree. Don't get me wrong, it's all friendly banter, but that night it just…" He paused. "You know that they're both amateur photographers and they've both been entering the same landscape photo competition for years?"

"Yes, go on," Walker urged.

"That competition has been a real flashpoint between those two. They are both so competitive, and Richard couldn't handle the fact that Bran was winning year after year. And Bran wouldn't let him forget it. That night, he just kept goading Richard, on and on. We begged him to stop, but once he gets the bit between his teeth there's no stopping him. That's what their relationship was like. Every time they got together socially, sooner or later they would end up in a row, especially when alcohol was involved."

"So probably not a good idea to bring the topic up at the party then?"

Morton shrugged. "Well, no, but as I said, we were all a bit wasted, so a bit oblivious to any red flags or elephants in the room."

"Your colleague said that it was you who started the conversation."

"What?" Morton said, looking wounded. "Who said that? That's not true. I might have joined in a little at the beginning, thinking it was funny, but it was clear pretty soon after that the tease was turning sour. Thinking back, I'm pretty sure it was Richard who brought it up," he said. "He was blotto, too."

"And were you involved in the fight that developed out in the street?"

"No, of course not! That was all down to that maniac, Kinross, pushing Richard's buttons."

"Did Jones throw the first punch?"

"Not at all. Richard was trying to reason with Bran and calm him down. I think at that point he finally realised things had gone way too far. But Bran just carried on, accusing Richard of stealing his photographic ideas, gate-crashing locations, and trying to scupper his chances of winning that stupid bloody competition."

He glanced up at the detective. "Like I said, they had some kind of love-hate relationship based on their mutual passion for nature photography. I totally get the rivalry, though. The model army community is rife with petty jealousies. I stay well clear as much as I can."

"Would you say their rivalry was toxic then?"

"Wait, I'm not saying their rivalry was so intense it would result in Bran actually killing Richard. That's completely absurd," Morton protested. They were friends and colleagues but they just had that kind of relationship. They pushed each other's buttons when they wanted to."

"The colleague said that when you were all out in the street, you were encouraging the two of them to fight."

"Well, Dawn is talking utter nonsense," Morton snapped. "Why would she say such a thing? The drink has fogged her memory, clearly. I was trying to calm things down and then I actually stepped in."

"Yes, your colleague also confirmed that. She said you were 'stirring it', her words."

"I can't believe this. That's really upsetting." Morton rubbed his taut knuckles across his mouth. "It started as a bit of a laugh, and I admit at first I was going along with it, bearing in mind I was pretty sozzled, too. But it was clear things were going too far, and that's when I tried to stop it. I don't know where Dawn was at that point, but that's what I did. I couldn't stand to see the two of them actually throwing punches at each other. It was horrible."

"So, what you're telling me is you were the hero of the night?"

"I wouldn't put it quite like that. We were all idiots that night and should have known better than to get so drunk."

"One more question, if I may. Where were you on the early morning of the twenty-first of June?" Walker asked.

"Here, right here," Morton snapped back, his eyes widening. "I always come up first thing before breakfast. It helps me get my brain ready for the day. And then I went to work."

"Okay, Mr Morton. That's all for now, thanks for your time," Walker said curtly.

"The person who did this needs to be locked up for a very long time," Morton shook his head. "It's just so evil."

"That's our objective, Mr Morton. Don't get up, I'll see myself out… or down," Walker returned to the hatch.

As she slowly climbed back down the ladder, she watched Morton pick up one of the infantryman and a paintbrush. He glanced back at her and smiled.

On her way past one of the upstairs rooms, she quickly stuck her head around the door. It was a neat and tidy bedroom with a single bed and a small study desk tucked under the window. On top of the desk was a framed photo. Glancing over her shoulder, she went in for a closer look. It was a photo of Morton and Jones standing together, arm in arm, with Stonehenge looming in the background behind them.

Adjacent to the bed was a half-sized bookcase with books squeezed in along the shelves. She knelt and scanned the rows. There were mainly geography textbooks, but on the top shelf, there were history books on various wars and famous battles including World War One and the Napoleonic Wars. Resting next to a hardback copy of *The Art of War* by Sun Tzu was an audiobook CD box of *Beware of Imitations* by the impressionist, Rory Bremner.

She got up to leave but noticed the wardrobe was open. Inside there were identical grey suits racked up in a neat row, but then on the end, there was a single blue suit that looked tailored and more expensive. A thump sounded above her head, and she jumped. She dashed out and went back downstairs.

In the hallway, Mrs Morton showed Walker out. "I hope you find the wicked person who did this soon, Detective."

"We do, too, Mrs Morton," Walker replied. Halfway down the path, she stopped and turned. "Just one more thing."

Mrs Morton pulled the door open again. "Yes?"

"Where was your son on the night of the twentieth and the morning of the twenty-first of June?"

"What?" Mrs Morton recoiled in surprise. "Please don't tell me my boy is a suspect?"

"We're just trying to establish a clear picture," Walker replied with one of her well-versed professional smiles.

"He was at home here with me," Mrs Morton returned immediately.

"Are you sure? I mean, sometimes it can be quite difficult to remember what we were doing at specific times. I would be a terrible witness. I can barely remember one minute to the next, never mind days and weeks in the past."

Mrs Morton thought for a moment. "Yes, I'm sure, and I remember because that's *Bake Off* night and we watched it together. We're both huge fans." She paused again. "And then he helped me upstairs, with my bad knees, you know, and we went to bed."

"So you left him and went to sleep?"

"Well, I don't sleep very well and I could hear him thumping about in the loft with his soldiers, and his music playing quietly. That went on for quite a while."

"So you couldn't say with one hundred percent certainty that he was in the house all night?"

"Well, no, but I would have heard him go out. As I said, I'm a very light sleeper and he was home all night," Mrs Morton said, her agitation growing. "And then in the morning he went to school as usual." She took a deep breath. "You're beginning to upset me with these questions, Detective. My son looked up to Richard. He was his hero and dear friend. It is, quite frankly, offensive of you to even suggest he might have had something to do with Richard's disappearance."

"Okay, thank you, Mrs Morton. I'll leave you now." Walker said, cutting her off.

Mrs Morton slammed the door.

Back at the car, Walker took a few deep mouthfuls of air. She'd underestimated the potency of the paint fumes in the loft and was feeling lightheaded. She climbed in and sat for a moment to recover. Perhaps it was the effects of the solvent, or Mrs Morton's intense reaction, but she couldn't shake Morton's smile from her mind. After a few moments, she started the car and headed back to the main road.

NINETEEN

Michael and Alice waited for Bone at his ex's front door.

"Hi," Alice said with a modest nod. "God, you look awful."

"Cheers," Bone replied. "Migraine."

"Do you want to pick Michael up tomorrow?" she asked.

"No, Mum. I want to go now," Bone's six-year-old son complained and pulled his hand out from her tight grip. He jumped down the step and grabbed his dad's leg.

"No, I'm fine. We're good to go, aren't we, son?"

"Yay!" Michael hollered.

"Don't forget your bag, Michael." Alice handed Bone a holdall stuffed to bursting.

"Bloody hell, what have you got in here?" Bone asked, struggling to lift it over his shoulder.

"Just his usual stuff, and a few of his favourite toys," Alice attempted to tie back her errant locks. She looked a little flustered. More than usual.

"Everything all right?" Bone asked.

"Fine."

But Bone sensed something was up.

"What is it?" he pressed.

"She has a boyfriend," Michael jumped in, pulling a face at his mum.

"Michael!" Alice exclaimed in horror. "He's not a boyfriend. We're just going out for a meal and a few drinks."

Bone tried to conceal his feelings. "So how long have you been seeing this guy?" he asked and failed miserably.

"That is none of your business," she snapped back.

"Of course. No. You're right. Sorry." Bone took his son's hand. "See you tomorrow."

"Tomorrow? I thought Michael was staying over for a couple of days as we agreed."

Bone suddenly realised he'd forgotten to ask "Oh, shit. It's just that I need to go in first thing. We're in the middle of this investigation."

"You're always in the middle of this investigation or that investigation. Maybe you should just stay here, Michael, and let your dad do whatever he bloody likes." She shook her head in dismay.

"No, Mum, please. Dad, I want to stay at yours."

Bone knelt. "Listen, Michael, I'm really sorry, but you can only stay tonight, but maybe Mum will let you come over on Saturday and we can have a boys' weekend."

"Yay!" the boy jumped up and down, swinging his dad's arm back and forth.

"You can't just make this up as we go along, Duncan. That's the whole point of mediation and access arrangements."

"I'm so sorry, Alice. It completely slipped my mind to call you. But if Michael comes over on Saturday it will give you a bit more time to, you know, socialise." He chanced his arm with a smile.

"I'll think about it. So when will you drop Michael back tomorrow?"

"Seven-thirty, is that okay?"

"Are you kidding?"

"Sorry. I need to get to—"

"All right, don't go there again," Alice cut in. She leaned over and zipped up Michael's jacket. "Be a good boy for your dad, okay?"

"We won't," Bone and Michael replied in unison, and Michael giggled.

Alice shook her head and shut the door, and father and son ran down the path and out to Bone's car.

Two hours of *Power Rangers*, a frozen pizza, and multiple bedtime stories later, Bone finally got Michael to sleep in the camp bed he'd set up in the spare room.

Returning to the living room, he crashed in the armchair, and his head fell back against the rest. Despite the exhaustion, having his son in the house seemed to clear the clutter from his brain. His migraine had vanished, and his anxiety levels had dropped. He let out a long sigh. After a few minutes of rest, he could feel himself drifting off. He forced himself up and retreated to bed.

He woke in a state of confusion. He opened his eyes and squinted through the gloom. It was still dark outside. But then his brain registered a strong smell of burning. He coughed and choked. He sat up and snatched at the bedside light. The room was full of thick, acrid smoke, pouring in from under the door.

"Fuck!" Jumping up, he reached for the door handle but stopped and placed his hand on the surface. It was still cool. He threw it open and stumbled out into the hall. The front door was ablaze with flames engulfing the ceiling above. He dashed into Michael's room.

Michael was sitting up, coughing and disoriented.

"Daddy," he cried.

Bone snatched him up into his arms and, grabbing a towel, he threw it over Michael's head. Back in the hall, the fire had now spread farther down the hallway. The flames had devoured most of the door, and between the flames, he could see the close beyond.

Bending over, he ran at the flames, rammed through the remains of the door, and out onto the landing. He put Michael down yanked the towel—now showered in flickering embers—from Michael's head and dropped it to the floor. Picking up his son again, he ran down the stairs and out into the street, followed by one terrified neighbour after another, in various stages of undress.

A fire engine turned into the street, its siren blaring loudly. It accelerated towards them and then pulled up with a deafening screech of brakes. Four firemen jumped out, and one approached Bone and the huddle of neighbours gathering around him.

"It's my flat, top floor. The door is ablaze," Bone said.

With a wave of his arms, the fire crew in full protective gear and masks ran into the flats, dragging a hose behind them. Michael cried as the shock hit him.

"We're okay, son." Bone pulled Michael tighter to his chest.

"What happened?" Michael spluttered.

"There was a fire. Hey, check out that fire engine."

He tried to distract him, but Michael continued to cry through his coughs.

"I want Mummy," he wailed.

"Yes, I'll take you back home."

An ambulance arrived on the scene, and two paramedics got out and approached.

"My son may have breathed in a bit of smoke," Bone wheezed and then coughed loudly.

"And you, too, by the sounds of things," the younger paramedic said. "We'll need to check you out,"

"Here?"

"No, the hospital."

"No, Dad. I don't want to go to the hospital," Michael cried out, now wriggling uncontrollably in Bone's arms.

Bone put him down.

"Hey, shall we go for a superfast ride in the ambulance?" the paramedic said, kneeling next to Michael. "We'll put the sirens on and everything, and I might even let you try out some of the gizmos in the back."

Michael fell silent.

"I have a feeling that Stephen, our driver..." She glanced up at her colleague and winked. "...has a secret supply of stickers somewhere."

Reluctantly, Michael gave in, and Bone picked him up again, and together with the paramedic, they climbed into the back of the ambulance.

A kindly A&E receptionist let Bone use her phone to call Alice. Ten minutes later, his distraught ex-wife rushed into the examination room, dishevelled and panicking, and dashed over to Michael who was being examined by a doctor.

"What happened?" She spun round and glared at Bone.

"Mummy. I went in an ambulance," Michael said as the doctor listened to his chest with a stethoscope.

"There was a fire at the flat," Bone said sheepishly.

"A fire? What in the hell, Duncan?" Alice kneeled next to her son. "Is he okay?" She brushed a few bits of ash from his hair.

"Could you give me a huge, big breath, Michael?" the doctor asked and pressed the stethoscope against Michael's bare back.

"Ouch, that's cold!" Michael complained.

"Do as the doctor says, Michael," Alice insisted.

Michael heaved in and let out a long puff.

Alice glanced back at Bone and frowned.

"Okay," the doctor said finally. "He'll be absolutely fine. There's no sign of any lingering smoke damage. Just keep an eye on him and his breathing over the next couple of days." He turned to Bone. "You next."

"I'm okay. There's no need," Bone replied.

"Are you sure?"

"I'm not coughing, and my chest feels fine."

"Right, I think we're done here then," the doctor said with a weary smile. "It was great to meet you, Michael."

The doctor held out his hand, and Michael shook it.

"And Spider-Man is definitely the best superhero." He raised his arm and zapped Michael with an imaginary web.

Michael returned fire, and the doctor was gone.

Alice removing a clean sweat top from her bag. "Come on, Michael, let's go home." She pulled it briskly over Michael's head.

Bone approached her cautiously. "Sorry, Alice. I don't know what happened," Alice bundled up the rest of Michael's things and, lifting him up into her arms, she pushed past him.

"Bye, Dad," Michael gave Bone a despondent wave.

"Can you just stop for a minute so we can talk, Alice, come on?" Bone pleaded.

But Alice carried on out into the corridor.

Bone followed them out. "Alice?"

She stopped. "It's late, Duncan. Michael needs to get to his bed."

"I'm not tired. I'm Spider-Man," Michael said.

"We'll talk tomorrow," Alice insisted. They disappeared through a set of double doors and out into the main A&E waiting room.

Bone let them go and headed out into the remains of the night, and to whatever horror story was waiting for him back at his burnt-out flat.

TWENTY

Back at his tenement, the fire engines and ambulances had gone, but there was a SOC van and a fire inspection vehicle parked up. A uniformed officer greeted him at the entrance.

"DCI Bone?" the officer said.

"Correct. How did you guess?"

"They're waiting for you upstairs." The PC let Bone past.

At the top of the landing, he was greeted by a second PC who guarded the burnt-out doorway of Bone's flat.

"Detective Bone?" the uniform asked.

"Is it that obvious?" Bone sighed wearily.

Just then, a fireman stepped through the gaping, charred hole in the door, clutching a clipboard. "You must be Detective Bone," he said, his body shifting inside his bulky, fire-repellent jacket.

"I'm going to start wearing a baseball cap with my name on it," Bone replied.

"Sorry?" the fire officer said. "I'm Arson Investigator Frank Copperfield."

"What have you found?" Bone interrupted.

"I've been examining the fire, and while we need Forensics to confirm, it's pretty obvious that some kind of accelerant was used to set the door alight," he said, shifting his clipboard from one arm to the other.

"So, deliberate?"

"Without a doubt."

"My son was here with me, the bastard," Bone growled.

"Indeed. But as I say, I'll have to wait for the SOC team to come back with their findings before I complete my report. They'll be here shortly."

Bone edged towards the blackened doorway, stepping over a sodden, muddy pile of burnt wood and ash.

"You might want to put on some protective gear, Inspector, as this is now a crime scene."

Bone ignored him and carried on.

"We've opened up all the windows, but I wouldn't advise staying here tonight, or even for the next few days until the smoke clears. That stuff is highly toxic," the inspector called after him.

Bone carried on down the hallway and farther into the gloom. The flat still reeked of smoke, and Bone coughed again. The hallway carpet squelched under his feet. The fire hoses had drenched the entire hallway, and the walls and ceiling dripped with blackened water.

"Jesus," he moaned.

He checked the kitchen, and aside from the same cloying smell of smoke, it was untouched by the fire. Carrying on to the living room, it was the same, with no sign of fire or water damage. He let out a sigh of relief.

In the bedroom, the first rays of morning light appeared through the open window, and the birds sang. He sat on the edge of his bed and retrieved his phone from the bedside cabinet. He was about to check his messages when he glanced across the room. There was something on the wall above the dressing table. He peered into the gloom and then got up for a closer look. The words LEAVE ALONE were spray-painted in blood-red capital letters covering almost the entire width of the wall.

"What the fuck?"

He pressed his forefinger onto the surface of the paint. It was dry.

A sudden voice had him spinning round.

"Inspector Bone?" A SOC officer appeared in the doorway, her pale, ashen face popping through her tight-fitting protective headgear.

Bone turned in surprise.

"I'm Forensics Officer Carol Drax," she said. "I'm in charge of the inspection tonight."

"Where's CFO Cash?" Bone asked.

"Even my boss has to sleep sometimes, sir," Drax said, and added "allegedly." the edges of her smile disappearing under the elastic hood. "Anyway, I prefer nights." Her deep-sunken eyes seemed to widen at the thought.

"I just found this." Bone pointed at the spray paint.

The officer shuffled over.

"I don't understand how this got here," Bone continued. "When the fire broke out, the fire crews were here very quickly, and the flat hasn't been left unattended since."

Drax leaned closer to the wall and sniffed.

"Difficult to tell with all this smoke still around, but at first glance, I reckon this was sprayed a few hours ago."

"So before the fire?"

"That is entirely possible. We'll run some checks on the paint."

Bone scanned the phrase back and forth a couple of times.

"See that?"

"Sorry, what?" Drax squinted at him.

"In the first word, there are strokes of paint joining up the letters, but in the second, the letters are completely unconnected," Bone said.

Drax peered at the graffiti for a moment. "You're right, that is odd. It's almost like two different styles." She turned back to him. "It would be worth getting a forensic handwriting specialist to have a look at this."

Bone nodded.

"There's something else I want to show you," she added.

Back in the hall, two SOC officers knelt by the front entrance, and a third was out in the close with a camera.

"If you could just stop there," Drax said. "We need to preserve the scene as much as we can." She hobbled over to her colleagues, her shoe protectors squeaking on the wet carpet. "The arson investigator said that he suspected some kind of accelerant had been used to start the fire." She stopped by the mound of charred remains. "At first glance, it looks like someone has poured an accelerant such as something like lighter fuel or even petrol through your letterbox." Kneeling, she removed a wooden spatula from her bodysuit and gently nudged the pile until the corner of the blackened brass letterbox plate appeared. "It's a dangerous game that, especially with petrol as it can instantly backdraft and blow up in your face."

"I wouldn't call it a game. My six-year-old son could have been killed," Bone retorted.

"Sorry, sir. Wrong choice of words. I would say, though, that whoever did this was not intent on killing you or your son, especially with that graffiti through there. Perhaps more of a warning?"

"Or a threat," Bone cut in.

"Yes, that, too," Drax agreed. "We'll carry on here, but it will take us a few hours to complete. I suggest you leave us to it."

Bone checked his watch. "I'll just get dressed. I'm not sure my pyjamas would go down well at the nick."

Drax smiled. "Sure, carry on, but try not to contaminate the site."

"I'd say the bastard who did this has won, hands down, on that front," Bone replied and left her to carry on with her work.

TWENTY-ONE

As Bone pulled up opposite the station, a tsunami of reporters surged towards the car, blocking his escape. He forced his door open, shoving bodies out of the way. He pushed through, ignoring the onslaught of questions. When he reached the bottom of the steps, Colin McKinnon's voice boomed out across the cacophony.

"Are you losing it again, DCI Bone? Set fire to a chip pan then?" he scoffed.

The gathered press burst into laughter. Bone stopped, forced his brain to resist leaping at McKinnon's throat, and turned to address them.

"We have nothing to report at this stage, thank you," Bone replied and leapt up the steps before he did something that would cost him his job.

"Morning, sir," the night sergeant said, clearing his things in preparation to leave. "You're early this—"

"Get Springsteen out of his cell and into an interview room, now."

"Sir," the officer said and dropped his bag back down on the desk.

Bone continued through and down the corridor to the incident room. He pushed the door open with such force it smacked against the wall. Harper, who was propped up at his desk staring vacantly at his computer screen, almost jumped out the window with fright.

"Jesus, sir, I almost had kittens there," Harper said. "God, what happened to you?"

"Some bastard tried to torch my flat with me and my son in it," Bone said. He clocked himself in the mirror by the coat hooks. "Jesus."

"What?"

"My son and I almost fried." He wiped at the smears of black ash streaked across his cheeks and forehead.

"What happened?" Harper repeated.

"Listen, are you the only one in?" Bone asked, ignoring him.

"Just me. I couldn't sleep again. I think it must be the painkillers they had me on," Harper complained. "The SOC team recovered Jones's laptop and phone from his flat, and they're with the digital forensics team. I thought I'd come in and give them a hand."

"Phone? I thought he'd have that with him when he went up into the hills?"

"Maybe he forgot it?" The DC shrugged.

"Okay, do that later, right now I want you to come with me." Bone ordered.

"Where are we going?"

"To throw the book at Bruce bloody Springsteen, downstairs," Bone snarled.

"Oh, right." Harper grabbed his jacket. "He's not violent, is he?" he asked on the way out.

"He'd cut off your balls and eat them if there was money in it for him," Bone replied. "Don't worry, if he tries anything, I'll bloody kill him. So here's hoping he does."

On the way, Bone stopped in the stairwell. "Oh, by the way, do you know anything about handwriting forensics?"

"No, but I know someone who does. My old uni friend is now a forensic document analyst, to use the technical term. She's done quite a lot of work for a few stations and units, mainly fraud but some serious crime stuff. She's good. I mean, really good."

"You star!"

"I aim to please, sir." Harper smiled and adjusted his glasses.

"Okay, when we get back to the incident room, could you contact her?"

"Sure, yes. What's it about?"

"I'll fill you in later. First, we have a lowlife to attend to."

They continued down the stairs.

When the detectives entered the interview room, Springsteen was by the table, flanked by two uniforms who had his arms in a tight lock.

"Mr Springsteen. Glad you could make it, and sorry to disturb you so early."

"I told you before, I'm not speaking to anyone without a fucking lawyer," Springsteen barked back and tried to free his arms.

The PCs shook him back and forth until he stopped resisting.

"Would you care to sit down, or would you prefer my colleagues to prop you up?"

"I want to go back to my cell," Springsteen moaned.

"Not a cat in hell's chance," Bone returned. "And don't worry, I only have one question for you, so it shouldn't take too long."

Reluctantly, Springsteen gestured to sit down, and the two officers lowered him onto the chair.

Bone hit the button on the recorder. "Interview commenced at…," he checked his watch, "Seven zero three a.m. Tuesday, the twenty-sixth of June. DCI Duncan Bone and DC Harper in attendance, along with PCs…" He glanced up.

"Gilfillan and Kerr, sir."

PCs Gilfillan and Kerr," Bone completed the preliminaries and turned back to the suspect. "Okay, that's the small talk out the way. Let's get right to it. Where's your brother?"

"No comm—" Springsteen started.

Bone slapped his palm down on the desk, and Springsteen looked up in surprise.

"Before you continue, just a quick reminder that refusal to cooperate will lead to a one hundred percent conviction for the assault and attempted murder of a senior detective. You were saying?"

Springsteen shuffled nervously in his chair. "I don't know where—"

Bone hit the table again, this time with a clenched fist, and with such force the table bounced off the floor.

"That's funny," Harper intervened. "A witness saw you and your brother on Craigend Ridge at the Kilmorgan Stone circle at approximately…" He flicked back through the notepad in front of him. "Nine twenty-six p.m."

Bone glanced over at the young detective.

"That wasn't us," Springsteen snapped.

"Well, our witness is extremely reliable, and I'm sure their testimony would hold up pretty well in the High Court," Harper added.

Springsteen huffed and shifted back and forth in his chair again. "We…"

"We?" Bone urged.

"The bastards have just abandoned us?" Springsteen continued.

"What bastards?" Bone asked.

"I can't… They'll kill me."

"Your paymasters?" Bone pressed.

Springsteen stared down at his hands.

"So these 'bastards' as you call them are happy to let you go down for a double life sentence. You really think you owe them your loyalty?" Bone continued.

"Look, they hired me and my brother to do a job," Springsteen said finally. "Find the nest, steal the eggs, and the male."

"So where's your brother?" Bone pushed.

"I honestly don't know. When we did a runner, I got caught, and he disappeared."

"He's in Kilwinnoch then?"

"He's probably back in London, I dunno." Springsteen shrugged again.

"So, he's sold you out as well?"

"No!" Springsteen snapped back.

The two PCs moved in.

"Last night, someone tried to torch my flat. My son almost died. Is your brother still doing your paymaster's bidding?" Bone snarled, his fists on the table, clenched and ready to swing.

"Jesus, no!" Springsteen returned in surprise. "He wouldn't… We would never do that."

"Unless they have his nuts in a vice?" Bone asked. "You do this one thing for us and we make sure your brother is protected."

"I don't see how when I don't know where he is." Springsteen huffed loudly. "This is bollocks. We didn't kill the teacher. We didn't set fire to your fucking flat. That's out of our league."

"One last time, who is your paymaster and where is your brother?"

Springsteen shook his head.

Bone stood. "DC Harper, do the paperwork."

Harper looked up at Bone and then clambered to his feet. "So, just to confirm, is that conspiracy to steal endangered and protected wildlife, resisting arrest, and assault of an upstanding member of our local community?"

"Might as well add perverting the course of justice and conspiracy to commit arson with intent to murder a child."

"That's fucking bullshit. I was in here. How could I possibly set fire to your house?"

"I'll think of something." Bone replied and marched out of the interview room.

On his way back to the incident room, Gallacher spotted him as he was attempting to unlock his office door.

"Duncan," he called and gestured for him to come.

Bone sighed and followed Gallacher into his office.

"Last night, well, I say last night, it was about three-bloody-thirty in the morning, I received a call from the station informing me that there had been an incident at your flat."

"A fire," Bone replied.

"First off, are you okay, because you look like shite?" Gallacher asked.

"So people keep telling me."

"Are you going to enlighten me or break just sit there like Dick Van Dyke the bloody chimney sweep."

"Someone poured petrol or some other delightful accelerant through my letterbox. My son was over. The first time he'd been to the flat since the Tennyson case." Bone scowled.

"Oh God. Is he okay?"

"Thankfully, he's fine, physically. I just hope there's no lasting mental scars."

"Thank Christ." Gallacher sighed. "So do you have any idea who would do this? Do you think it's in some way connected to the death of the teacher?"

"Well, whoever it was left a wee note sprayed on my bedroom wall that said *leave alone*, so taking a wild guess, I'd say yes."

"Where are you up to now with the case? You have a suspect in custody. How's that going?"

"We've just charged him with a list of things, but I'm just not sure if we're on the right path with him. The way things are going, our list of suspects is growing by the hour."

"What is it with this bloody town? Why can't we just have straightforward domestic bloody murders instead of this twisted madness all the bloody time?"

"That's Kilwinnoch for you." Bone shrugged. "Never a dull moment."

"Okay, so next moves?"

"Next move is to let me get on with my job." He glanced up and added, "With respect, sir."

Gallacher dropped his bag by his desk and sat. "I don't want you going off like a bloody firework over your boy," he warned.

"I'm channelling my rage, sir."

"Another word about your conduct, either from colleagues or that bloody local rag, and I'll pull you from this case, clear?"

"Yes, you have mentioned that before."

"And that's because I'm serious Duncan. And I would be doing it for you and not the reason I can see written all over your face."

Gallacher paused for a moment and studied his friend's furrowed features. "You're exhausting, Duncan." He sighed and tapped his finger on the desk for a moment, as though weighing up options. "Keep me updated." he gestured to the door.

"Sir." Bone nodded and left.

TWENTY-TWO

Brandon Kinross's house was located in a small mews development behind Kilwinnoch's high street.

"I remember when Fisher's bike shop was here," Bone said as he pulled the Saab into the designated parking space in front. "My dad bought me my first Chopper in there."

"What the hell is a Chopper?" Walker feigned ignorance.

"You don't know what a Chopper is? I'm going to have you sacked," Bone replied and glancing over at his colleague in disbelief.

"I'm only pulling your chain, of course I do. Isn't that the bike that Mozart composed his first concerto on?

"I'll be decomposing you in a minute," Bone retorted and climbed out. "There was a hardware store next door. My old man was never out of it." He scanned the bland, featureless shoebox townhouses, clustered claustrophobically together to maximise space and profits. "You'd think the architects would at least try to fit in with the surrounding buildings." He glanced over his shoulder to the backyards of the Victorian shops behind them.

"It's all about the dosh, not the design," Walker said, and followed hiim along the row.

"What number is it again?" Bone asked.

"Twelve. Right here." She pointed at a door in front, with silver-plated numerals screwed onto the stonework.

"Even the number's bland." Bone rapped on the door. He was about to knock again when he heard someone on the other side coming down a set of stairs. The door flew open.

"Yes?" Kinross answered. He was clutching an electric toothbrush that was vibrating noisily in his hand.

"I'm DCI Bone, and this is DI Walker from Kilwinnoch station."

They both flashed their lanyards.

"Could we have a word?"

"What now?" Kinross said, looking flustered.

"If you don't mind, yes," Bone replied.

"I have to get to school. I'm kind of late," Kinross said, with more than a hint of irritation.

"We have some news about your colleague, Richard Jones," Bone added.

Kinross stared at the two detectives for a moment and then, finally realising his toothbrush was still on, he grappled with the button until it stopped.

"You'd better come in then." He opened the door wider, ushering them in. "Please excuse the mess," he said as they ascended a narrow and extremely steep stairway that seemed rammed into the corner of the hall. "I'm in a bit of a rush this morning and I haven't had time to…"

The upstairs room felt equally claustrophobic, made all the worse by what appeared to be a full-scale weight-lifting gym that almost covered the entire floor space. Kinross snatched up a towel from the floor.

"You like to keep fit then?" Bone asked the obvious.

"You could say that. I find that if I don't do a couple of workouts a day I'm a basket case. So what's happened?" he asked removing his sweat-soaked T-shirt and wiping his armpits with the towel.

"Perhaps you'd like to get changed first," Bone asked, taken aback by Kinross's sudden exhibitionism.

"I'll just grab a fresh T-shirt if you don't mind," Kinross replied.

Walker noticed a pronounced pinkish scar running around Kinross's left shoulder and under his arm.

"That's quite a wound you've got there," she said.

"Ah, yes." Kinross glanced down and ran his forefinger along the line. "Climbing accident. I fell almost thirty feet off the side of Scafell Pike or Scarfell as I call it now, and landed on my shoulder."

"Ouch," Walker winced.

"The whole of this joint is now metal and my shoulder is permanently frozen." He disappeared through a door at the back of the living room.

"Weird," Walker whispered.

Moments later, Kinross was back, now wearing a tight, sleeveless Lonsdale T-shirt, his over-developed biceps and pecs pressing against the nylon fabric.

"Do you still climb?" Bone asked.

"A bit, but my injury curtailed my love of free climbing," he said. "So please, tell me what's happened."

"I'm sorry to tell you that the body found at Braeburn Falls is that of your colleague, Richard Jones," Bone said.

Kinross continued to stare at Bone, with barely a movement or emotion registering on his face.

"Did you hear what I said, Mr Kinross?"

"No, but, that's not right," Kinross finally responded.

"Perhaps you should sit down, Brandon," Walker cut in.

Kinross dropped down on a narrow armchair tucked between a rowing machine and a rack of weights.

"What? This can't be right. I just thought… How?"

"At this stage, we don't know the cause but we are treating his death as suspicious," Bone said.

"I can't believe it. I mean, I saw the reports of a discovery and all that, but I just thought it was maybe another drowning accident or something," Kinross rubbed his palm back and forth over one of his biceps.

"Would you like a glass of water?" Walker asked.

"I mean, we were… I just saw him," Kinross stammered.

"When and where was that, Mr Kinross?" Bone pressed on.

"I don't know… er… at school last Wednesday."

"And how did he seem to you?" Walker continued.

"I dunno, just his usual combative self, with me anyway."

"Tell me about your relationship," Bone carried on.

"Nothing to tell really. We had many an interesting discussion about all sorts. Our politics are very different. I told all this to your colleague who spoke to us at the school."

"So discussion, not argument?" Walker interrupted.

"Oh, sometimes it got a bit heated." He looked up. "But we never fell out. It was kind of the way we were together. Our colleagues used to laugh about it and said we'd make a great couple."

"Could you tell us about the dinner party on the twelfth of June?" Walker continued.

"You know about that?" Kinross asked in surprise.

"We do now, and you know you should have told us before," Bone interjected.

"Yes, well, on that occasion, things did get a little out of hand, but I think we'd all had a little too much to drink," Kinross said. "But we were just letting off steam, you know?"

"That's what your colleague said," Bone confirmed.

"Who, Oli?" Kinross asked.

"Yes, but it was Miss Chalmers who had the sense to tell us in the first place."

"There really was no need to mention it. It was a drunken night of stupidity. Haven't you ever had one of those?" he countered.

"Yes, plenty, but none that may have ended in the death of one of my work colleagues," Walker said.

"Both Miss Chalmers and Mr Morton said that you were brawling with Mr Jones on the front lawn outside his house, is that correct?" Bone persisted.

"I wouldn't say we were brawling. That makes it sound like some kind of Clint Eastwood film. We just got into a bit of a tussle. Like I said, too much booze, which was entirely my fault as Richard asked me to prep some cocktails and I think I used too much vodka in them."

"What was the fight about?"

"Hardly a…" Kinross's agitation was growing by the second. "It was a row about the photo comp we both enter each year."

"And how did it start?"

"Oh, I don't know," Kinross groaned.

"Are you withholding more information, Mr Kinross? Because if you are we can continue this conversation down at the station," Bone's irritation was increasing.

Kinross shook his head again. "I really can't remember. But my colleague and friend is dead. Surely that's more important?"

"Miss Chalmers has already told us that Mr Morton was, *'stirring it,'* as she described it, with the two of you for most of the night, and he continued to do so even during your tussle out front. Would you agree with her account?" Walker stepped in again.

"The only thing I remember was giving Richard a drunken hug at the end of the night and nursing a hangover from hell the next day, with my worst class thrown in for good measure. But that doesn't surprise me about Oli stirring, to be honest."

"What do you mean?" Bone asked.

"He can be an irritating little prick."

"Funny, that's what Mr Morton called you," Walker said.

Kinross laughed. "Well, that makes him even more of an irritating prick. Always hanging about Richard like a sycophantic creep. He can be so weird sometimes. He'd do these impressions of people at work that he thinks are funny, but I've always found them disturbing, to be honest, especially when he mimicked Richard, which was always so sickly smarmy. He even turned up at a staff do once, dressed in the same blue suit Richard wears and pretended to be him all bloody night. Funny for five minutes, then just plain pathological."

"So I take it you don't get on with him?" Bone asked.

"At long arm's length, he's just about tolerable, but I couldn't stand the way he was constantly sucking up to Richard. It's unhealthy. But Richard went right along with it, even when Oli was the only teacher in the entire school who got hauled over the coals when the inspectors landed and trashed his lessons. Somehow the wee prick managed to get Richard to take the flack. That's the kind of guy Richard was."

"So Wednesday Twentieth was the last day you saw Mr Jones?" Walker asked.

Kinross nodded. "Yes, at work. And as I said, he seemed absolutely fine to me."

"So you were on speaking terms again?" Walker continued.

"Of course we were. Neither of us bear grudges. After so many years, we both understand how it works between us."

"Finally, where were you on the evening of the twentieth and twenty-first of June?" Bone asked.

Kinross looked up. "I was up at the Corriemurran Cairn and Standing Stones, to try and catch the solstice for the photographic competition."

"How did you get up there?" Bone persisted.

"I drove up in the night."

"When did you arrive and when did you leave?"

"I don't believe this," Kinross snapped back. "I had nothing to do with Richard's death."

"We're just trying to establish everyone's whereabouts, Mr Kinross. No one is accusing you," Walker reassured.

"I got there about one in the morning, set up, and then I left later that morning, early enough to get back for work."

"And did anyone accompany you, or do you have proof you were up there?"

"I went alone. I drove up. I camped on my own. I drove home. That's it."

"So no one else at the stones? Druids or sun-worshippers?" Walker asked.

"There was a small group of travellers on the other side of the valley, but I didn't go near. My kit is worth thousands, and I don't trust any of them."

"No stops for petrol or food?"

"Oh come on, Detective. This is beginning to upset me now," Kinross complained. "No, I drove straight there."

"What about photographs? Wouldn't they have a time stamp on them?" Walker persisted.

"I didn't take any in the end. I set up and waited but in the end the light just wasn't working for me, so I packed up and drove home." He looked at his watch. "I'm really sorry, Detectives, but I do have to go to work. I have a class of second years first thing who will burn down the school if I'm not there."

"Okay," Bone said. "Thanks for your cooperation. And in the meantime, if you think of anything else, please don't withhold it, or I'll have you up at Sheriff Court faster than you can say instant dismissal, you understand?"

Walker handed him her card. "That's a direct line to the incident room."

Kinross took the card and stared at the Police Scotland logo on the front. "I can't believe this is happening. It seems so..." He tailed off, lost for words.

"Right, we'll let you get off. We'll see ourselves out," Bone said.

The detectives left.

Back at the car, Bone opened the door and stopped. "Thoughts?"

"Vain, egotistical, cold, a little highly strung, and completely lacking in social etiquette," Walker replied.

"Strange to go to work after such devastating news about his colleague," Bone said, climbing in.

"And a very shaky alibi." Walker got in and closed her door. "I mean would you hump all that gear up that mountain and not take a single shot?"

Bone glanced over at her. "Our killer?"

"Physically capable. I wouldn't like to get in a 'tussle' as he called it with him, put it that way, even with the Robocop shoulder. But I'm struggling with the why."

"Maybe he's on steroids. Those could make him aggressive," Bone suggested.

"He doesn't seem the kind of guy who would cheat like that. More of a rule book, Gestapo type."

"Oh God, this case!" Bone moaned.

"Yes, but we love it, don't we?" Walker sneered.

Bone reversed the Saab out of the cul-de-sac and back onto the main road. Reaching down, he pressed the button on the retro 70's cartridge player attached to the underside of the dash panel.

"What are you doing?" Walker asked.

"I bet you can't guess what I picked up at a car boot the other day." Bone smiled.

"Please don't tell me you're going to play one of your jazz classics again?"

"Oh, a bit more up to date than that," he said and pushed the play button.

The machine clacked, and the car filled with the opening bars of Glen Campbell's 'Rhinestone Cowboy'.

"You've got to be kidding," Walker complained over the din.

"Two quid, the box is in the door next to you," Bone cleared his throat and sang along badly to Campbell's smooth twang.

"Oh dear God, this is what hell must be like." Walker turned over the thick, yellowing cartridge box with a faded picture of Campbell straddling a horse while playing a guitar.

"Come on, you know you love it," Bone cried out above the sweeping sound of strings.

Walker giggled.

"There you go, you see, it's infectious," Bone said.

"No, it's not that. I'm thinking of the Billy Connolly version," Walker snorted.

"You remember that?" Bone asked.

"My dad was a huge Connolly fan. He'd get us all to sing along to his version," she said and sang even ruder alternative lines.

Bone laughed and joined her in the chorus, Big Yin style.

He took the next turning onto the high street and accelerated down the hill, both of them now singing at the top of their lungs.

The car approached the junction at the bottom and the lights changed to red. He hit the brakes. Nothing. He pressed the pedal again, but the Saab continued to accelerate.

"Red light," Walker cut off her singing and nodded towards the junction.

"I've no brakes," Bone replied and pumped the pedal frantically.

The junction loomed up ahead with traffic streaming across in both directions.

"Pull the handbrake," Walker urged. She slammed her fist into the cartridge player and stopped Glen mid-yodel.

Bone complied, but the car continued to race down the hill like a runaway train. A mother pushing a pram stepped out onto the road just ahead. Bone blasted his horn at the woman. She glanced up, and her face filled with panic. She yanked the pram back, but the wheel caught on the kerb. Bone swerved, and the car shot past within a hair's breadth of colliding with them both.

"Force it into second," Walker shouted over the roar of the engine, the panic clearly rising in her throat.

Bone yanked at the stick, and the gearbox crunched and screamed, but it refused to lock. The car careered through the lights and hit the bottom of the hill with such force the front sent sparks flying into the air.

"Fuck!" Bone roared, and the Saab shot straight across the junction, narrowly missing a white van crossing immediately in front.

A bus screeched on its brakes as the terrified detectives bounced past, but the front clipped the back corner of the Saab and the car spun around, tipped onto two wheels, and clattered up onto the pavement, alongside to the pedestrian crossing. Luckily, those waiting for the lights to change had just crossed. The car crashed down onto its four wheels with a loud clatter and finally came to a standstill. Bone and Walker sat in silence for a moment, staring out of the window.

A few pedestrians rushed over.

One knocked on Bone's window and mouthed, "Are you okay?"

Bone wound down the window.

"Are you okay?" the burly builder repeated, who'd just clambered out of his white van.

Bone glanced over at Walker, who blew out her cheeks with relief. They both slowly clambered out of the Saab. Bone held up his hands. They were shaking.

"What the hell happened?" Walker asked and pushed her hair back from her face.

Bone shook his head.

"That bloody car. I've told you so many times it needs to be scrapped," Walker protested.

Bone looked back at the builder. "Was that you in the van?"

"Aye, I thought we were both goners," the builder said, bewildered. "Jesus Christ, did ye no' see the red light?"

"Brakes," Bone said and he staggered towards the bus that had parked up by the side of the road, just beyond the junction. The driver climbed out of his cab.

"I'm so sorry. My brakes failed," Bone said.

"I clipped your rear end," the driver replied, clearly shaken up.

The Saab had a large dent in the back corner. "Are your passengers okay?"

"The bus is empty, thank God. I was on the way back to the depot," the driver replied, rubbing at his neck.

Just then, a wailing squad car approached and pulled up across the junction to block the traffic. Two PCs climbed out. Bone went over to them.

"The brakes failed on my car," Bone repeated and pointed to his pride and joy, which was resting at a despondent angle half off the kerb.

"Inspector Bone?" one of the officers asked.

"Yes, Detective Walker and I were on our way back to the station," Bone acknowledged.

Walker appeared next to him.

"Looks like you were all pretty lucky to come away uninjured. The witness who called it in said you were going like the clappers when you hit the junction."

"Brakes failed at the top of the High Street." Bone shook his head.

The second PC approached, clutching a breathalyser.

"I'm sorry, sir, but I'm going to have to do this," the young officer said, her face a little flushed with embarrassment.

"Oh, come on. Is that necessary? We're on duty."

"I'm afraid so, sir. If I don't, then we could be accused of preferential treatment or worse."

"Okay, I see your point."

"I thought you detectives had to use the station pool cars," the first PC said, grimacing at the Saab. "God, I'd love to drive that GTI you have access to in there."

The female officer fiddled with the breathalyser for a moment and handed it to Bone. "Sorry, sir. If you could just give this a long puff."

Bone took the instrument and put it to his lips. Just then, a man pushed through a small crowd gathering round the scene, held up a camera with a telescopic lens, and snapped Bone in action. Walker spun round.

"Hey!" she shouted.

The photographer continued to snap. She raced over, but the man retreated through the crowd. She gave chase. The man ran to a car and jumped in, and Walker ran after it. But it accelerated away with a blast of its horn. Walker stopped, gasping for breath. An arm appeared from the driver's window, and a hand gave her the finger.

"McKinnon," Walker puffed, realising it was one of his lackeys. "Shit." She returned to Bone to deliver the news. "I think you might be the top story in the *Chronicle* tomorrow," she said.

He sighed and shook his head. "Bloody McKinnon."

"You tested negative, sir," the female officer said with a soft sigh of relief.

The other PC, who was now hovering at the back of the Saab, called the detectives over.

"Have you seen this, sir?" he said, and kneeled by the rear door.

The scratched-out words LEAVE ALONE were keyed into the paintwork.

"It appears my car is not to blame here after all," Bone said. "Could you call in a truck to have it taken back to the station for Forensics to take a closer look?"

"No bother, sir."

"Someone seems pretty determined to scare us off this case, sir," Walker said.

"Oh, how little they know us, Rhona," Bone growled.

He turned back to the message on the paintwork. At first glance, though the scrawl marks were all over the place, the style appeared similar to the graffiti on Bone's bedroom wall, with discrepancies in style between the first and second word.

"Right, I think a cup of coffee is in order after that joyride, don't you?"

"I think so." Walker nodded. "My shout,"

"You bloody bet it is." Bone smiled.

TWENTY-THREE

When Bone and Walker arrived back at the incident room, Baxter called over from her desk.

"Sir, Forensics was looking for you. They've just completed an initial post-mortem on the victim."

"No rest for the righteous," Bone said with a sigh. "Okay."

"Sir, I've been over to digital forensics," Harper said.

"And?"

"The laptop was clean, just work emails and files, and Jones's search history was all environmental searches along with geography-related topics. However…" He gestured for Bone and Walker to approach his desk. "The USB recovered from behind the bath had some interesting content."

He waited until the pair were in front of him before he continued.

"Go on," Bone said, intrigued.

"There was only one folder on the stick, unnamed. It was password protected, but after a bit of fiddling, we managed to get in."

"*You* managed to get in, you mean," Bone said.

"We found a series of video recordings. Hold on." Harper tapped his keyboard, and moments later the monitor filled with a grainy, bird's eye view of a street at night, with a figure standing under a streetlight.

"Is that Jones's street?" Bone asked.

Harper nodded. "It's my guess that footage was taken from Jones's living room or bedroom window." He pressed the fast-forward button. "There are quite a few, and the dates and times of each recording are displayed at the bottom, every few days, usually around midnight."

"The calendar," Walker said.

"That's correct, yes. Forensics matched the entries on the calendar with the recordings."

Bone peered at the gloomy moving image. "Can we ID the figure?" he asked.

"We ran the recording through a few clean-up applications, but unfortunately, the individual is wearing some kind of face covering, a scarf or balaclava, to hide identifying features, and the all-black outfit at night doesn't help either."

"Bugger," Bone whined. "Did you manage to find time to contact your handwriting specialist mate?"

"I did indeed, and she has requested more info, images, and if possible, samples of any suspects' writing so that she can run a comparative analysis."

"Can you action that, then head up to the school and ask Jones's colleagues to provide some writing samples?"

"What shall I say if they ask why?"

"Just say it will help eliminate them from our enquiries."

"Yes, sir. I'll get on it."

"Good work with the video, DC Harper. You'll make a great detective one day." Bone smirked.

He headed back to the door.

"Would you like me to come with you to see the man in black, sir?" Walker asked.

"To hold my hand?"

"Something like that, yes." Walker smiled.

"I'm a hardened, world-weary murder cop, I can handle it," With a grimace, Bone about turned and left.

TWENTY-FOUR

As usual, Cash loitered in the corridor outside the examination room, dressed from head to toe in his black, wipe-clean butcher's gown and matching over-trousers.

"Good afternoon, Duncan. We meet again," he said as Bone approached.

"Indeed," Bone replied.

"Do come in," Cash said, ushering Bone inside.

Bone shuddered and followed Cash across the dimly lit room to an examination table with the naked corpse laid out under a bright surgical spotlight.

"Sorry that it's taken us so long. It was an absolute nightmare trying to get this poor sod off the hillside without contaminating the body and any lingering evidence. However, here he is," he said, gazing down at the greying, bloated body in front of him.

Bone recoiled. "And here we are." He took a deep breath.

"So, as you can see we cut him open and had a rummage around." Cash pointed to the deep scar sewn together with what looked like bootlaces, running from his thorax to his belly button and then across his chest. "You'll be relieved I did a quick cross stitch before you arrived, to save you a trip to my bucket over there." Cash grinned.

"I've never thrown up, have I?" Bone asked in surprise.

"Well, there was that time when we had to go through the liquidised remains of that pensioner. I think that was a particularly low point in my glittering career."

"Oh Jesus, don't remind me. That sound when you submerged your hands." Bone gagged.

"Isn't it so odd to think of all that life and love and ambition and desire reduced to a bucket of malodorous jelly?" Cash shook his head.

"Right, enough reminiscing. Shall we crack on?" Bone attempted to head off another of Cash's existential crises.

"There is a fracture to the supraorbital foramen, just above the left eyebrow, here." Cash tapped the skull lightly with his gloved finger.

"Was that the cause of death?"

"Hold on," Cash interrupted. He twisted the neck sideways until the head was tilted at an unnatural angle. "You may wish to come round here for a better look," he added.

Bone reluctantly complied.

"Here you can see a second blow, with a pronounced fracture to the parietal bone. The shape of the penetration mark here indicates a blunt object, such as a hammer."

"So which came first, front or back?" Bone stared down at the gaping hole in Jones's skull. "Which was the fatal blow?"

"Neither," Cash replied. "Examination of his vital organs clearly shows that Jones drowned to death. I'll show you."

He went over to an ominously large fridge and pulled at the double lever. As the door swung open, a plume of ice fog emerged and surrounded him like a special effect in a *Hammer Horror* film. He returned with a tray and placed it on an inspection table next to the slab. Two neatly severed lungs rested side by side in its centre. He leaned in and, picking up one of the lungs, he gently squeezed it. Bloody, yellowish liquid flowed out of the severed tubes.

"His lungs are full to the brim with water, indicating that our victim drowned to death, though the fracture to the back of his head would have probably killed him in the end anyway."

"In the waterfall pool?" Bone asked.

"I can't be a hundred percent sure on this, and we are running checks on the lung fluid, but I would say that he was still alive, though possibly unconscious, when he was crucified on the wall behind the waterfall. The killer may have tilted his head so that the flood of water pouring down on him drowned him, and also irritatingly, washed away much of the forensic evidence we need."

"So you're saying Jones got lamped, and still alive, either fell, stumbled, or was dragged into the pool, hoisted up onto that platform, and was nailed to the cliff, then left to drown?"

Cash shifted down the body. "See these scratch marks here on the victim's knees?"

Bone leaned in.

"This is just a professional guess at this stage, but looking at the type and the state of the scratches, I would say our man here may have clambered up onto the ledge himself." Cash continued.

"So not dragged up?"

"Think about it, Duncan. You're in a deep pool of water, there's a few thousand gallons per second of water pouring down on you. Would you drag an unconscious male of above-average build and weight front first onto a slippery ledge?"

"He was trying to get away from his killer then?"

"That's a more realistic and likely scenario." Cash clicked his teeth. "But there's one more thing,"

"There's always more." Bone rolled his eyes.

Returning to Jones's bruised and battered skull, Cash tilted the neck back, and with a spatula, prised open the mouth.

"You remember I asked the divers to have a quick look in here?" he said. "Well, when I dived in, so to speak, I found that two centimetres of the front of the victim's tongue is missing—a clean, even slice, like a scalpel through skin. Can you see that?" He reached up and adjusted the lamp.

Bone peered into Jones's gaping mouth. "What was the thing dangling out that we saw on the video?"

"Ah yes, more intrigue," Cash said. "Hold this for a second." He invited Bone to take the spatula.

Bone reluctantly accepted it, and while he continued to lever Jones's jaw open, Cash returned the lungs to the fridge, then went over to a row of drawers below the body storage unit. He slid one out, removed a second tray, and placed it on the inspection table. Bone's hand was shaking, and Jones's jaw jittered up and down as though the victim was trying to speak.

"Are you okay with that?" Cash asked.

"Just get on with it," Bone urged.

Cash retrieved the spatula from Bone, removed it, and gently pushed Jones's jaw shut. Bone let out a quiet sigh of relief.

"Okay, so I removed this cable tie from the back of what is left of the victim's tongue," Cash said, and with a pair of tweezers, he picked the object up from the tray. Gently tugging at the strip, he flipped it over.

Bone spotted some tiny marks on the underside.

"Is that a letter L?" he asked.

"Yes, there's a message. I took a couple of close-ups." Turning back to the wall, he switched on a monitor and adjusted the angle for Bone to see. He picked up a remote and pushed a couple of buttons.

The screen remained black.

"Shit," Cash exclaimed. "I had this thing set up for you. Wait a sec."

He continued to fiddle, and then the screen burst into life. The glare from the examination light obscured Bone's view.

"Let me pull this a bit farther over," Cash said and shifted the extendable mount across the body until the screen was right in front of them.

A close-up shot of the cable tie filled the screen, and the water-smudged words LEAVE ALONE handwritten along its length were now clearly visible.

"Shit," Bone muttered.

"Forensic analysis of the lettering indicates this has been written with a very fine permanent pen, hence it survived the deluge." Cash looked up. "It would appear Mr Jones may have upset someone."

"Upset enough to kill him," Bone added.

"Indeed." Cash nodded.

"But what does this *leave alone* mean?" Bone asked, almost to himself.

"Leave me alone, leave it alone, leave whatever you're doing alone, or else?" Cash shrugged.

"And why go to all that bother in the middle of a bloody waterfall to crucify someone, then sever his tongue and attach a bloody cable tie to it?"

"Lunatic, obviously, but maybe it's some kind of idiomatic reference, you know, like cat got your tongue or…"

"Loose tongues cost lives," Bone interrupted.

"There, that one, yes. Someone is playing silly buggers."

"Anything else?" Bone asked with another sigh.

"Aside from the tragic violent cycle of the human condition that we have to witness day in, day out, that's all for now." Cash's frown deepened further. "I always find it so staggering the depths of depravity human beings can sink to. I mean, here's a man in the prime of his life, a well-loved local hero, butchered, for what?"

"One of the usual suspects, no doubt; money, love, envy, greed," Bone suggested.

"Round and round we go, like some demonic, deadly Ferris wheel," Cash whipped the cover back over the body, like a slightly deranged magician, and shoved it back into its makeshift coffin in the wall. He turned back to Bone. "We are flawed and broken as a species." He slammed the storage door shut.

"Okay, thanks, and keep me updated," Bone said trying again to stop another classic Cash rant.

"I mean, what are we really?" Cash shrugged. "Instruments of sadistic evil."

"I'll let you get on then," Bone said and made a quick exit.

Bone marched into the incident room and he ran straight into Baxter who was lurking behind the door. He pulled back in surprise.

"Bloody hell, Sheila, don't do that,"

"Sorry, sir, I was coming to find you. Emergency services just received a call from the property of Oliver Morton. There's been some sort of incident."

"What sort of incident?" Bone asked.

"The caller reported an intruder."

Bone hurried back along the corridor. He was about to call Walker when he spotted her climbing out of one of the pool cars.

"Morton's place, now, you drive," Bone hollered across to her.

Walker climbed back in.

TWENTY-FIVE

When they reached Morton's house, two squad cars were already on the scene. Walker pulled up, and the detectives jumped out and raced across to a PC, who ran up the street towards the house.

Bone raised his lanyard. "What's going on?" he asked the hot and bothered uniform.

"There's been a break-in and an assault on the occupants. We're trying to find the attacker," the officer said between breaths. "The owner thinks he ran out the back. No sign up there."

The detectives dashed into the house, the door wide open. A PC turned to stop them.

"DCI Bone and DI Walker," Bone shouted.

"Sorry, sir. One of the residents, a Mr..." the PC began.

"Morton, yes, we know," Bone interrupted.

"We found him out in the garden with a head wound, very distraught. He's in there." The PC pointed to the kitchen. "And a second resident, his mother, I believe, is upstairs in a bedroom with a female officer. Mr Morton thinks the intruder legged it through the back door about twenty minutes ago."

The detectives ran into the kitchen. Morton paced up and down with blood pouring from a deep gash on his forehead.

"He went that way," Morton yelled and pointed out the open back door. "Is my mum okay?"

"Where is she?" Walker asked.

"She's upstairs having a lie-down."

Bone gestured for Walker to go and check while he ran out into the back garden. A uniform was by the back wall.

"Two of my colleagues have jumped over and are checking the pathway and field, sir," the PC said.

Bone stretched up and peered over the top of the wall. The uniforms at the far end of a field ran around like headless chickens. They both disappeared into a clump of trees.

On his way back in, Bone noticed that one of the glass panels on the back door had been knocked in, with glass scattered on the linoleum floor. Inside, Morton still paced the floor.

"You need to sit down, Mr Morton, and let me get something for that nasty cut," Bone said. He spotted a kitchen roll and, snatching it up, pulled a couple of sheets. "Sit down, please." he repeated.

"No, I need to find out if my mum is okay!" Morton shouted and pushed past him.

A paramedic appeared and blocked his path.

"Whoa there, where are you going?" the paramedic said, staring at the bleeding wound.

"Where's my mum, is she okay?"

"My colleague is attending to her. She's okay. We need to sort you out. Come back in," the paramedic insisted.

The paramedic took Morton's arm and led him back into the kitchen, sat him down, and started dressing the wound.

The two PCs came back in from the garden.

"No sign," one of them said.

"Have you put a call out?" Bone asked.

"Yes, sir," the PC confirmed. "Hopefully, he won't get too far in broad daylight. The path up there is a dead end."

Bone turned back to Morton. "What happened, Oliver?"

"Are you sure my mum is all right?" Morton asked the paramedic again.

"Let's just get you sorted, okay?" The paramedic attended to Morton's wound.

"Oliver," Bone repeated.

"I was up in the loft and I heard a hell of a commotion. On my way down the ladder, I saw a man in a black hoodie tracksuit attacking my mum on the landing. I tried to grab him, but he hit me with something and knocked me over. When I got to my feet, I saw him running downstairs. I chased after him, but he was too quick. He ran out the back and over the wall. I called nine-nine-nine on my mobile and went to see if Mum was okay, but she had locked herself in her bedroom. I pounded and pounded on the door, but she didn't reply. I hope she hasn't collapsed or he's hurt her. Please tell me he didn't harm her."

A second paramedic appeared at the door. "Your mother is fine, Mr Morton. She's just in a bit of shock."

"Oh, thank God, can I see her?" Morton started to get up.

"No, you sit yourself back down, Oliver. We just need to check you're not concussed."

Bone went back out into the hallway. Walker came down the stairs to meet him.

"She's pretty shaken up," Walker said.

"Did she say what happened to her?"

"Very little. She said she didn't see the intruder so no ID. She has a pretty nasty shiner. I think the paramedics are going to take her to hospital for observation."

Bone carried on out the front. Another squad car had arrived, and more PCs ran around, from one end of the street to the other.

Up on the main road, a car drove past with lights flashing and sirens blaring.

Walker appeared at the front door. "Sir, come and see this."

Bone followed her back in.

In the living room, she stepped over books and papers scattered on the floor to reach a small dining table at the back.

"This," she said.

Bone joined her and glanced down at the table. Scratched across the surface of the wood were the words *Leave Alone*. He kneeled by the scrawl.

"Busy psychopath, isn't he?" he said, finally.

"Very," Walker replied.

He stood and checked his watch. "Right, let's get the SOC team in and formal statements from Morton and his mother asap."

TWENTY-SIX

In the incident room, Bone called his team over, but before he could speak, Harper interrupted.

"Sir, some news," he said. "Police divers have just recovered a camera from the waterfall pool. They're sending it over to digital forensics."

"Oh, bloody hell. They'll just sit on it for a few days and come back with nothing. As soon as it comes in, get down there and tell them to prioritise, under my order."

"Okay, will do," Harper replied.

"And then when they've wasted enough time…" Bone added.

"I'll have a look at it." Harper smiled.

"Indeed, Mr GCHQ," Bone turned back to the team. "Rhona and I have just come back from Oliver Morton's house. This afternoon, an intruder broke into his house and attacked him and his mother."

"Are they hurt?" Mullens asked.

"Minor injuries and shaken up, but okay. The intruder escaped before officers arrived. A manhunt is underway, but as yet, no sign."

"So that's Morton off our invitation to the party list then?" Mullens grumbled.

"It would appear so, yes." Bone approached the incident board. "The intruder left this same message scratched into their dining table." He pointed at the graffiti images. "The SOC team should be on their way over there, so hopefully they might pick something up, but so far, our prolific psychopath seems to be pretty competent at covering his tracks."

"Only a matter of time," Walker said.

"Yes, but time is what we don't have," Bone replied. "The post-mortem found that after the killer struck Jones over the head, Jones survived the blow and tried to escape his killer by stumbling or falling into the pool then clambering up onto the ledge behind the waterfall. The killer followed, struck him again, rendering him unconscious, and then pinned him to the wall with climbing pitons, positioning his head to allow the waterfall to pour down his throat."

"So he drowned?" Baxter asked.

"Yes."

"What a weird fucking bastard thing to do." Mullens flinched.

"Bloody psychotic," Baxter added.

"That's not all," Bone continued. "The killer sliced off the front of Jones's tongue and attached a cable tie to the remains." He pinned the photocopied images of it to the incident board.

The team closed in.

"The same bloody message. Are we sensing a pattern here?" Mullens joked.

"We are dealing with a seriously unhinged individual," Bone said.

"You're telling me," Baxter agreed.

"It's looking like we're all lucky to be alive."

"Including your son," Walker added. "Though, sounds like that was the killer's intention, to scare us off."

"Yeah, like that's going to fucking happen," Mullens said.

"We need to work fast here before our friend strikes again," Bone pressed on. "Any news on the elusive Springsteen brother?"

"Nothing yet," Baxter replied. "We've issued a warrant for his arrest, and all stations in the area have been alerted, though it's pretty likely he's gone to ground."

"Or his paymasters have got to him first," Mullens said. "They might be getting a bit twitchy about the other Bruce in the clink downstairs, that he might spill his guts." Mullens winced again. "Oh, why did I say guts?" He rubbed at his stomach. "This is worse than that time my old man ate that off curry and I had to go round to clear up his spray-tanned bathroom."

"For God's sake, Mullens!" Walker exclaimed. "Just have something to eat and put us all out of our misery."

"You have no idea of the sacrifices I'm making," Mullens complained. "And anyway, I promised Sandra I'd be good." He pinched his sides again.

"When did that ever stop you before? We won't tell her, just eat! And if she finds out, you can say your diet was affecting your work and your boss ordered you to stuff your bloody face," Walker said and glanced hopefully at Bone.

Bone raised is hand. "I'm not getting involved." He turned to his grumbling colleague. "Right, Mullens. It is admirable that you are so loyal to your wife, and quite frankly somewhat surprising, but if you are going to persist with your diet, just keep your moans to yourself, clear?"

"As my colon, sir," Mullens huffed.

"Okay." Bone nodded and turned to Baxter. "How long do we have left before we have to let the brother go?"

"Four p.m. today," Baxter replied.

"Can you ask Gallacher to request an extension?"

"On what grounds?"

"Make something up!" Bone snapped. He took a deep breath. "Sorry."

"Okay, sir."

"And any more on Jones's private life?"

"Aside from the incident at his party, nothing."

"No other skeletons or dirt?" Bone pressed.

"Clean as a whistle."

""All roads lead to dead ends." Bone ran his finger down the length of his scar. "We'll just have to keep digging as we always do," he said.

TWENTY-SEVEN

When Bone finally escaped the station, instead of heading straight home, he took a detour to Alice's house to check up on how his son was doing and to see if Alice had calmed down a little yet. He rapped on the door. Michael's familiar thumps approached down the hall. After a moment or two, the door finally opened, and Alice stepped out, pulling the door closed slightly behind her.

"Duncan," she said, looking surprised.

"Sorry to just drop in on you, but I was worried about—"

Michael's head appeared around the gap in the door, and he squeezed his body through.

"Dad!" He wrapped his arms around his dad's legs.

"How's my wee fella doing today?" Bone asked and picked him up.

"Fine." He looked straight into Bones eyes and beamed a wide smile. "I made a Lego Batmobile. Jeff helped me."

"Who's…?" Bone started.

"You can't keep doing this," Alice interrupted.

Bone looked up.

"Doing what?"

"You know what. Showing up uninvited."

"Uninvited? I'm just a concerned dad checking on how his son is doing."

"And whose fault is that?" She leaned in on the other side of Bone to try and mask her voice from her son. "You put his life in danger," she whispered.

"You know I couldn't be more sorry about that but he's still my son."

Michael wriggled around, and Bone tickled him.

"So who's Jeff then?" Bone asked.

"Stop!" Michael giggled and let out one of his signature mid-giggle farts.

Bone stopped and dropped Michael back down.

"Who's—?" Bone repeated.

"I heard you the first time," Alice snapped back.

Just then, the door swung open, and a tall man appeared.

"Everything okay?" the man said, his voice deep and authoritative.

"Duncan, this is Jeff. Duncan is my ex-husband."

"Jeff's Mummy's new boyfriend," Michael jumped into the fray.

"He's not." Alice blushed. "We're just friends."

"None of my business. Nice to meet you, Jeff." Bone extended his hand and tried to conceal his jealousy.

"Jeff Bassett. It's a pleasure to meet you, Inspector," he said and shook Bone's hand vigorously. "But such a terrible thing that's happened to Richard."

"Jeff's a teacher at the school, Duncan," Alice said.

"What?" Bone asked, stepping back slightly.

"I teach English so I didn't know Richard very well," Jeff explained. "But the whole school is just devastated. He was such a well-loved member of staff."

"Alice, could I have a quick word?" Bone urged Alice to follow him to the front gate.

"I'm in the middle of cooking dinner, Duncan. What is it?"

"It won't take a minute," Bone smiled at Jeff, who smiled back exposing a set of perfect white teeth.

"You wait here with Jeff, Michael," Alice said to her son.

"Aww, I want to go with Dad," Michael complained and grabbed Bone's leg again.

"Only a wee minute," Alice repeated.

Jeff held out his hand. "Come on, Michael, let's go back and put the rocket boosters on Batman's car."

Bone winced.

Michael looked down the path at his dad and then at Jeff's extended fist, and reluctantly, he went back in. Alice followed Bone out to the street.

"What?" she asked, impatiently.

"What?" Bone retorted. "A teacher from Kilwinnoch Academy has just been murdered, and you decide to date one of his colleagues?"

"Not that it's any of your bloody business, but Jeff wasn't one of Richard Jones's close colleagues. He barely knew him. He works in a different department. And we're not 'dating'. This isn't bloody *Grease*, Duncan."

"It is my business when three members of the teaching team at the school are on our persons of interest list, and Jeff is in there now playing daddy to our son."

"So he's the killer, is that it?" Alice shot back.

"You know what I mean. This is not good, not right now."

"Are you sure this is about protecting our son, which you haven't exactly shined at recently?"

"This is all about my son, our son. "I don't..." He took a breath. "You don't know this guy from Adam. Maybe just leave off for the next couple of weeks, until we put this case to bed."

"Leave off? You sound like some disapproving Victorian father." Alice shook her head. "Our marriage is over, Duncan. It's time you moved on. I think it's you that should leave off, leave right off!" She stormed back up the path, slamming the door behind her.

"Bugger," Bone groaned and, fishing his phone from his pocket, he called Baxter.

"Can you ring the head at Kilwinnoch High and ask her about one of her teachers called Jeff Bassett?"

"Anything in particular you want me to ask?"

"Oh come on Sheila, use your nowse," Bone replied. "Any links to the case, relationship with Jones, the usual." He took a long deep breath.

"Are you okay, sir?" Baxter asked.

But Bone had already hung up.

TWENTY-EIGHT

Back at his flat, Bone recoiled as he approached the makeshift plywood door that the SOC team had installed. The scorch marks and blackened walls around the frame were still visible. A PC stepped out from the gloom of the landing.

"Evening, sir," she said with a nod.

"Have they gone?" Bone asked.

"Forensics?" she asked and glanced back at the crime scene tape stuck to the door.

"No Dominos pizzas," Bone growled. He glanced up. "Sorry, long day."

"Aye, sir, a couple of hours ago, I believe."

Bone pushed at the door and squeezed under the tape.

"I'm not sure you should be going in there. The smell of smoke is still pretty bad," the PC said, following Bone to the door.

He ignored her, continued into his burnt-out hallway and pulled the door shut. His shoes squelched under the still-sodden carpet, and the stench of smoke clung to the back of his throat. He spluttered again. Luckily, the damage was minimal and mainly superficial smoke damage. in the living room, he kneeled by his beloved Dansette record player and he checked its condition, along with a pile of LPs stacked up alongside. There was no sign of damage. He sighed, but the smoke caught the back of his throat and he coughed again. He rushed over to the window, opened it wider and took a few deep clean breaths.

Removing his jacket and rolling up his sleeves, he went to the kitchen and dug a bucket out from under the sink, filled it with water, and grabbed the dishcloth. Back in the hall, he set the bucket down by the door and soaked the cloth. He was about to start washing down the blackened walls when he stopped. A sudden searing pain shot across the front of his head. He staggered backwards, dropped the cloth and kicked over the bucket, spilling its contents onto an already soaked carpet. He toppled backwards against the wall and slid down.

"Are you okay?" the PC called out from the other side of the door.

Bone pressed his palm into the scar on his temple and closed his eyes to try and stop the room from spinning. His breathing shortened, and panic rose in his throat. *Hyperventilation.* He reached for the wet cloth he'd dropped at his feet, pushed it against his face and took three or four deep breaths, in and out,

out and in, while slowly counting down from ten to one, as his counsellor had taught him.

"Sir?" the uniform called again.

At last, his breathing calmed and the searing pain dropped to a dull, thumping headache.

"Fine, I'm fine," Bone gasped back.

After a few more deep breaths, he clambered back to his feet, and using the wall to steady himself, he stumbled through to the bathroom. Ransacking the cabinet, with bottles, shavers, and packets spilling out onto the floor, he located the ibuprofen and at the sink, he turned on the tap full and gulped down mouthfuls of water. When the panic receded further, he returned to the living room and dropped down onto an armchair. Within a few seconds, he was asleep.

He woke in a cold sweat, his soaking shirt clinging to his chest. The nightmare he was experiencing was still roaring in his ears. Alice was standing over by the graffiti-covered wall clutching a can of spray paint. She turned and sprayed a second message on the wall. Bone tried to stand, but his legs felt paralysed. He peered through the gloom. Alice smiled, and blood streamed down her face. The message read, *I will always win*. She raised her hand and offered Bone the can. Then the dream dispersed, and the room, the smells, and the sounds of reality returned.

Bone checked his watch. 5:42 a.m. He'd been asleep for over seven hours. When he tried to escape from the armchair, his neck and shoulders refused to move. He painfully stretched and turned, and with a loud groan, corkscrewed himself out of the chair. He forced his legs to take him through to the bedroom. Switching on the ceiling light, he sat on the end of the bed and was about to remove his shirt when he caught sight of the graffiti scrawled across the wall, the two words with disparate styles glaring at him.

In the living room, Bone fired up his laptop and ran a search on the history of handwriting styles. As a kid, he had been taught print script style but was always envious of the previous generation's beautiful cursive-style calligraphy. And now, his son was learning this style, too.

A few more clicks, and Bone opened a blog post on literacy and the Scottish curriculum, and scanning down, spotted a header, The Resurgence of Cursive Style. He scrolled through and stopped on a graph showing the chronology of styles, with dates of changes to the curriculum plotted on a timeline. Scrolling further, he landed on 1992, the year when cursive style was formally reintroduced back into the curriculum.

He saved the page and went back to the bathroom for a shower and a quick change.

TWENTY-NINE

By the time Bone arrived at the station, his medication had shifted his migraine almost completely. But the familiar dull hammering quickly returned when he spotted the press crew gathered outside the entrance.

"Oh bugger," he muttered.

He turned the pool car into a side street and parked up. Climbing out, he was about to take the alleyway round the back, which led to the station's rear entrance, when McKinnon, the *Chronicle* reporter, appeared from nowhere, with his paparazzi photographer by his side.

"DCI Bone," he called and raced towards him. The photographer raised his camera and started clicking.

"I see that downpour earlier has flushed you out of a drain, McKinnon," Bone snarled, pushing past him.

McKinnon pursued after him. "Any progress on your investigations, Detective?"

"There will be a full progress statement later today," Bone replied curtly.

"Kilwinnoch residents are getting extremely impatient. Mr Jones was a local hero, whereas you, Inspector…" McKinnon sneered.

Bone stopped and turned around.

"So were you over the limit, then?" McKinnon's sneer turned into a fill-blown gloat.

Bone stepped towards him.

"Careful, Inspector. Unless, of course, you like seeing yourself emblazoned across our front pages."

"You are a pariah, McKinnon. Just leave me alone." Bone spun round and carried on up the lane.

"So, your bosses still have full faith in your abilities?" McKinnon persisted. "And completely satisfied with your handling of the case so far?"

"I feel sorry for you," Bone said, stopping again. "It must be so hard going through your life with a face like a shrivelled-up, empty scrotal sack."

"Takes one to know one, Inspector." McKinnon smirked.

"And you can tell your photographer if he ever comes near me again, I'll ram that box so far up is arse he'll be shooting his tonsils for the rest of his sad, miserable life." Bone marched on.

"Always love these little intimate moments we have together, Inspector," McKinnon called out.

Bone cut down onto the lane and through the back gate of the station. Once in the building, he let out a loud roar. A PC passing by looked over in surprise.

"You okay, sir?" the alarmed uniform asked.

"Argh!" Bone raged again.

The PC hurried off down the corridor.

Gallacher's door flew open, and Bone's boss stepped out. "DCI Bone, my office, now!" he ordered.

"Shit," Bone muttered.

"What in God's name is this?" Gallacher threw the *Chronicle* down on his desk with such force it hit his row of pens, scattering them in all directions. "Are you determined to shut down the unit and drive me into an early grave?"

"Yesterday morning, DI Walker and I were on our way back from interviewing a potential suspect and the brakes failed on the Saab." Bone started to explain.

"That wreck!" Gallacher bellowed. "I don't know how many times I've told you to use one of the pool cars. It's against regulations to drive a private vehicle. Jesus!"

"I believe someone tampered with the brakes. The same person who nearly killed my son." Bone protested.

Gallacher slumped back down in his chair and smoothed his Brylcreemed hair.

"Please tell me you were under the limit?" Gallacher asked.

"Of course I was."

"I just never know where your head's at, Duncan. I know that if someone tried to harm my son I would be off the scale with rage."

"I'm channelling my *'rage'* as you call it, into catching the psychopath or psychopaths who killed

Jones and are trying to intimidate us," Bone retorted. "So you think I've hit the bottle, is that it?"

"No, of course not. But just look at this. It would have been a hell of a lot easier to deal with if you'd totalled yourself—this is an even bigger fucking car crash." Gallacher thumped the paper with his fist, and more pens tumbled off the desk. "Christ," he muttered and bent down to pick them up.

"This is just another of that sewer rat McKinnon's vendettas against me, sir."

"What is it with you and this bloody journalist?" Gallacher said, realigning his pens on the desk.

"I've no clue, but I'd happily do twenty years in Braefells Prison just to watch the tapeworm die."

Gallacher shook his head. "Well, you're going to have to speak to the press and set things straight as we are looking at fucking Hiroshima and Nagasaki combined here. I've already had head office on the phone demanding your suspension and removal from the case."

"Okay, sir. I'll speak to them later."

"You need to do it right fucking now. I'll try and calm things down with head office, but I can't guarantee they won't pull you or send over internal."

"Not that again, really?" Bone protested.

"Yes, that again." Gallacher sat forward. ""To be honest, Duncan, I'm getting really bloody tired of having the same conversations with you. I let you come back last year, but every day that goes by I'm regretting that decision."

"We solved the case and saved the unit."

"Yes, you did, but at what cost? I'm beginning to think Head Office is right. You're a liability, and I never thought I'd say that about you."

"That's totally unfair, sir. That prick has set me up. You can't pull me. Some evil bastard nearly killed my son, and I want to string the bastard up by his gonads."

"That's exactly why I should sign you off sick again. You're angry, and anger is not where a DCI should be, especially one with your baggage." He stared at Bone. "I mean, you're shaking now."

"I'm fine. What are you on about?"

"Your hands," Gallacher said.

Bone held up his hands, and the fingers juddered back and forth. "It's been a busy few days. I'm tired, that's all."

"I say this as a friend and not your boss. You need to calm the fuck down. My main concern is your health above everything else. Just be very careful, Duncan, please."

Bone stood and turned to leave, but a figure stood by the door, blocking his way out.

"What are you waiting for?" Gallacher asked.

Bone moved towards his apparition, but it refused to shift. He stopped again.

"What's the matter with you?" Gallacher barked at him.

The figure raised its head, and its charred, decomposing features emerged from within the hood. A smile curled upwards on burnt, torn lips and yellow-and-black teeth. Bone inched closer. The creature opened its eyelids, exposing empty black sockets. It mouthed the word *loser* and smiled again.

"Are you okay, Duncan?" Gallacher tried again.

Bone turned back to his boss, and then back to the door. The creature was gone.

"Sorry, I thought I had something else to tell you," Bone lied.

Gallacher shook his head, and Bone left.

Bone rushed down the corridor, into the toilets, slammed a cubicle door shut, and retched down one of the loos.

At the sink, he splashed cold water on his face until the nausea finally passed. Collecting himself, he headed slowly back to the incident room. But before he could reach the door, he was intercepted desk sergeant Brody, who appeared extremely flustered.

"Sir, DS Baxter's husband just called in. She didn't come home last night, and he is extremely worried about her." he said.

. "What? When?" Bone stuttered.

"DS Baxter's husband just rang," Brody repeated.

"Shit," Bone exclaimed, his brain finally surfacing from the thick red fog. "Okay, could you ring him back and say we're on our way to him now, and send a squad car over as well?"

"Sir," Brody replied and marched off.

Bone rushed to the incident room. "Walker, Mullens, come with me," he said urgently.

"Aw, sir, I'm right in the middle of—"

"Drop it, Mullens. Move your arse."

Mullens pulled a face, and the three detectives headed out to the car park.

"What's going on?" Walker asked, trying to keep up with Bone.

"Baxter's husband just rang in and reported her missing," Bone replied.

"I was wondering where she was. I couldn't believe I'd beaten her in," Mullens said.

They headed for the Golf, but Walker veered off towards the BMW.

"This one will get us there quicker." She threw open the driver's door and jumped in.

Bone clambered in next to her, and Mullens squeezed into the back.

"Why do I always end up in the back?" Mullens complained.

"Not now, Detective," Bone snapped as Walker started up the high-performance chase car and roared out of the car park, scattering a cluster of journalists huddled by the gate.

THIRTY

DS Baxter's red-stone Edwardian semi was located in Kingsburn village about three miles out of Kilwinnoch. Baxter's husband, Jim, used to work in the city, but ill health had forced him into early retirement. As they rushed up the front steps, he appeared at the door in a dressing gown and a state of agitation, wisps of what was left of his greying hair blowing around wildly in the breeze.

"She just went out for a cigarette. I don't understand. It's just not like her," he said, his tone rising with his panic.

"It's okay, Jim, just calm down and tell us what's happened," Bone said and took a hold of Jim's arm.

Jim turned and retreated back into the house, and the detectives followed. He took them into a galley kitchen and stopped by the back door. He now seemed out of breath as though he was on the brink of hyperventilating. Walker pulled over a chair and got him to sit down.

"Mark, maybe you could wait outside for a minute? It's a bit crowded in here," Bone said, winking back at Mullens, who nodded and retreated back down the hall.

"She wouldn't just…" Jim began but ran out of air.

"Just slow down a minute, Jim," Walker said. "Just catch your breath."

Jim inhaled deeply a couple of times and was about to say something again.

"A couple more," Walker urged.

Jim complied.

"Would you like a glass of water?" Walker asked.

"No, I just want to know where my wife is," Jim shifted his hands up and down on his knees.

"Okay, Jim," Bone cut in. "Just talk us through exactly what's happened."

"Last night, Sheila went out for her usual before-bed cigarette. She doesn't smoke in the house anymore after my illness, you know?"

"And what time was this?" Walker asked.

"Er… about ten, ten-fifteen. I remember the news was on, and that's when she usually goes. She can't stand watching the news. She calls it a busman's holiday."

"Me, too," Walker said with a smile.

"So she went out where?" Bone continued.

"Just out into the back garden. I'm forever emptying her bloody ashtrays. Filthy habit, but she's a total addict. I can't tell you how many times she's tried to quit."

"So, then what happened?"

"Well, she was gone for a bit longer than usual, so I went to see what she was doing, but she wasn't there."

"She'd gone out?"

"Sometimes she'd take a notion and pop down to the local off-licence for a wee nip of something, if we were out, but we had plenty of her favourite tipple in. Believe it or not, she loves Advocaat."

"Do they actually still make that stuff?" Walker asked.

"And anyway, she'd always tell me she was going," Jim added.

"So what did you do?" Bone asked.

"I got dressed again and went down to the village store to see if I could spot her en route."

"I assume you didn't, but did you see anyone else?"

"Just a couple of local teenagers looking like they were gearing themselves up for an attempted underage alcohol purchase."

"So what then?"

"I wondered if she might have popped into the Golden Fleece for a quick one. She's been known on the odd occasion to drop in, usually when a case is getting to her, but there was no sign of her there either, and the landlord said he hadn't seen her."

"Was the pub busy?" Walker asked.

"This is Kingsburn, Detective. It's only busy when the specials are on," Jim sniffed. "No, I came back home and called a couple of her pals, old lawyer mates she still meets now and then, but they were none the wiser either."

"And then?"

"I went to bed and hoped she'd just turn up with a carton of Golden Virginia and a bottle of Advocaat. But I waited and waited, and by the time the sun came up, I was in a right state. Then I rang you."

Mullens appeared at the door. "Sir, the squad car has arrived."

"How many officers?" Bone asked.

"Three, I think."

Bone got up and approached him. "Okay, door to door and tell them to work their way down towards the village centre," he said. Then leaning in, he whispered, "But tell them not to alarm anyone."

He turned back to Jim, who had also stood, looking anxiously towards the detectives.

"It's okay, Jim, we'll find her, don't worry," Bone said, trying to reassure everyone, especially himself. "Could you take us to where Sheila usually has her smoke?"

"Aye, sure," Jim said briskly as though happy to finally have something to do. "Through here."

He took Bone and Walker out through the back door and round the corner of the house to a small patio area with a rusting metal bistro table and two chairs.

"If the weather's kind she normally sits here, and when it's raining she ducks under the eaves over there." He nodded over to the back of the house.

Bone looked down at the ashtray in the centre of the table, overflowing with cigarette ends.

"Where does that go?" Walker pointed at a narrow concrete path running across a lawn in need of cutting.

"Just down to the end of the garden," Jim replied.

"Can I have a look?"

"Aye, of course, but I've already been down to check."

Walker set off down the path while Bone disappeared around the side of the house. The path meandered through the grass until it reached a high brick wall and a six-by-six shed.

"You checked in here?"

"Aye, but it's rammed to the gunnels."

Walker unbolted the door.

"Careful," Jim warned.

She slowly eased the door open, but a deckchair tumbled out between the space and landed at her feet.

"I'm not the tidiest of gardeners." Jim huffed.

Bundling the chair out of the way, Walker peered inside. The shed was rammed to the roof with garden equipment and clutter with no room for anyone to squeeze in. She stepped back and grappled with the deckchair.

"Leave it," Jim urged.

Walker dropped it back down. "So what's on the other side of your back wall here?"

"Just into the primary school playing field. The wee menaces throw their apple cores and crisp packets over the wall. I'm forever cleaning them up."

Walker ran her hand across the surface and, finding a foothold, shimmied herself up. The playing field stretched out towards a prefab and the main Victorian stone building behind. The school perimeter was surrounded by a high fence. She jumped back down.

"Are the school gates locked every night?"

"I think so, aye. We've never had any intruders over that wall, if that's what you're thinking."

Just then, Bone appeared. "Anything?" he asked.

Walker shook her head. He fished his phone out of his pocket and tried Baxter's mobile again. A faint ringing sounded from across the other side of the garden. Bone looked up at Walker, and they walked towards the sound. It stopped.

"Damn," Bone rang her number again.

They continued across the lawn as the ringing grew louder.

"It's definitely her phone," Jim said anxiously.

"It sounds like it's coming from that far corner," Bone said.

They rushed over. He dialled her number again. The ringing sounded behind the wall.

"What?" Walker exclaimed in confusion.

"Over here," Jim said and he dashed to a half-sized, rusting iron door in the bottom corner of the wall.

"What's this?" Bone asked.

"It's the old coal store. We haven't used it for years."

Bone yanked at the handle, but it wouldn't budge.

"Wait, there's a way to open this," Jim said and, pushing his shoulder into the door, he heaved the handle upwards, and the door swung open with a loud scream. A waft of damp, musty air belched out.

Bone peered in, but it was pitch-black.

"Sheila, are you in here?" he called, but there was no reply.

Fiddling with his phone, he flicked on the torch. The beam revealed a narrow brick tunnel like a sewer running about ten feet ahead.

"Sheila?" he called again and, bending low, he crawled inside. The light flicked back and forth as he shuffled deeper into the space. "Sheila!" he called out.

The beam flashed past an object at the very back of the empty store. Bone redirected the light, and the beam caught Sheila's face.

"Jesus!" Bone cried out and stumbled to her, banging his head on the ceiling.

She was on the ground. Her hands and feet were bound, and her mouth was gagged. Her head bled from a three-inch wound on her forehead.

"Sheila!" he held up her head, which flopped up and down. "Sheila, can you hear me?"

Baxter moaned and slurred a few words.

"Walker, in here!" Bone cried out.

Moments later, Walker appeared.

"Help me get her out. She's hurt."

Together, they dragged Baxter out of the coal store into the garden.

"Oh my God, Sheila!" Jim cried out and rushed over.

"Get this crap off her."

They pulled and tore at the packing tape around her hands and feet, then carefully removed the gag from her mouth.

"My poor love, what happened to you?" Jim dropped to his knees and held her face gently in his hands.

Walker dialled for an ambulance.

"Sheila, can you hear me?" Bone said, kneeling next to Jim.

For a moment, Baxter's head continued to flop around, but then she opened her eyes and looked around at her husband and then at Bone.

"Are you okay?" Bone repeated.

"My head hurts," she muttered, shaking.

"You've a nasty cut on your head, and you may be in shock," Bone said.

Jim took off his dressing gown and draped it over his wife's shoulders.

"What time is it? Who...?" Baxter continued.

"Don't try to speak."

Baxter licked her lips. "I need a fag," she said finally.

Bone glanced over at her husband. "I think she's okay," he said and smiled.

A few minutes later, an ambulance arrived, and as the crew lifted Baxter out of her front door on a chair, Mullens came rushing up the street.

"What's happened?" he asked.

"More intimidation," Bone said. "Call off the search party, we've found her."

"Oh, thank Christ," Mullens said with a sigh of relief. He went over to the crew who were manoeuvring Baxter up the ramp and into the back of the ambulance, with Jim following behind. "Bloody hell, Sheila. What happened to you?" he asked from the side. "Did you get lamped by a Golden Virginia lorry?"

"Don't mention cigarettes," Sheila moaned. "I'm bloody gasping."

"Well, I have to say, I'm a bit disappointed with your choice of pyjamas. I always thought you slept in Harris Tweed," he joked.

Baxter shook her head then moaned with pain.

"Let them get on, Mark," Bone ordered.

Mullens stepped back. The crew jumped in, and the ambulance disappeared up the street.

"This is getting seriously out of hand," Bone groaned.

"Understatement of the year, sir," Mullens replied.

"We need to catch this this bastard before someone gets killed."

"Aye, one of us, by the looks of things." Mullens blew out his cheeks.

Just then, Bone's phone rang.

"What the hell now?" he stabbed at the button.

"Sir, Brody here," the desk sergeant said.

"What?" Bone snapped back.

"There's a Ms McKenzie here to see you."

"Who?" Bone asked.

"The forensic document examiner. She wants to talk through her initial report with you."

"That was quick. Okay, we'll be there in ten," Bone said and hung up.

THIRTY-ONE

On his way back to the station, a squad car accelerated past Mullens's car and flagged him down. The two cars pulled into a lay-by. A uniform climbed out of the driver's side and approached. Mullens wound down his window.

"Sorry to stop you, sir. The station has been trying to get a hold of you."

"What's up?" Mullens asked. "And before you say anything, I've not eaten a thing since breakfast, so just get on with it."

"What?" the PC replied. "No, er... the station received a call from an officer in attendance at your father's house. Apparently, there's an ongoing incident in progress."

"Oh Jesus. What's happened now?" Mullens muttered to himself. "What sort of incident?"

"I don't know, sir. I was just told to intercept you en route to the station."

"Okay, thanks." Winding up his window, Mullens roared out of the lay-by, spraying gravel up onto the PC's hi-vis jacket.

Turning into his dad's road, he spotted two squad cars, an ambulance, and a fire engine parked up outside the house, and it looked like most of the neighbours were outside, lined up behind a makeshift cordon.

"Bloody hell." He stopped the car and jumped out.

"What's going on?" he asked, approaching one of the PCs standing by the cordon.

"DS Mullens?" the uniform asked.

"No, George Clooney. Who else?" Mullens returned and held up his lanyard.

The PC stepped to one side to allow Mullens to pass. At his dad's gate, he was met by a second PC.

"DS Mullens?" she asked.

"What is this, some kind of Pin the Name on the Detective's Arse Day? Yes!" he bellowed. "Now would you please explain to me what is going on?"

"Earlier this afternoon, a neighbour reported a man on the roof of your father's house. They said he looked like he was a jumper."

"What, suicide? My dad? Are you kidding?"

"No, it's a young man. He's at the back of the property. There's a specialist officer on the ground now, trying to talk him down."

"Christ's sake, let me through." Mullens attempted to push past.

"Sorry, sir, I've been instructed to send you round the side of the building so that you can liaise with the incident officer."

"Where's my dad?" Mullens barked.

"Presumably inside the property, but I'm not sure."

Mullens charged up the side path and spotted a PC at the bottom of the back garden staring up at the roof.

The PC dashed over. "DS Mull—?"

"Shut it!" Mullens interjected. "Just tell me what's happening." He held his hand to his eyes to shield them from the glare of the sun and peered up.

Tim, the young care nurse, was perched at the very top of the roof, clinging to the chimney, his blue plastic NHS apron flapping in the breeze.

"It's okay, son. There's an officer coming up to help you get down."

"I'm not going back in!" Tim hollered.

"Don't worry, if you'd like to talk a bit more, that's okay. The main thing is that you're safe."

"I'm not safe!" Tim replied.

"Just stay calm. We can help you feel safe again. We'll look after you."

"No, it's him in there. He's going to kill me," the nurse cried back. "I'd rather take my chances and jump than go back inside."

"No one is trying to kill you." The PC glanced over at Mullens.

"Oh yes there is!" Mullens interrupted and ran to the back door.

"Please don't, sir, we have specially trained officers who can deal with this."

"He's not a bloody jumper, he's my dad's care worker. I'd be out there as well, if it was me."

"Da!" Mullens cried out. He dashed through the kitchen and down the hall. "Where is he?" he muttered to himself. "Da!" He took the stairs, two at a time.

A PC appeared from the back bedroom. "Sir, please leave this to us," she urged.

"Where's my father?" Mullens insisted.

"Er… he's in his room next door. We told him to stay in there for his own safety."

"For your own safety more like." Mullens ran across the landing to his dad's bedroom. "What the hell have you done?" he asked when he spotted his dad in another of his wrecked armchairs pushed into the corner.

"Nothin'," his dad said, feigning innocence.

"So you just fancied a wee game of rounders is that it?"

"What, this?" George said. He picked up a baseball bat by his side and tapped the end on the floor. "That's just for my personal protection. That pervert was in at my gonads and places I didn't even let your mother go."

"Da! Too much!" Mullens exclaimed. "Did you lamp him one with it?"

"Nah, just a wee reminder not to get tore into my tackle."

"He's got a lump on his head the size of Mount Vesuvius."

"He did that fallin' over my wheelchair."

"Da, this is serious. You've just threatened an NHS nurse, you bloody lunatic."

"Hey, he's the lunatic, always at me with his cold, mingin' flannels."

"He's just doing the job you can't do anymore," Mullens said with a sigh. "The whole street is out to watch the spectacle, and a bunch of experts are out there who think our friend is trying to top himself."

"I wish he would."

"Da! That's enough. Give me the bat." Mullens tried to prise it from his dad's clenched fist.

"Hey, sir, that's my wee bodyguard." George continued to resist.

"It's the rest of us who need protection," Mullens said and finally snatched it from him. "Thank you. Now wait there while I go back and try and salvage what little I can from this nightmare and apologise to that poor sod on the roof."

Mullens returned to the back bedroom where the PC leaned out of the window, attempting to talk to the nurse.

Mullens pulled the PC back in. "Let me speak to him."

"I'm not sure that's a good idea."

Ignoring him, Mullens leaned out of the window as far as he could until he could just see the nurse.

"Tim, it's Mark here. I've confiscated the baseball bat, and my dad is trapped in his armchair. The coast is clear."

The nurse looked down and almost slipped off the roof. "Your dad's a bloody madman. He chased me up here with that... weapon."

"Aye, for an infirm senior citizen with dementia, he can move like a bloody panther when he wants to," Mullens chuckled. "Come on down."

"I'm not going back in there," Tim said.

"No, don't move. Let the fire crew get you down, and I'll meet you at the bottom, okay?"

"As long as you keep him away from me."

"Don't worry, I'll sort him out."

Reluctantly, the nurse nodded his agreement, and Mullens waved for the fire crew to elevate their ladder.

When the nurse was finally rescued from Mullens's dad's chimney stack, a paramedic checked the lump on his head and gave him the all-clear.

"So sorry, Tim. I did warn you that my dad would be a challenge for Genghis Khan and his entire army," Mark said.

"I underestimated his stealth."

"Aye, we've all done that."

"I just want to get out of here and go home," the shaken nurse said and retreated towards his Fiat 500 parked across the street. "Don't worry, I'm not going to press charges or anything like that. It's his dementia, I understand that."

"I'm not sure you'll have a say in that. If the PCs on duty decide to report it, then it might go farther."

"Well, I would rather just forget the whole thing and quit while I'm still alive."

"That's very good of you. I'm not sure I'd be so charitable." Mullens smiled.

The nurse jumped in his car and drove off, past the various emergency vehicles.

"Show's over!" Mullens hollered to some neighbours still lingering by the cordon.

The suicide prevention PC approached Mullens.

"Before you say anything, my da has mid-stage dementia with aggressive tendencies."

"You're telling me. That poor nurse was frightened out of his wits."

"He's an absolute liability," Mullens groaned.

"Well, the time might have arrived for you to consider putting your father into a care home where professionals can deal with him and he'll be less likely to harm anyone in the future."

"I seriously doubt that. But yes, end of the road, I think. Wish me luck."

"You're going to need more than luck with him. I suggest a suit of armour," the PC joked, and with a shake of his head, returned to his squad car.

THIRTY-TWO

A young woman dressed in an ankle-length tartan skirt and checked waistcoat greeted the detectives in the station foyer.

Bone extended his hand "Good morning, Ms McKenzie" Bone said and held out his hand.

"I take it you're DCI Bone?" she asked, shaking his hand lightly.

"Yes. Let's go through," Bone said.

She followed the detectives through the security doors into the rear of the station.

In the incident room, she spotted Harper. "Will!" she exclaimed and went over.

Harper clambered to his feet and hobbled round his desk to greet her.

"It's good to see you again after all these years," she said.

They embraced.

She stepped back. "You look well. How are you?"

"I'm glad someone thinks that," Harper said. "I'm doing okay, Catriona." He smiled. "Thank you for dealing with this so quickly."

"You may not be thanking me when I give you my report," she said.

"Oh, dear," Bone said. "Would you like a drink, a coffee or anything?"

"Coffee would be great, thanks." Her Southside Glasgow accent twanged.

Walker approached.

"Catriona, this is my colleague, DI Walker," Bone said. "Rhona, this is Catriona McKenzie, the forensic document examiner we hired to run a handwriting analysis of the graffiti."

"Good to meet you," Walker said. "Will speaks very highly of you."

"Oh, he's a sweetheart, isn't he?" McKenzie glanced over at Harper and he blushed.

"Sorry, that wasn't very professional of me. Will and I were at uni together," McKenzie explained.

Walker smirked. "I know, we heard."

"Let's go to my office," Bone said. "Could you get the coffees, Will, and then perhaps you could join us?"

Harper nodded enthusiastically.

In Bone's neglected office, he cleared the piles of papers and files from a chair and pushed it over to his desk.

"Please take a seat, and sorry about the mess. I don't use my office much. I prefer to be on the shop floor, as it were." He spotted a blackened banana skin dangling from the corner of his desk and quickly flicked it into the bin.

"Do you have a screen available? I've made a few notes and added some observations to the images Will sent over," McKenzie said as Will slipped into the room with the coffees precariously balanced in his hands.

"Yes, I think…so…?" Bone glanced over at Walker, then Harper.

"I'll sort it, sir," Harper said. He hobbled over to a TV monitor attached to the wall above the door.

"While we wait, how did you get into this line of work?" Bone smiled politely.

"Ah, that's what everyone asks, and to be honest, I'm not really sure what happened." She laughed. "I did an undergrad degree in chemistry, and then I took a shine to forensics. I found that I had an aptitude for the chemical analysis of documents. And while I was doing my PhD, one of our tutors was Professor Frank Dobson." She stopped as though waiting for a reaction.

Bone shrugged. "Sorry, I don't know who that is."

"The world's leading authority on handwriting analysis," Harper interrupted. "Okay, I've set this up." He tapped the remote, and the screen came to life.

McKenzie rummaged around in her briefcase and produced a USB. She handed it to Harper.

"Thanks, Will," she smiled at him again.

Harper blushed again and plugged the stick into the unit housed on a shelf to the right of the door.

"Could you open the file named Kilwinnoch, please?" she asked.

Harper complied, and after he tapped the attached mini keyboard, the folder appeared on the screen. He located the correct file from the list and clicked it open.

McKenzie went over to the screen. "Okay, before I go through this, I need to say that while the forensic report on the chemical composition of the spray paint is helpful, my analysis is limited as I am working from images rather than a physical document such as a handwritten letter. So please be aware of this."

She moved closer over to the keyboard next to Harper.

"Which button do I press?" she asked.

Harper looked up.

"To run the sequence, I mean?"

"Oh, yes, er… this one," Harper stuttered and pointed to the down arrow.

She turned back to Bone and Walker. "I've conducted a detailed analysis of the three images of handwriting samples Will sent over, but to be honest, it's somewhat insufficient to give you any kind of definitive results that might be considered reliable to be used in a court of law." She tapped the key and the first image, the graffiti scrawled across Bone's bedroom wall, appeared on the screen.

"In each of the photos taken at crime scenes, I worked through twelve characteristics, which I won't bore you with. What I'm searching for essentially are consistencies to establish whether the writing was done by the same author. Results here are inconclusive. There are a number of stylistic differences between the first and second word." She clicked the image, and it zoomed in on the letter *a* in the word *leave*. "Here you can see signs of a connecting stroke." She clicked again, and a circle appeared around the faint flourish. "And this is pretty consistent in all the images," she continued. "There is also a second and more pronounced connecting stroke visible between the *n* and *e* in the word *alone.*" She clicked again, and the screen displayed a close-up of the word scrawled into the paintwork of Bone's car.

Bone winced.

"This is where things get tricky," she said. "In my professional judgement, the letter *a* that occurs twice in both words, *leave* and *alone* are indications that the connecting stroke is forced. On the other hand, the connecting strokes between the *n* and *e* appear to be authentic, again in my judgement."

"So, the long and the short of it?" Bone asked.

"I'm afraid that based on the samples provided, results are inconclusive. There's simply insufficient evidence to indicate whether the author's style is cursive or block. I'm so sorry. That's probably not the answer you wanted to hear."

"No, not really." Bone shrugged.

"However," she continued, "when I ran a comparative analysis using the samples provided, I found a couple of interesting characteristics."

"Go on," Bone said.

"So in Sample A…" A paragraph of handwritten text appeared.

"A is Brandon Kinross, sir," Harper interjected.

"I identified three similarities in style," McKenzie continued. "Writer A's calligraphic style is predominantly cursive, and I found three consistent matches in pen strokes between letters."

"So the graffiti could be Kinross's?" Bone asked.

"I didn't say that," McKenzie replied. "Again, there is insufficient evidence to jump to that conclusion. And things get even more complicated when we look at sample B."

"Oliver Morton," Harper added.

The image switched again to a second paragraph.

"Writer B is a block writer with a clear separation between letters and zero link strokes. Here, I identified two stylistic similarities that were consistent in the graffiti."

"Oh Jesus." Bone rubbed his head. "So where does that leave us?"

"It leaves you back where we started with inconclusive results that wouldn't hold up in court."

"What's your professional opinion?"

"Off the record?"

Bone nodded.

"I'd say that we are either dealing with someone with high levels of handwriting forgery skills, or someone trying to cover their own handwriting. Either way, the graffiti is a closest match to Writer A, but don't quote me."

Bone sighed. "Okay, thanks. And with regards to styles, I read cursive was introduced in schools in nineteen ninety-two, is that right?

"Not exactly. Cursive and block have been taught in primary schools for years, and it's up to individual schools to choose their preferred method. In recent years, a hybrid style has been adopted by many schools, which is somewhere in-between both styles."

"So, trying to connect someone's age to their chosen style of handwriting is pointless?"

"For people over sixty it might be possible, but anyone under, it can be all over the place, to be honest." She stopped. "Oh dear, more vagueness, sorry."

"Okay, thanks," Bone said.

"I'm not sure I deserve thanks. I wish I could be more helpful."

"No no, it all goes in the mix. Thanks for coming in," Bone stood.

"I thought it best to explain face to face," McKenzie said, seeing as it's so inconclusive.

"And see your old friend, too?" Walker added.

"Well, yes. She glanced over at Harper, who tried to conceal his smile from his colleagues.

Removing the USB, Harper handed it back to her. "I'll call you later, maybe we could catch up with a drink?"

"Sure, great." McKenzie replied. "I'll see you later then." She turned back to Harper's grinning colleagues, nodded, and left.

"Sir, could I have a quick word?" Harper cut in before Bone could comment. "As we thought, digital forensics drew a blank with the damaged large format camera, however…"

"Here we go," Bone groaned.

"As soon as they were done with it, I signed it out to check it over myself, hope that was okay?"

"Fill your boots, Will," Bone said.

From a cabinet drawer by his desk, Will removed an evidence bag and, clearing a space on his desk, placed it down and withdrew the bashed and twisted remains of the camera.

"Forensics said that the SD card had been removed and the camera's hard drive was too badly damaged to recover any files. But I just thought I'd have a wee go. So after a bit of fiddling and unscrewing, I managed to fish the hard drive out of the camera." He reached into the evidence bag again and removed a tiny black box. "As you can see, it's a bit worse for wear."

Walker joined them. "Did you get in, then? she asked.

"No."

"Talk about anti-climax." Bone exhaled.

"But I used to work with a guy at GCHQ who specialised in restoring hard drives in way worse states than this. He talked me through what to do, and it was actually a lot simpler than I thought. All you have to do is—"

"Harper, please!" Bone interrupted. "Just tell us what you bloody found."

"The SD card was missing, but the hard drive had a few stored images from Jones's visit to the falls."

"Don't tell me he snapped his killer?"

"I wish. Sadly, no, a couple of great landscape shots, though. But with further digging, I found a tiny fragment of recorded sound that I managed to salvage. The time signature registered as seven oh three a.m. on the twenty-first of June, the day of Jones's death." He tapped at his keyboard again. "I transferred it here. It's very quick, only a few seconds." He pressed play.

The computer speakers hissed, and a rasping growl cut through the white noise. The recording stopped.

"What was that?" Walker asked.

Can you isolate that sound from the background noise?" Bone added.

"I ran this original recording though a clean-up app. Actually, I tried three or four, and this was the best of the bunch." He clicked a second file and hit play.

The speaker rasped again, but then the white noise dispersed, and after a moment's silence, a voice cut in.

"Loser," it snarled, and the recording stopped.

Bone stepped back from the screen, taken aback by the familiarity of the voice.

"Are you okay, sir?" Walker asked.

"Play it again, louder," Bone ordered.

Harper rewound and pressed the button.

'Loser,' the voice hissed again.

"It barely sounds like a human being," Walker said.

"More like a snake if it could talk," Bone winced.

"Sorry, I can't get it any cleaner, that's the best I could do," Harper said.

"Why would that be on there? Is it a video camera as well?" Walker asked.

"Most of these large format cameras have video functions and are capable of short recordings. I think sometimes photographers use them to check light conditions," Harper said.

"So why sound only?" Bone asked.

"At a guess, I'd say maybe when Jones was attacked, the record button got pressed, but the lens cap was on. Hence, sound only."

"Bloody good work, Will. Those life-threatening injuries seem to have done wonders for your abilities as a detective." Bone praised.

"Thanks, you say the nicest things, sir," Harper adjusted his glasses.

"Well, if that's our killer, is it more likely he knew the victim?" Walker asked.

"It does look like that, but unfortunately the recording is too distorted to make any kind of positive ID." Bone said.

"Well, maybe this rivalry thing got the better of Kinross. I mean, it did that night at their end-of-year celebration," Walker speculated.

"Then there's the shit-stirrer, Morton." Bone replied, "but the assault rules him out."

"It does, but I still didn't like the way he smiled at me when I interviewed him."

"Oh Jeez, why did I agree to come back and put myself through this again?" Bone grumbled.

"Is it your happy-go-lucky outlook?" Walker joked.

"Bugger," Bone said.

"What?" Walker asked.

"I've completely forgotten to speak to the press. I promised Gallacher I'd do it first thing this morning."

"Well, we have been kind of busy. Would you like me to do it, or accompany you for moral support?" she offered.

"That would be good. A show of strength."

"And Gallacher, too, for a united front?"

"Oh Christ no, that's one sure way to make me look guilty."

"What, even guiltier than usual?"

"I'll put you on bread and water if you're not careful." Bone smirked.

The group of reporters and TV crews had swollen from the hardy few to a First Division football crowd. As Bone and Walker emerged from the station, they surged up the steps and crowded around the entrance, pushing for prime position. A TV cameraman stumbled on the step and almost fell into Walker.

"Okay, enough." She raised her hands. "Please step back and respect our space!" she shouted over the barrage of garbled questions.

The press crews ignored her and continued to surge forward.

"Good afternoon," Bone bellowed.

After a moment or two, the mob hushed.

"Thank you!" Bone roared again, and the hysteria finally abated. "On Monday, twenty-fifth of June, a body of a white male was recovered from the Braeburn Falls. Following forensic examination, the deceased was identified as a Mr Richard Jones, a teacher at Kilwinnoch Academy."

"Was it murder?" a reporter asked.

"At this point, we are treating the death as suspicious and investigating a number of leads."

"Do you have any suspects?"

"Our thoughts are with the family, colleagues, and friends of Mr Jones at this time."

"What about your car crash? Were you drunk at the wheel?" a voice cried out.

Bone immediately recognised *Chronicle* reporter, Colin McKinnon's nasal whine.

"We are also investigating this incident, and the car involved has been impounded for examination."

"Were you pissed?" McKinnon called out again, squeezing through to the front of the group.

The rest of the rabble burst into laughter.

"Breathalyser tests are taken as a matter of routine. I urged the officer to administer the test."

A TV reporter squeezed in next to McKinnon. "Mr Jones was a well-loved member of the local community. Don't you owe it to the residents of

Kilwinnoch to solve this tragic crime as soon as possible?"

"We are working round the clock, day and night, to resolve this case," Bone's impatience was escalating.

"And do you have any suspects?"

"As I said, we are treating the death as suspicious and are investigating a number of leads."

"Was your car crash on the high street a sign that you're still unfit for duty, Detective?" McKinnon persisted. "Is your PTSD continuing to hinder your abilities and slowing down the investigation?"

Bone stepped towards the sneering reporter, but Walker caught his arm.

"Thank you very much," she said. "We will update you with developments as and when we have them. Thank you and good afternoon."

She tugged at Bone's jacket, and they retreated into the station.

"That shrew-nosed skid mark!" Bone snarled.

"Not worth your energy, sir," Walker said. "He's trying to get a rise and another photo opportunity."

"Well, he succeeded. Just let me at him for one minute. That's all the time I would need to rip the rat-turd's head from his neck."

"Well, it'll keep Gallacher at bay for a bit, so job done."

"McKinnon is right, though, about one thing," Bone said as they headed back to the incident room. "We have a long list of possible maybes that amount to absolutely bloody nothing."

Blood Water Falls

THIRTY-THREE

That evening when he arrived back at his flat, the sight of the fire damage was like rubbing salt in a wound that wouldn't heal. Attempting to ignore the carnage in the hallway, he headed straight for the living room and the safe harbour of his Dansette. If ever he needed some soothing music to calm the fireworks going off behind his eyes, it was now.

Kneeling, he flicked through his collection and picked out *Chet Baker Sings*, one of his go-to-in-a-crisis favourites and an album he turned to again and again when he felt the world caving in around him. He put the needle to the vinyl, dropped down in his armchair, and closed his eyes to shut out the madness for a moment. Baker's soft trumpet swooned once again, and within a few bars, he was adrift.

Walker's voice calling from the hallway stirred Bone from his trance-like state. He sat up. The record had ended, and the needle clacked back and forth. He checked his watch. An hour had passed.

"In here!" he called out.

She appeared at the living room door. "Sorry, sir, the door was…"

"Burnt to a crisp?" Bone quipped, rubbing his eyes. He got up and switched off the record player.

"Sorry to disturb you, but I thought it was best to call in with this one."

"What one?" Bone asked. "Would you like a drink of something, coffee, tea, whisky and Irn Bru?"

"Whisky and what? You've got to be joking."

"It was my dad's favourite, and I've taken a bit of a shine to it."

"You are a seriously strange man, sir. No, you're okay. I'm good." She winced.

"You don't mind if I do?" Bone asked.

"It's your house, definitely not mine." She glanced round the smoke damaged walls.

"So what is this news you have that can't wait until the morning?" Bone reached into a side cabinet and removed a bottle of Macallan single malt.

"Well, first up, the report came back on your car with confirmation that the brake cable had been cut, but no prints or DNA. On the plus side, they fixed the dent but couldn't get a match on that ridiculous colour to remove the scratched message. It's waiting at the station for you."

"I told you it wasn't her fault. You have more?"

"I've been studying that stalker footage again—you know that we recovered from behind Jones's bath…" She paused. "Please don't tell me you're going to annihilate that work of liquid art with Irn Bru."

"My house," Bone grinned and poured a generous measure of malt into a glass. Then, pulling a can out from under the unit, he popped the top and filled it close to the rim.

Walker watched as the soft drink obliterate the whisky and shuddered. "There was something about it that I just couldn't put my finger on," she continued.

"You watched all of it?" Bone turned in surprise.

"Pretty much, over and over. Luckily, Will had edited it down, so that made it a bit easier, but I just couldn't get a handle on what I was actually trying to find. But then on a fourth or fifth pass, it dawned on me," she said and recoiled again when Bone took a sip of the offending cocktail. "I'll show you what I mean. I've brought a copy over."

"Let me get my laptop." Bone disappeared into the bedroom.

While he was on his way back to the room, Walker picked up Bone's glass, sniffed the contents and pulled another face.

"I'll pour you one if you want," Bone said when he returned.

"That is horrific. A total betrayal." Walker exchanged the glass for the laptop. "Okay, so…" She put the laptop on the dining table, flipped the lid, and the machine slowly came to life. "Where's the USB port?" she asked, leaning over to check the sides of Bone's ancient computer.

"On the back."

"Bloody hell, this is old. You should ask Gallacher for a new one."

"I'm sure he'd rather just sack me."

"Right, let's start again," she said and locating the port, she waited until the laptop booted up.

Moments passed.

"In your own time," she tapped the table impatiently.

Finally, the machine stopped groaning, and Walker opened up the MP4 file. The video montage played. Bone pulled up a chair.

"So here is our lamplight lunatic on day one, day two, et cetera." She doubled the speed on the video, and the figure's position under the streetlight shifted around as the video ran through each nightly capture. "I stared and stared at this… and then Can you see it?" she asked Bone, who was transfixed by the moving image.

"Other than change of positions and weather conditions, nope."

"Let me play one more time." She rewound the recording and play again. "Okay, you know when we interviewed Kinross, we asked him about that shoulder injury with the pretty dramatic scar." she continued.

Bone nodded and carried on studying the footage.

"And he said he had a permanently frozen shoulder?"

"Aye?"

"Look at the figure's stance."

Bone leaned in a little closer to the screen.

"In every shot, the figure is leaning slightly to one side, with the left shoulder down."

"Bloody hell, you're right," he exclaimed. "That's Kinross's stance, his frozen shoulder. He's our bloody stalker."

"It's definitely a fit of some kind," Walker added.

"Well spotted, Rhona. Right then, we need to get the bastard in for questioning. We might have just hooked our killer," Bone said triumphantly. "Let's put him on the rack and see if he'll crack."

"Is this sufficient to warrant his arrest?"

"This and the fight story, absolutely."

Walker frowned. "But what about the day of the murder? Mullens said that the whole department, including Kinross, were at work as usual. Could he really bump Jones up at the Falls and make it back in time to get changed and himself together for the head's morning meeting?"

"Remember what Roxburgh said. I reckon an experienced mountaineer like him could get back to his house from the Falls in an hour, easy. So if he set off, say, even an hour after sunrise, say five a.m., he'd be home, showered, and guilt-free by seven-thirty tops."

"It still feels like we're stretching it, sir. Shouldn't we wait a bit longer and find a bit more dirt before—"

"We have the strongest lead in the case so far, Rhona. We have to follow this up." He grabbed his jacket.

"What, now?" Walker asked, surprised by Bone's urgency.

"I'm in the mood to nail the bastard who nearly killed my son, but you go home, I can deal with this."

"Are you serious?" Walker protested. "I'm coming with you."

"Okay, but I don't want this to get between you and Maddie. You have a lot to talk through."

"It's nearly eleven o'clock, it already has, sir."

"Okay. You ring Mullens, and I'll face the wrath of disturbing Gallacher and ask him to authorise an armed response unit. Let's go."

"Armed response?"

"We need to go in hard on this," Bone said.

They marched out of his flat.

THIRTY-FOUR

At Kinross's house, an armed unit was already pulling up on the next road adjacent to the cul-de-sac. The detectives jumped out and approached a Land Rover. Bone flashed his lanyard at the driver. Three officers clambered from of the back and tooled up. One handed Bone and Walker body vests.

"Really?" Bone said to the thick-built policeman.

"Yes, really!" he ordered.

Reluctantly, Bone wrestled the vest over his head.

"Who's your OIC?" Bone asked as a second vehicle arrived and stopped just ahead of them.

The officer pointed. "That's her," he said and disappeared round the other side of the Land Rover.

They went over as a tall, middle-aged woman in full-body armour and helmet standing by the van.

"DCI Bone and DI Walker," Bone said.

"I need you both to keep well back while we enter the property," the OIC ordered. Two officers ran past carrying a heavy, black metal ram.

Bone and Walker followed the officers into the cul-de-sac. The two with the ram approached Kinross's front door flanked by another two wielding Heckler and Koch rifles, and more backup lined up behind them with extendable batons.

"A bit full-on this, isn't it?" Walker whispered to Bone as they crouched behind a wall.

"If it scares the living shite out of him then all the better for us," Bone replied.

"Police!" one of the group hollered and the officers pounded the door with the ram.

It flew open, the lock and chunks of wood scattering in all directions. The lead kicked the door down completely, and the assault team rushed in.

A commotion inside filtered out, and then the commander's radio crackled to life, and a voice rasped, "Secured."

The commander gave Bone the nod, and they ran over to the house and went in. Kinross was in the living room, facedown on the floor with his hands cuffed behind his back. An armed officer knelt on his kidneys, his rifle pointing at Kinross's head. The commander came in behind the detectives.

"Stand down, Officer," she said to the over-enthusiastic mountain on Kinross's back.

Bone went over to the prostrate teacher and knelt by his head.

"What's going on?" Kinross mumbled through a mouthful of rug.

"Mr Kinross, I'm arresting you under Section one of the Criminal Justice Act twenty sixteen for the murder of Richard Jones."

"What? No!"

"The reason for your arrest is that I suspect you have committed an offence and I believe that keeping you in custody is necessary—" Bone continued.

"This is ridiculous!" Kinross interrupted.

"—and proportionate for the purposes of bringing you before a court or otherwise dealing with you in accordance with the law. Do you understand?"

"No, I don't fucking understand. Let me go!"

"You are not obliged to say anything, but anything you do say will be noted and may be used in evidence. Do you understand?" Bone repeated.

"I haven't done anything… I couldn't…" Kinross pleaded.

Bone stood. "Take him back to the station."

Two officers picked him up from the floor and manhandled him out of his house.

On the street, some of the neighbours were out, and a few filmed the action.

"Guess where that footage will end up?" Bone said to Walker as they removed their body armour. "Go on home, Rhona. I'm going to let our friend sweat in a cell until the morning."

"You sure?"

"Your partner needs you. Go. That's an order."

"Sir," Walker headed out to the cul-de-sac. She stopped and turned. "How will you get home?"

"I'm going to walk. I could do with the air."

Walker nodded and left him.

After Bone had alerted the station to the imminent arrival of his prime suspect, he set off for his flat. On the way, he ran the case over in his mind. Something lingered like a bad smell—it all suddenly seemed too easy. He chased the thought out of his head, and spotting Sandino's Chip Shop lights, headed for a culinary distraction.

THIRTY-FIVE

The next morning, Bone ran the gauntlet of press outside the station, now in full-on hysteria mode. He pushed through, ignoring the barrage of questions about last night's activities. He spotted McKinnon in the throng but was through the front door before he could intercept him.

"Morning, sir, I see you survived Beatlemania out there?" the desk sergeant said, about to plunge into a Lorne sausage and fried egg bap.

"Is Walker in yet?" Bone asked.

"Aye, and there she is now," Brody said and nodded at Walker who appeared from the corridor.

"Morning, sir," she said.

"I think we should speak to the press," Bone said to Walker.

"What, now?" she asked, clearly beginning to feel like a stuck record.

"The tittle-tattle is only going to get worse, and at least we have some good news for a change. Wipe the smug, smarmy grin off that clinger-on's sphincter."

"Don't you think we should wait until we've interviewed the suspect?" Walker urged.

But Bone was already halfway out the door. He turned and gestured for her to follow him.

When the press pack saw the detectives emerge, they surged forward in a wave of flailing arms and legs and eruption of flashing lights.

"Good morning, ladies and gentlemen," Bone called out.

Walker stepped up beside him, looking a little shell-shocked.

Cameras and mics and flapping mouths pressed in towards them. Bone held up his hands, and Walker pushed a couple of journalists back.

"In the early hours of this morning, a thirty-three-year-old white male was arrested in connection with the murder of Richard Jones," Bone continued.

For a few moments, the noise died down, but when Bone paused, the mob erupted again with questions.

"At this stage, the man is helping us with our enquiries. As yet, no charges have been made, and our investigations continue."

"Why have you arrested Brandon Kinross?" a whiny voice cut through the rabble. McKinnon emerged from a line of journalists and shouldering his way up the steps to within punching distance of Bone. "Did Mr Kinross kill our local hero?" he persisted.

"We have no further information at this time. We will update you again as soon as the situation changes, thank you," Bone turned to go before temptation got the better of him to thump his nemesis in the face.

"Is he the killer or are you just looking for a commendation medal, Inspector?"

Bone stopped on the top step.

"Sir," Walker urged.

"Cat got your tongue, Inspector?" McKinnon yelled up.

Bone clenched his fists.

"Come on, sir," Walker repeated nervously.

After a glare at McKinnon, Bone followed her back into the station. "One day," he snarled.

"But not today," Walker replied and exhaled.

"How's our friend been?" Bone asked the desk sergeant.

"The night officer said he was noisy," Brody replied and wiped the greasy remains of his hastily dispatched bap from his chin. "But all is quiet now."

"Could you organise a couple of PCs to take him down to one of the interview rooms?"

"Will do, sir." Brody disappeared through the back.

"Shall we see what our suspect has to say for himself?" Bone said.

"I've been thinking about all those dates when Jones filmed his stalker," Walker said as they headed onto the stairwell. "That's quite a lot of alibis the guy's going to need."

"What are you saying?" Bone asked.

"I mean, could you say for certain where you were on all of those nights and have witnesses or evidence to prove it?"

"That's easy. I'd either be here or at my flat—rock and roll."

"Aye, and the neighbours could testify to the cacophony coming out of that prehistoric record player." She paused. "To be honest, the whole thing is still not sitting quite right with me."

"For God's sake, Rhona. We have a suspect in custody. Let's just take this one step at a time, then once we're through this then we lay the doubts on the table okay?"

"That's the problem. I think we're jumping two or three at a time right now."

Bone sighed. "Let's just see what he says. He might surprise us with a confession."

Approaching the interview room, Bone spotted Kinross up ahead, flanked by two PCs. He was protesting loudly and jostling between them.

"This is going to be fun," Walker said.

When they got to the interview room, Kinross was still arguing with the uniforms at the door. Unshaven and dishevelled, he looked like he'd been dragged through a hedge backwards.

"Go in and sit down," one of the PCs ordered.

The second grabbed Kinross's arm and tried to escort him in, but Kinross jerked away.

Bone interrupted the potential altercation. "Mr Kinross, good morning."

The incensed teacher spun round. "You!" he snarled.

"Please do as the officers say and take a seat."

"I want you to let me go," Kinross continued.

"Well, the sooner you take a seat, the sooner this will be over," Bone insisted.

Kinross stared at him with fury in his eyes. He glanced back at the chair next to the interview desk and reluctantly sat.

"Good, thank you," Bone said.

He nodded to the two PCs, and one stepped out while the other stood guard by the door.

Bone and Walker sat opposite.

"What is all this about?" Kinross asked. "I was dragged out of my bed at gunpoint, handcuffed, and thrown into a police van. And I've been in a cell all night practically freezing to death with no food or an explanation—"

"Would you like me to get you a cup of coffee?" Walker asked.

"Just totally out of fucking order," Kinross said, ignoring her.

Walker got up and asked the PC outside to bring Mr Kinross a coffee.

Kinross looked up at Bone. "I didn't fucking kill him, if that's what this is all about."

"Mr Kinross, you have a right to legal representation. Would you like to make a call?" Bone asked.

Walker sat back down and turned on her tablet.

"Why? I don't need a lawyer. I haven't done anything," Kinross protested. "The only reason I might need one is to sue your fucking arses for assault and psychological torture."

"So, you're waiving your right to the presence of a lawyer?"

"I'm innocent. Yes!"

"Okay." Bone turned on the recorder and ran through the preliminaries, while Kinross continued to protest his innocence.

"Let's go back to the night of the dinner party," Bone started.

Kinross threw up his hands. "For God's sake I've told you everything that happened that night."

"Why did you wait for us to ask for information about the fight when we interviewed you on the twenty-sixth of June instead of offering it prior to that when you were first questioned at the school?" Walker asked.

"I told you. It wasn't a fight. It was nothing, just drunken stupidity."

"If it was nothing, why the secrecy?" Walker pressed.

"I wasn't being secretive. Jesus!" Kinross protested. "I just thought it might seem a bit—"

"A bit…?" Bone cut in.

"Odd. You know, us all having a stupid barney and then Richard goes and…"

Kinross's face fell. "We were just having a laugh about that bloody competition. Just a daft drunken laugh, but that wee shite, Morton, kept stirring it. I've told you all this before."

"We just want to go through it again so that we're sure in our minds exactly what happened," Bone said.

"Nothing happened. I don't know how many ways I can say it," Kinross growled. "Yes, we had a bit of a scrap, but that doesn't mean I killed him or give you the right to stick a fucking loaded rifle in my face." His anger was at boiling point.

Just in time, the PC arrived with a coffee and placed it on the table.

"Drink that," Walker said.

Kinross stared at the detectives for a moment and then guzzled down a couple of gulps of the hot drink.

"We had a bit of a wrestle. That's all it was," he continued. "We were both too drunk to actually do anything serious to each other. And we ended up both on the grass laughing about it. That's how we always were with each other."

"Staunch rivals?" Bone asked.

"No, friends. Good friends." Kinross put the coffee cup down on the table "I didn't kill him. Please let me go home," he said, suddenly looking weary and deflated.

Walker opened her folder. "I'm going to show you some images." She removed three A4-sized pages. "For the DIR, I'm showing the suspect evidence documents F-twelve, F-eighteen, and G-twenty-three. "Do you recognise any of these?" she asked, and placed the pages down in a row in front of Kinross.

Kinross scanned the photos. "That's my marking there," he said, tapping the middle image.

"So you confirm that document F-eighteen is your handwriting," Walker asked.

"Yes, of course. I gave it to one of your colleagues a few days ago."

"And what about the second and third images Do you recognise those?"

Kinross studied the prints again. "What is that, graffiti or something?" he asked, peering at the spray-painted message across Bone's bedroom wall.

"Did you write these statements, Mr Kinross?" Walker asked.

"What?" Kinross sat up. "No, of course not. I've never seen these before. What are they?"

"For the record, you are denying that images F-twelve and G-twenty-three are your handwriting?" Walker pressed.

"This is nothing like my writing. Am I the only one in the room who hasn't swallowed a stupid pill?"

"They look pretty similar to me." Bone leaned towards him. "After you set fire to my property, almost killing my son, you then sprayed this message on my wall."

Walker looked over at her boss, anxiously.

"Bullshit, what?" Kinross exclaimed.

"You then cut the brake cable on my car and scrawled the same message here, on the side!" Bone tapped the third image.

"Absolute garbage." Kinross frowned.

Bone slammed his fist down on the table and glared at the teacher.

"We'd like to show you some video footage," Walker cut in, attempting to turn down the heat. "For the DIR, we are going to show the suspect video evidence F-eleven."

"This is CCTV footage taken at Cromer station on the twentieth of June, the night Richard Jones disappeared," Bone stated.

Walker opened the laptop, located the MP4 file, and pressed play.

"You can see Mr Jones leave the train and exit the station via the ticket office tunnel," she said. "Moments later, a second person with their features obscured by a hoodie exits a carriage farther up and follows Jones out of the station." The video stopped. "Is that you, Mr Kinross?"

"No, it is not. Where did you say this was?"

"Cromer station at ten forty-one p.m. on the twentieth," Walker replied.

"That couldn't be me. I was at home getting packed up and ready to leave for Corriemurran I was going to capture the solstice at the stones up there."

"And can anyone verify that?"

"Like who? I live alone. But I drove up in the early hours and stopped at a petrol station. I have the receipt here." He reached down. "One of your officer's took all my stuff. You have my wallet, but you can check it," he said, his desperation rising.

"We would now like to show you more video footage," Bone continued, ignoring Kinross's claim.

Walker clicked on the second file.

"For the purposes of DIR, we are now playing video evidence F-twenty-two for the suspect," Bone said.

Walker clicked the file and the stalker video played.

"What's this now?" Kinross asked, staring at the screen.

"This is edited footage taken by Jones from his bedroom window, over a series of nights from first of May to fourteenth of June," Bone continued.

Kinross shook his head. "I don't understand. Who's that?"

"We believe this person was following or stalking Jones. We found these recordings hidden in his flat," Bone leaned over and paused the recording.

Kinross looked up. "Someone was stalking him?"

"Was it you?" Bone asked.

"What?" Kinross retorted. "I don't know what this is. Are you saying you think that guy there is me? If anyone is going to stalk Richard it would be that weirdo, Morton."

"When we interviewed you on the twenty-sixth of June you told us about your injury and your frozen shoulder," Bone said.

Kinross shook his head and rubbed at his legs, as though he couldn't take much more.

Walker pressed the play button, and the video rolled again.

"Do you notice the way the figure under the light is standing, with his left shoulder down slightly, and if we speed up the tape, you can see his position is pretty consistent throughout."

"I see where this is going, and that's not me!" Kinross protested.

"Would you say this peculiar stance indicates a frozen shoulder?"

"Are you fucking serious?"

"I'd say it's a pretty decent match, wouldn't you?" Bone pushed on.

"That could be anyone. I mean, a frozen shoulder isn't exactly a rare condition. Or the guy might have one leg shorter than the other. Fuck if I know. But that is…" He leaned closer to the screen.

"Mr Kinross?" Bone asked after a few moments of silence.

Kinross jerked back. "That's Morton!" he suddenly exclaimed. "He's mimicking my posture so that you think it's me. What an utter bastard! He's trying to set me up for Richard's murder."

"And do you have any evidence to support that theory?" Bone asked.

"I told you before he was into these weird impressions, copying mannerisms. His relationship with Richard was dysfunctional, toxic. I'm telling you, that's him! He's trying to cover his arse and bury me in the—"

"Your relationship with Jones wasn't exactly functional, Mr Kinross," Walker interrupted.

"I know Richard and I had the fight and that doesn't look good, but we were friends. I'm telling you, Morton, he's a total pariah," Kinross continued his claim.

"But Oliver Morton and his mother were attacked in his home, and there is evidence that the person responsible for Jones's death committed the assault," Bone said.

"What?" Kinross said in surprise.

"That's right, Mr Kinross. You can see why we don't buy your theory. what we do buy, is that after we turned up at your house, you broke into the Morton's house and assaulted Oliver Morton and his mother."

"Why would I do that?" Kinross shrugged.

"That uncontrollable rage of yours, Mr Kinross. Morton was speaking out of turn about you, and you didn't like that one bit," Bone suggested.

Kinross blew out his cheeks.

"The same rage that led you to murder Richard Jones." Bone pushed harder.

"This is just insane. Listen to yourselves!" Kinross barked.

"Mrs Morton, a frail seventy-six-year-old pensioner suffered multiple head injuries and is still too frightened to return home because of what you did, Brandon," Walker added.

"I'm telling you, Morton's the one you should be cross-examining. He's a total fruit loop," Kinross insisted. "And a fucking loser," he muttered.

"What did you say?" Bone interrupted.

"Well, that's what he is and always has been, but Morton took the meaning of loser to another level."

Bone glanced over at Walker. "An interesting choice of words. "Though I'd say that only a loser would concoct some feeble allegation against an innocent man to save his own skin."

Kinross threw up his hands again.

"Would you say Richard Jones was a well-loved member of the community?" Bone persisted.

"What is this now?" Kinross retorted.

"Isn't that something you desire but will never have? "You win all these competitions and it seems you usually win all the arguments, perhaps even fights too, but you'll never win the popularity contest. People don't like you, and you hated Jones because they love him."

"Rolling out the 'O' grade Psychology nonsense now?" Kinross snapped back "So, you think I was jealous of him and that drove me so insane with rage and hate, I murdered him? That's just utter codswallop.

"I put it to you, Mr Kinross, that your rivalry with Richard Jones finally got the better of you," Bone carried on. "Your hatred drove you to stalk and then to finally murder Richard Jones at Braeburn Falls, where your anger boiled over and you proceeded to mutilate his body."

Kinross turned to Walker. "You believe this tripe as well?"

"And following your crime, you carried out a campaign of intimidation, threats, and attacks on myself and my colleagues." Bone pressed on.

"This gets more insane by the minute. What did I do?" Kinross smirked, obviously no longer able to cope with more accusations.

"You think what you did is funny?" Bone asked.

Walker looked over at her boss.

"It's so ridiculous, it's actually hilarious now." Kinross laughed. "I'm all ears, so tell me, what's the next atrocity that I committed?"

"I'll tell you what you did," Bone replied. "You nearly killed my son, you sneering bastard!"

He jumped up and lunged at Kinross, pulling the lapels on his jacket. Walker quickly intervened. She grabbed Bone's wrists and pulling her enraged boss off him. The PC at the door dashed forward and stopped Kinross from leaving his chair.

"That's assault!" Kinross yelled.

Bone stormed out.

Walker stared at the door for a second. "For the benefit of DIR, DCI Bone has stepped out of the interview room."

"After assaulting me," Kinross interjected.

"I have here a set of dates for you to look at," Walker said and removed another A4 sheet from her notes.

"Oh, so we're going on, are we?" Kinross balked. "I'd say your colleague is more capable of killing Richard than I am. He's deranged."

"These are the dates and times Jones made the recordings of the figure outside his property," Walker said, ignoring Kinross's rant. "We'd like to give you some time to check through the list and think about where you were on or around each of those."

Kinross then turned to the PC still lingering behind him, then finally he scanned the sheet in front of him.

Walker signalled to the DIR that she was going to leave the room.

"So if you're going as well, am I free to leave now?"

"I strongly suggest you study those dates very carefully, Mr Kinross, because right now, things are not looking good."

Walker continued to the door.

"Jesus Christ, after all that, you're not letting me go? Your boss just thumped me one. I'd say things are not looking good for him!" Kinross bellowed. "Let me go now!"

But Walker had already left.

"Where is he?" Walker asked the uniform outside the door.

The PC nodded to the bathroom at the end of the corridor.

"Okay, take him back to his cell. I think we need some cooling off time here."

"Ma'am," the uniform said, and with a grimace went in to face the cacophony of Kinross's complaints.

Walker opened the loo door and called in. "Sir?" There was no reply.

She ventured in and peeked her head around the wall to check in case any other male members of staff were in. Bone was at the far end leaning on a sink.

She approached him. "What happened in there?" she asked quietly.

Bone continued to eyeball himself in the mirror.

"Sir," she repeated.

"I saw him sneer and I just lost it," Bone said finally.

"Is this about your son?"

Bone spun around. "Of course it's about my son! The bastard in there tried to kill him."

"Sir, if I may speak honestly."

Bone nodded, finally.

"I think we're clutching here," she said.

"He was fucking laughing at me in there," Bone retorted.

"He's terrified, sir. He's not laughing, that's one hundred percent, total fear."

"So, what are you saying?"

"We don't have enough to charge him. It's all just circumstantial."

"But the video, the injury."

"He's right when he says that an injury like that is common. We have no facial recognition on any of the footage, at the station or Jones's house." She paused. "I think…"

"Spit it out," Bone urged.

"I think it's a case of wishful thinking."

"On my part, you mean."

"I can understand why you want to nail this guy. We are under so much pressure, and you need closure for the attack on your son, but, sir…"

"Go on."

"Could your family circumstances, you know, access to your son, all of that, be affecting your judgement here?"

"You mean my guilt?"

"Well, if the cap fits, sir."

Bone turned back to his reflection in the mirror. "I'm still a bit of a wreck, aren't I?"

"More of a reclamation project," Walker said with a smile. "But lamping a suspect is not good."

"For a second there I wanted to kill him."

"Well, he does have a face you want to punch, but let's see if he comes back with anything on the dates I've given him. You never know, I could be wrong about this, and I'll gladly punch the bastard as well."

"Aye, right." Bone shrugged. "When are you ever wrong?"

Just then, the door opened, and Mullens walked in.

"Oh, intimate, I like it," he said when he spotted the two of them.

"Inappropriate, Mullens!" Walker snapped back at him.

Mullens picked up on the seriousness of the conversation and backed up.

"I'll use the ladies," he said and disappeared.

Walker rolled her eyes.

"Okay, I'll press on here. I think you need to go and see your son and talk to Alice."

"I can't leave you with all that right now."

"Sir, I'm all over it. You go. Time out. Any developments, and I'll call you."

Bone shook his head.

"That's an order," she insisted.

Bone finally went to leave.

"And if Gallacher sticks his beak in, I'll tell him you're following up on a lead, okay?"

"Thanks, Rhona," Bone smiled back.

"Just sort it out, and don't hit anyone on the way out," she joked.

Bone left, taking the stairs to the back exit. Walker stood for a moment and let out a long, deep sigh. Then, clocking the urinals and remembering she was in the gents alone, she rushed out and headed back to the incident room for a full mug of strong coffee.

As Bone headed across the car park, he spotted Baxter, lurking by the fence, her slouched frame half subsumed in a thick cloud of smoke.

"Why the hell are you back in, Baxter?"

"I can't be doing with lying about in bed. I need to be working," Baxter replied, dropping her cigarette and stubbing it out with the toe of her shoe.

"But haven't you got a concussion or something?"

"I'd rather have a concussion here than at home."

"Well, don't overdo it, Sheila. The last thing we need is another ambulance arriving."

"What?" Baxter asked.

"Harper'll fill you in." Bone shook his head and carried on to the rear gate.

"Oh, sir," Baxter called back.

Bone spun round. "Aye?"

"Before my wee holiday in my coal shed, I followed u your request and rang the school to ask about the teacher Jeff Bassett."

"Oh aye, what did you find?"

"Not a lot really. Thirty-eight years old, English teacher, worked at Kilwinnoch Academy for eight years. The head did say he was professional friends with the victim but wasn't sure if that extended beyond work," she continued. "But was sufficient for me to dig a bit deeper."

"And?"

"So he's married—"

"I knew it!" Bone interrupted.

"Sorry, now divorced, two years ago," Baxter corrected.

"What grounds?"

"Er…" She paused and rubbed her head. "Yes, got it. Adultery."

"Bastard!" Bone exclaimed.

"No, it was his wife who was accused of adultery. They settled out of court. But besides that, no record or run-ins with the law. He's a member of the local gym and running club." She paused again and frowned. "Oh, and he's involved with the council in a scheme to improve literacy for kids from poor backgrounds. And a bit of dish, if you don't mind me saying." She smiled.

"Stop, okay, I get it," Bone interrupted again. "He's an upstanding member of the community."

"Pretty much, yes."

"And any more links with Jones?"

"Aside from working at the same school, I can't find any. No political affiliations that I can find or into campaigning like Jones. Just a quiet, fit-looking guy."

Bone exhaled. "Right, fine. Thanks."

"Would you like me to pin his lovely face to the incident board when I go up and brighten it up a bit?" Baxter asked, raising an eyebrow.

"That won't be necessary, Sheila. As you were."

"Sir," Baxter said, her face falling, and she disappeared through the back door.

THIRTY-SIX

"Michael is in class, Mr Bone," the tight-mouthed school secretary said, leaning through the reception hatch.

"I know, I just wanted to check that he was okay."

"Oh yes, I read about that in the paper. So awful. You must feel terrible about that," she added.

"There are no words," Bone replied. "Anyway, can I take him out for an hour? Would that be okay?"

"One moment please." The secretary closed the sliding hatch window.

Bone checked his watch.

Moments later, the hatch opened again.

"I'm sorry, Mr Bone, the school has been instructed to not allow you contact with Michael." His lips tightened further as though preparing for an incoming verbal assault.

"Instructed by whom?" Bone retorted.

"We have to abide by the rules. I'm very sorry I can't help you."

"Did my ex-wife, Alice, tell you to do this?"

"I'm very sorry, Mr Bone."

"Bloody hell, I'm Michael's father. I have a right to see my own son," he pleaded.

"I suggest you speak to your ex-wife, thank you," the secretary said, and she slid hatch closed with a loud thud.

He rapped on the window. "Wait, come on. This is ridiculous."

She could still see her moving around beyond the opaque pane.

"Please!" he rattled it again.

But the hatch remained shut.

"Bloody hell!" Bone roared and stormed out of the school and jumped back into his car.

Checking his watch again, he did a quick U-turn and set off up the street, heading for Alice's work.

He drove at speed out to the new business centre on the outskirts of Kilwinnoch. Driving to the end building on a row of gleaming silver-and-glass units, he pulled up and raced into the foyer.

"I'm looking for Alice Bone." Bone

The receptionist slumped behind her desk sat upright with a start, as though she hadn't seen a human being for days.

"Who?" she asked vacantly.

"Alice Bone?"

"Ah, do you mean Alice Fitsimmons?"

"Yes," Bone replied, surprised that Alice had shed her married title.

"And you are?" The receptionist squinted at him suspiciously.

"I'm her husband, Duncan Bone."

"Ah, yes. Hold on." She buzzed through and alerted Alice that Bone was there.

Moments later, Alice emerged from a door at the back of the foyer.

"Duncan, what are you doing here?" she said, approaching him.

"What are you playing at, Alice?"

"I'm not playing at anything, Duncan. I'm at work, and you shouldn't be here." Alice returned, already annoyed with him.

The receptionist pretended not to be listening.

"I called in at Michael's school to see how he's doing, and they wouldn't let me see him."

Alice glanced over at her earwigging colleague "Let's go outside," she said.

"Did you tell them to do that?" Bone wouldn't relent.

"Duncan, not here. Come on," Alice marched out of the foyer and into the car park.

Bone followed her out. "Well?" he accused her again.

"Let's go round the side. It's more private."

"I don't give a shit who hears this. It's totally out of order," Bone came at her again.

Alice spun around. "If you're going to get abusive, I just can't deal with that," She marched round the side of the building to a section of lawn that looked out across fields and the Campsie Hills in the distance.

"Sit down a minute." She directed him to a bench facing the view.

"I don't want to sit down, I want you to tell me the school got it wrong and this is a mistake."

"Listen, Duncan. I've been bending over backwards to accommodate you and keep you happy—"

"How do you work that out?" Bone interrupted.

"Let me finish." She took a deep breath. "We agreed on access rights and a timetable, and I basically gave you what you wanted."

Bone shook his head.

"But it's never enough for you, is it?" she looked at him, rage and sadness in her eyes.

"He's my son. Of course it's never enough."

"I was willing to compromise and let things go, for the sake of Michael, but you just kept pushing and pushing it, and interfering in my life."

"We have shared history, Alice. We can't erase that."

"But this is the here and now. Our history is over, Duncan. *We* are over. That's why it's so important to abide by legal agreements to keep things civil."

"I just miss him," Bone appealed.

"But he could have died in your care."

"I know and I feel so terrible about that."

"It's your job that's the problem, Duncan. Your job nearly killed him. Michael isn't safe with you. That's why I instructed the school to refuse you access."

"You can't do that." Bone protested.

"I can and I did. I spoke to my solicitor, and she told me I was well within my rights."

"Don't do this, Alice, please," Bone pleaded again.

"I can't trust you with him on your own anymore."

"So no weekend sleepovers?"

"Are you serious?" Alice retorted. "From now on, if you see him it will be on my terms and never alone, not for the foreseeable."

"I never thought of you as a heartless cow," Bone growled.

"I'm looking after the well-being of my son, Duncan. One of us has to," Alice bit into her lower lip.

Just then, Bone's phone rang.

"This will crush me, Alice." He said over the shrill.

"Is that along with all the other things in your life that are crushing you?" Alice sighed.

Bone's phone continued ringing.

"Work calling, Duncan," Alice said and shoved past him.

"Wait, shit," Bone said. He fumbled with the handset and hit the cancel button and chased after her.

"Please don't do this, Alice," he tried one more time.

She stopped and turned, but his phone started up again. She shook her head and returned to her office.

"Fuck!" Bone roared and answered the call. It was Walker.

"Sir, sorry to disturb you," she said. "We've followed up on Kinross's claims, and his alibi holds up. He was in Oban on the twentieth and twenty-first.

Baxter called the hotel he stayed at, and they confirmed."

Bone said nothing.

"Sir? Are you there?"

"Here," Bone answered, finally. "And there's no way he could have sneaked back to Jones's property in the night?"

"He attended a cèilidh in the hotel bar until two a.m., so impossible."

Bone pressed his forefinger hard against his scar.

"Sir, we need to release him. He's not our man."

Bone stood in silence for a moment.

"Sir?"

"That leaves us back at ground zero," Bone replied at last.

"We have to let him go," Walker repeated.

"Yes I know." Bone conceded. "Do it, I'm on my way back."

THIRTY-SEVEN

At the station, an ambulance was parked up outside the entrance, and a couple of PCs tried to keep the press back. Bone stopped the car, jumped out, and ran over. When reporters spotted him, they surged forward, almost overwhelming the officers' precarious line. Bone ducked through before they could reach him and leapt up the steps and was about to go in when the doors flew open and paramedics emerged carrying a stretcher.

"Out the way," the medic at the front hollered at Bone.

He stepped to one side. As the stretcher passed, he caught a glimpse of Robert Springsteen laid out with an oxygen mask over his face and tubes sprouting from his arm. A third medic precariously balanced a bag of fluids while trying to maintain pace with the stretcher. Walker appeared behind the medics.

"What's going on?" he asked.

"Springsteen's been stabbed," Walker replied.

"What?" Bone spun round and clocked the medics lumbering the stretcher into the back of the ambulance.

"Earlier, some lawyer arrived and visited Springsteen in his cell. After the lawyer left, a PC found Springsteen on the floor, bleeding profusely from a stab wound to the stomach."

"Jesus Christ!" Bone exclaimed. "Is he going to be okay?"

"It's serious, could be fatal."

"This just gets better and better." Bone marched into the station.

The desk sergeant was in front of his desk, with all the appearance of a man at the end of his last day on death row.

"What the hell happened, Brody?" Bone barked. "Who let this so-called lawyer in to see Springsteen?"

"Sir, she said she was from Hitchcock and Partners, that hotshot London Law firm. You know, the ones that defend all the celebs," Brody said.

"Did you check her credentials?"

"Of course. She had ID, posh London accent, sharp suit, all the trappings, and everything seemed in order."

"Well, everything was clearly not in order. And why are they carrying him out the front door, for Christ's sake, through all those vultures?"

"Sorry, sir, the ambulance crew had access issues with the back door."

"So, who found Springsteen then?"

"The lawyer was here for only about twenty minutes, and she left. The PC who let her out the cell said Springsteen appeared to be okay at that point."

"And then?"

"A second PC checked on him about half an hour after that, and he was on the floor."

"Where's the PC who found him?"

"I'll summon him, sir." Brody returned to his desk.

"Where's Gallacher?" Walker called over to the desk sergeant.

"Head office meeting, ma'am."

Walker glanced back at Bone, and he blew out his cheeks.

"A moment's reprieve while we try to sort out this bloody mess," Bone said.

A few minutes later, a flustered young constable appeared from the stairwell.

"PC Glennon, sir," the uniform said.

"You found the suspect in his cell, is that correct?" Bone asked.

"Yes, sir. I was doing the rounds, checking everyone was okay, and found the suspect on the floor of his cell with a nasty wound in his stomach."

"You didn't see his visitor, the lawyer, arrive or leave?"

"No, sir."

"Was he conscious when you found him? Did he say anything?"

"Yes, sir." The young officer confirmed. "He said, 'For my brother,' and then he passed out."

"Nothing else?"

"No, sir. Then I raised the alarm, and we called emergency services."

"That's all for now," Bone dismissed him.

"Sir," the officer said and retraced his steps back to the stairs.

"This is an absolute bloody nightmare. We're about to let our number one suspect go, and now this?" Bone said. "Thank God Gallacher isn't here right now, because I'm sure he'd set the armed unit on us."

"We should have some security footage of this lawyer, shouldn't we?" Walker asked, distracting Bone from the cliff edge.

"Aye, ma'am." The desk sergeant pointed at the camera by the door. "And in the cell corridor downstairs," he added. "I'll dig that out."

"Seal off the cell and call the SOC team," Bone said.

"On it, sir," the desk sergeant replied and picked up the phone.

Bone turned back to Walker. "This is a warning to the Springsteens to keep their traps shut. This has got to be about more than just stealing osprey eggs. Those lowlifes must be connected to Jones's death, surely."

"We don't know that, sir," Walker said.

"And once we ID that lawyer, she'll lead us right to their gangmasters," Bone continued, ignoring Walker.

Before she could reply, he stormed off up the corridor and back to the incident room.

Harper looked over from the window. "What's going on? I heard an ambulance siren, but a PC in the corridor told me to return to the incident room. Who was that getting carted out?"

Bone marched across the room and into his office.

"Springsteen's been stabbed," Walker said.

"In custody?"

Walker nodded, knocked on Bone's office open door, and went in.

"Sir, I'm not sure we have anything tangible linking the Springsteens to Jones's death."

"What do you mean? This is a clear warning," Bone snapped back.

"With respect, sir. I don't think we should go in like a bull in a china shop again, like we did with Kinross."

"A bull in a china shop? We had cause, DI Walker," Bone retorted. "Okay, let's look at what we've got. We have one suspect at death's door, who now appears to be another victim, a second on the run and a third we've just released as he is completely fucking innocent," Bone raged. "So if you haven't got any better ideas, I think we should run with the bull in a fucking china shop option, don't you?" He pushed past her and marched out of his office and over to the incident board.

Walker sidled up to him. "You okay?" she whispered.

"What is okay about any of this?" Bone snarled, staring at the board.

"I agree that all roads seem to be leading us to the Springsteens, but it still could be coincidental."

"In case you haven't noticed, right now, the Springsteens are all we have."

The door of the incident room flew open, and Gallacher appeared.

"DCI Bone, a word!" he ordered.

"Well, that's just great," Bone muttered and followed Gallacher out.

Gallacher slammed the door of his office, and before Bone could sit down, his boss launched at him.

"I was on my way back from head office when I received a call from the deputy chief constable informing me that one of your suspects was in hospital fighting for his life."

"Sir, it would appear that—" Bone started.

"In custody," Gallacher snapped back.

"A woman who claimed to be his lawyer got through our security and attacked Robert Springsteen."

"Just got through? This is a fucking police station. People just don't *get through.*"

"I don't know what happened. DS Baxter went missing yesterday and—" Bone started to reply but Gallacher cut him off.

"So you've lost one of your team now, as well? I'm out the station for five minutes and it's like the set of Apocalypse fucking Now."

"She's been found, sir. We believe Jones's killer abducted and assaulted her."

"Oh dear God." Gallacher slumped down at his desk. "You couldn't make this shite up," he growled. "And what about the teacher you're holding? Are you going to charge him?"

"He now has a double alibi, sir, so no. We had to let him go."

"So help me understand this please." Gallacher stood again. First, you arrest half the population of central Scotland, then let them go without charge. Then you total the town's high street and end up on the front pages getting breathalysed."

Bone shook his head.

"You accuse Kilwinnoch's number one employer and chair of the Chamber of Commerce of murdering a local hero—"

"We are just doing our job, sir," Bone tried to explain.

Gallacher raised his hands and continued his rant. "And who is now threatening to sue us."

"That's just bloody ridiculous—"

"I'm not finished," Gallacher stormed. "You announce to the world's press that you have caught the killer, and then ten minutes later you release him."

"New evidence came to—" Bone said.

"I won't tell you again, Inspector." He cut him off again. "And then to top it all, like shit-smelling icing on a rotting Christmas cake, your last remaining suspect is stabbed in custody."

Bone remained still.

"And guess what? Internal are now on their way over from Edinburgh. Again!"

"I hope this time they don't try to blow me up."

"This isn't funny, DCI Bone," Gallacher returned. "This is a total fucking mess."

"Yes, sir, it is. That's because serious crime is messy," Bone replied. "And we're in the middle of it, dealing with lowlifes and scumbags and psychopaths, living with violence and intimidation, kidnapping and life-changing injuries that never heal. This is what we do. We put our lives on the line day after day after fucking day." He paused for breath. "With respect."

"if you're not up to the game then stop playing, Duncan. It's as simple as that."

Just then, there was a loud knock at the door, and Harper appeared.

"Sorry to—" Harper began.

"Not now!" Gallacher hollered.

Harper closed the door.

"Even for you, this is on another quite extraordinary level."

"We're just trying to do our job, sir."

"What job is that, demolition crew? You're a human wrecking ball, Duncan, and this comes after the Peek-a-boo fiasco and its sequel."

A knock on the door sounded again.

"And you seem hell-bent on shutting down the RCU and putting me in an early grave," Gallacher continued, ignoring the persistent rapping, growing louder by the second. "You are completely out of—What is it?" he roared at the door.

Harper appeared again.

"This better be worth it, Detective, or you'll be facing a future with your head detached from your neck."

"Sorry, sir," Harper started.

"Just get on with it!"

"Mrs Morton is here, sir," Harper said to Bone.

"What?" Bone turned in surprise.

"She said she wants to speak to you as a matter of urgency," Harper added.

"Sir, can we pause this conversation," Bone asked. "Mrs Morton is the mother of Oliv—"

"We are not done here, DCI Bone," Gallacher said.

"Sir, this could be vital to the case," Bone appealed.

"Just get out my sight." Gallacher slumped back down at his desk and running his palm across his heavily perspiring brow.

"She's pretty upset, sir," Harper said, hobbling along, trying as best he could to keep up with Bone.

"Where is she?" Bone asked.

"We took her to the counselling room, as far away as possible from the SOCO who are all over the basement area. DI Walker is with her now."

"Okay. You get back to the incident room. I'll take it from here."

"Sir," Harper about-turned.

When Bone reached the counselling room door, he stopped, took a long deep breath, and then stepped in. Mrs Morton sat in one of the armchairs with Walker on the sofa next to her.

He approached the pair. "Mrs Morton," he said and glanced over at Walker who shook her head.

Mrs Morton attempted to get up.

"No, please, you sit. I'll pull over a chair." Bone positioned himself opposite.

Mrs Morton began to cry.

"Oh dear." He reached over to the coffee table for the strategically placed box of tissues. "What's happened? I hope you didn't have to walk through all the reporters out there."

"No, it's not that," Mrs Morton sniffed.

"So, how are you? I hear you've been feeling pretty traumatised after the incident at your house, and you've been too fearful to go home, is that right?"

Mrs Morton's sobbing intensified.

"Would you like a glass of water or a cup of tea?" Walker asked.

"It was him," she said through the sobs.

"What was him?" Bone asked.

"My son, Oliver. He denied it, but I knew. A mother knows."

"Knows what?" Bone pressed.

"He was the intruder. I didn't think he'd actually do anything, but he hit me so hard…" She broke off in another fit of crying.

"Okay, let's start again," Bone said. "So, your son, Oliver, faked the break-in and the assaults, is that what you're saying?"

Mrs Morton looked up, her face wet with tears and smeared with mascara. "He loved Richard, Detective." She dabbed at the end of her nose, trying to find her composure. "Like a brother, I mean, but somewhere along the line his deep admiration became something of an obsession." She paused and took another shaky breath. "He would talk about him all the time. He even got me to help him buy similar clothes. I just thought it was some kind of hero-worship and he'd get over it. But it got worse and worse, and then he did this." She pointed at the black-and-purple bruise around her eye.

"Did your son kill Richard Jones, Mrs Morton?" Bone interrupted.

Mrs Morton stopped crying suddenly and sat upright. "He's not well, Inspector. Deep down, he's still a good boy, but he's sick."

Bone gestured to Walker, and she ran out of the counselling room. Moments later, a female PC arrived.

"Thank you, Mrs Morton. The PC will look after you, while we go and find your son."

"Please don't hurt him," Mrs Morton shouted after him.

Bone was already halfway up the corridor.

THIRTY-EIGHT

Walker slammed on the brakes outside Morton's house. Jumping out, the detectives raced up the path. Bone had called for backup, but it hadn't arrived yet. He hammered on the front door, but it swung open.

Bone edged his head around the frame and peered down the gloomy hallway. There was no sign of movement. They both went in, creeping slowly along the wall. Bone pointed to the kitchen. Walker carried on, and Bone started up the stairs. When he reached the landing, he squinted into the bathroom. Empty.

The loft ladder was down. He inched his head up for a peek above the hatch. The room was in devastation. Tables were upturned, and Morton's prized collection of antique military soldiers were scattered in all directions. The lamp at the far side of the loft was on and swinging wildly from one side to the other.

"Police. Come out," Bone called, but there was no sign of him. Bone climbed in. "There's no point hiding, Oliver, come out," he repeated and inched closer to the lamp, the tiny metal figures crunching under his shoes. When he was within a few feet, he leapt around the debris and yanked aside a tabletop leaning against the back wall. But there was no one there.

"No sign of Morton, sir," Walker said from the top of the ladder.

"Jesus, Rhona," Bone said, steadying the lamp. "He's gone totally crazy in here."

"The rest of the house is the same. A complete meltdown by the looks of things," Walker replied.

Just then, a voice called up from the hallway, "Sir?"

"Backup," Bone said and clambered back to the hatch and following Rhona down the ladder.

"The suspect has been spotted on Garrell Road," the PC said, still clutching his radio.

"Driving?" Bone asked.

"No, on foot," the PC confirmed.

Bone rushed past, with Walker behind.

"Quickest way?" Bone asked, jumping into the car.

"This," Walker said.

She slammed the car into reverse and took off at speed, backing out of the cul-de-sac. It careened onto the main road and she performed a textbook reverse handbrake turn and accelerated up the street. Bone exhaled, and with shaking hands, buckled up.

"Is that something you learnt to do on a tractor at your dad's farm?" Bone joked, nervously.

When they reached Garrell Road, two squad cars and a police van were already on the scene with police swarming all over. As they climbed out, Bone spotted Mullens running up the street towards them.

"I picked up the message, sir," Mullens said, his breathing laboured. "I've been right down to the end and up the next road, but I can't see him."

Bone scanned the long line of grey, featureless council flats stretching from end to end. A PC's whistle sounded from behind the row.

Bone frantically searched for a gap in the building. "How do we get over there?"

"This way, sir," a uniform called over to the detectives and disappeared through a narrow space obscured by a single fruitless apple tree.

The detectives raced over, following the PC. The whistle sounded again. Out into the back close, Bone spotted a PC on the ground clutching his stomach. The PC waved and pointed as they approached.

Walker ran over to the officer down, and Bone and Mullens continued across the back green, through a rear exit, and out the other side.

The garden ended abruptly, and they found themselves on the next street.

"You go that way," Bone ordered.

The pair ran off in opposite directions.

At the end of the road, Bone turned into the adjacent street, but there was still no sign of Morton. He spotted an alleyway and made a beeline. A bin crashed over just ahead and the lid rattled on cobbles. He raced on and turning a corner back towards the main road, he spotted a figure disappearing into one of the storage outhouses lining the alleyway.

"Got you, you bastard," Bone panted.

At the outhouse door, he stopped, held his breath, and pressed his ear to the surface. He could just make out the faint sound of someone breathing near the other side of the door. He stepped back and was about to pull the handle, when the door suddenly flew open, and the suspect rammed him full in the face, knocking him backwards onto the cobbles.

The suspect leapt over him and Bone tried to grab his ankles, but he was too quick. Bone jumped to his feet, but the suspect spun round and thumped him again in the side of the head with a metal bin lid, knocking him off his feet again and sending him sideways into the outhouse. The door slammed shut behind him, and the outhouse was plunged into darkness. Before he could scramble back to the door, the bolt rattled. Blind, he reached out into the dark, and when his hand connected with the wooden frame, he pushed at it with all his strength, but it wouldn't budge.

"Fuck. Fuck. Fuck!" Bone raged. He tried his shoulder, but it still wouldn't move.

He searched his pocket for his phone and the light button, but the door opened and light flooded back in. A shadowy silhouette filled the gap. Bone ran at it, in full rugby-tackle position. The figure swerved out the way.

"Whoa, tiger!" Mullens cried out and caught Bone before he tumbled across the alleyway into another set of bins.

"What happened to you?" Mullens asked spotting a line of blood running down Bone's cheek.

"I had him," Bone rasped and wiped the blood from his cheek. "But he got the better of me."

"I can see that," Mullens sniggered. "There's no sign of him up the other end either."

"The bastard's got away again," Bone complained.

"Seems like it. For now anyway. But we'll get him in the end."

"Aye, but what will he do in the meantime? That's what I'm worried about." Bone spat out a string of blood.

"You might want to get that checked out. " Mullens said.

"I'm okay. Next time I'll bloody nail him."

"Aye, right," Mullens laughed again. Then added "Sir," with a smile.

Two uniforms ran over to the detectives.

"Don't stop, keep searching!" Bone hollered at them.

They continued on down the lane.

"Phone the station and tell them to redirect more officers here before he slips out of the area completely."

"Sir," Mullens replied and fished his phone out of his pocket.

Bone pressed the wound on his cheek. "Fuck, this does need stitches," he said.

"I'll take you down to A and E."

"No, you need to carry on here."

"Well, a squad car then, no arguments," Mullens insisted.

"Stop bloody fussing. It doesn't suit you," Bone complained. "I can't afford to be in there for hours on end while this lunatic is still at large."

"Aye, but your face looks like Sauchiehall Street on a Saturday night. Just say you're on duty and they'll let you skip the queue. That's what I do."

Bone cursed, and Mullens whistled for one of the PCs to come over.

THIRTY-NINE

Once Bone had been stitched up, he resumed his search, with units from three other stations joining the manhunt. But after hours of searching, Morton was still nowhere to be found. By five a.m., with dawn on the brink, Bone's head pounded, and he went back to his flat for his medication. At the entrance to his close, he was greeted by a PC.

"Morning, sir," the young officer said.

"What are you doing here?" Bone asked.

"I was ordered to remain here at your flat, sir, while the suspect is still at large."

"There's no need for that. Stand down."

"Sir, Detective Superintendent Gallacher issued the order," the young PC said, looking flustered.

"Well, I'm giving you a new order. Wouldn't you rather be tucked up in bed than out here in the cold?"

The PC hesitated for a moment and then with a formal nod, he headed off into the murk of the new day. Bone let out a long sigh and wearily shuffled through the close, up the stairs, and unlocked the bolt on his temporary door. Avoiding eye contact with the state of the hall, he headed straight to the bathroom. Rifling through the medicine cabinet, he found his pills and popped a couple, washing them down with a few gulps of tap water. He glanced up at his bandaged and bruised face. His left eye was swollen, and he now sported the first flush of a full-blown shiner.

"Jesus," he muttered and pressed his finger against the bloodstained mesh taped below his cheek.

In the bedroom, he slumped down on the end of the bed. Finding his phone, he called Walker.

"Sir, are you okay? Mark said you'd gone to A and E with a face wound," Walker asked immediately.

"I'm fine," Bone replied. "Anything new?"

"Nothing, sir, sorry. The teams are still out and have now widened their search. We think he might have slipped through and got on a train to Glasgow. One of the team said they spotted him near Kilwinnoch station."

"Bugger," Bone cursed. "If he's managed that, then he could be anywhere."

"Absolutely. All we can do is keep searching. He's bound to turn up somewhere sooner or later."

"Okay, but you need to go home and rest, Rhona."

"I'm okay, sir. I'm good for another couple of hours."

"Right, let's reconvene in an hour, before you go off duty, and hopefully we'll have caught the bastard by then."

"You should be resting up, sir. Take care of that head of yours."

"God, you're worse than Mullens. It was only six stitches. I've been blown to smithereens, you know?"

"Ha, indeed you have. Sorry, sir."

Bone hung up, and a searing pain shot across his forehead. He pushed the ball of his palm against his skull, but that seemed to make it worse. He lay back on the mattress and closed his eyes. Within seconds, he was asleep.

A noise woke him from a restless dream to a dark room. His head spun, and his breathing was fast. Reaching for the edge of the mattress, he rolled onto his side and searched in the gloom for a glass of water, but the side table was bare. He slowly pulled himself up. His head still pounded. A movement in the farthest corner had him turning. A hooded figure lurked in the shadows.

"Ah it's you, back so soon?" Bone said to his unwelcome visitor.

The figure moved closer. Now Bone could hear breathing other than his own rapid gasps.

"You just couldn't leave it, could you?" the figure said.

Bone sat upright. "Morton?"

"Why wouldn't you just stop?" Morton moved closer still, his face emerging from the darkness.

"How did you get in?" Bone shifted slowly up from the bed.

"I would stay down if I were you," Morton threatened. His hand emerged from the dark clutching a hammer.

Bone sat back down. "You need to listen to me, Oliver. Whatever this is, you won't win."

"I gave you every opportunity, but you wouldn't stop."

"What is it you want?" Bone asked.

"It's too late for what I want. It's what I need," Morton hissed.

"And what is that?"

"Redress. You denied me my future, so I'll deny you."

"This was about your job? You killed your boss for his job?"

"For my life," Morton protested.

"That's pathetic," Bone retorted.

Morton raised the hammer. "Don't say—"

"All you had to do was go for a promotion in another school, not butcher your mentor and frame everyone in Kilwinnoch. Wouldn't that have been easier?"

"A monarch's reign reaches its natural end, but the king would not abdicate," Morton replied.

Bone slid his hand along the mattress, and his finger connected with an empty glass.

"I was a loyal and patient servant, but still he wouldn't go. That left me with only one option."

"And what was that, murder and mutilate his body?" Bone asked.

"It's called revolution." Morton shot back. "And I have to say, I was quite proud of my little smoke screen. Nothing like some good old ritualistic killing to point the finger at organised crime."

"Ah, I get it now. You're just a sad, pathetic wee man with a Napoleon complex." Bone chuckled. "I bet you've a small dick as well."

"I'd say that particular glass slipper is a perfect fit for you, Inspector," Morton sneered.

"You're nothing but a loser," Bone cut back.

"Don't call me that!" Morton snapped.

"If your tiny glass slipper fits, loser," Bone persisted.

"You stupid people!" Morton roared and, raising the hammer, he lunged at Bone.

Bone snatched up the glass and hurled it at his assailant, clipping the corner of his head, and it smashed against the back wall. Bone jumped up and rammed into him as he roared towards him. Morton swiped his hammer through the air, missing Bone's skull by millimetres. They toppled backwards into the dressing table, its contents flying in all directions.

On the floor, Bone grappled with Morton's flailing arms, dodging the hammer as the demented teacher swiped it wildly from side to side. Bone managed to climb on top, but Morton kneed him hard in the groin, and Bone slumped forward in agony. Morton slid out from under him, clambered to his feet, and raised the hammer again. Bone reached out and grabbed Morton's legs, and he toppled forward into the door, catching his head on the doorknob on the way down.

Scrambling upright, Bone ran over to Morton who was splayed out in the doorway, motionless and flat out on his face. He was about to snatch the hammer from Morton's hand, when Morton suddenly sprang to life and stumbled forward into the hallway.

Bone gave chase, but Morton spun round, swung the hammer, and smashed it into Bone's injured cheek. Bone screamed in agony and the blow knocked him sideways against the wall, and he onto the floor. Morton raised the weapon again, and Bone covered his eyes. But then he stopped, staggered backwards, turned, and ran down the hall and out of the flat.

Partially recovering, Bone set off after him but almost fell headfirst down the stairwell. He careered out into the street and scanned both directions. A car screeched past him, and he caught sight of Morton in the driver's seat.

"Stop!" he roared in vain.

He ran across the street, he threw himself into the pool car and set off in pursuit. Grappling with gears and his phone, he called the station.

"DCI Bone. In pursuit of a suspect on Riddrie Road. Yellow Fiat 500 heading north out of Kilwinnoch. Send armed response unit now!" He dropped the phone onto the passenger seat and hit the accelerator.

Morton was ahead, but he was losing him.

The Fiat suddenly took a left into a narrow lane. Grabbing the wheel, Bone forced the pool car to follow, and with a loud wail of complaint, it just made it. The Fiat weaved past rows of bins, but Bone's car was too wide and clipped every one on the way past, sending rubbish and metal flying. At the end of the lane, the Fiat turned right onto the high street and tore off towards the lights. Bone followed, and when he saw the fast-approaching junction he shuddered, remembering his last encounter with it.

Blood was now pouring from the reopened wound on his cheek. As the two cars raced to the junction, the lights changed to red. The Fiat ploughed on through, and Bone was about to follow, but he spotted a car approaching from the right. He slammed on the brakes but the wheels skidded through the junction, narrowly missing the oncoming vehicle. The car bounced over the kerb and Bone hit the accelerator again. As the two cars reached the outskirts of town, the Fiat turned up onto the Campsie Road. Bone was losing ground.

"Come on! Don't let a bloody Fiat 500 beat you!" Bone raged and pressed his foot to the floor.

On the hillside road, the Fiat turned again.

Bone fumbled with his phone again, found Walker's number, and punched at the buttons.

"Walker!" Bone hollered when she answered. "He's heading out towards the falls."

Walker shouted down the line, but he couldn't hear her for the scream of the engine.

Four miles out, the Fiat took a right into Monklands' farm and raced up the long tree-lined drive. Bone followed, the car's headlights bouncing up and down on the gravel track, beaming across the arch of trees and the Fiat up ahead. As they approached the main farmyard, the Fiat pulled in, the door swung open, and Morton jumped out. He ran off across the yard and into the darkness.

The security light on the adjacent barn came on, and Bone picked him up running over the same field he and Walker had taken to the falls earlier that week. Bone hit the brakes again, and the car skidded on the gravel and came to a stop. He leapt out and followed Morton, taking the same route across the yard. When he got to the gate into the field, he started to climb it, but it swung open and he almost fell on his back.

"Shite!" he cursed, and regaining his balance, continued on over the field. The path along the edge was now even muddier, and as he ran, his shoes disappeared farther and farther into it, collecting around his feet and slowing him down.

Glancing up ahead, he could just make out Morton's shadowy figure taking the stile at the other side. Finally, Bone reached the other side, and gasping for breath, climbed the stile and carried on down the steep slope towards the waterfall. Halfway down, the roar of water came from up ahead, but Morton was no longer in sight.

He jumped, slid, and stumbled on, and when he reached the bottom, he ran to the trees, stopped, and scanned the faint outline of darkened sky between the branches.

Nothing moved. Morton was nowhere to be seen.

He inched forward, trying to control his breathing, continually checking ahead and behind. He stopped again and listened. A loud crack made him turn.

Someone moved between the trees.

He raced forward, and the figure took off to the right. Forcing his way through thickening branches and undergrowth, Bone reached the spot where the figure had been, but again, there was no sign of him.

A second crack. This time on the opposite side.

"How the hell did you get over there?" Bone muttered. He retraced his faltering steps and moments later found himself out in the open, the river and the top of falls straight ahead.

Morton's silhouette perched on the very edge of an outcrop. Bone approached.

"Stop!" Morton called out, his face illuminated by the slow creep of dawn light. He smiled.

"You need to give it up, Oliver," Bone said between gasping breaths. "An armed unit is on its way, and believe me, they won't hesitate to shoot you."

"I don't think you'd want them to do that. Not until I let you in on my little ruse."

"What ruse?" Bone inched closer.

"Stop!" Morton repeated. "Last warning."

"So you're going to chuck yourself off, is that it?"

"You ruined everything for me. All my strategies and designs. I was ready to accede to the throne. I would have made a worthy successor. He trusted me with his legacy."

"What legacy?"

"His life. His selfless sacrifice. He would have wanted me to have what was his, but you snatched it away from me."

"That's because you are a loser, Morton. That's what Richard called you just before you killed him. That's his legacy to you," Bone said, sick of listening to Morton's nonsense.

Morton stepped back towards the edge. "I guess your son will be waking up soon and getting ready for school, won't he?"

"What have you done?" Bone shot back, panic rising in his chest.

"My Trojan Horse," Morton replied, his grin widening.

"Tell me!" Bone roared.

"He's such a lovely little boy. Michael, isn't it?" Morton sneered.

"What have you done to my son!" Bone took another step towards Morton.

"Steady. Don't you want to hear the end of my wee tale?"

"You fucking—" Bone raged, his fists clenching, ready to leap on him.

"I bumped into him this morning with his new daddy, Jeff. You know, my colleague from school? A lovely man, by the way, bit of a drip, but hey, the ladies like him for that."

"What have you done to him!" Bone bellowed at him.

"There were so many people out looking for me. Fame at last, but not a single uniform near your son's school. Pretty slack policing there, if you ask me. So me and handsome Jeff had a wee chat about your boy's packed lunch."

"So he *is* in on this, too?" Bone retorted.

"Who, Mr Gosling? Oh dear, no." Morton let out a high-pitched laugh. "An innocent lamb to the abattoir. Anyhow, where was I?" He sighed.

"Fucking tell me!"

"I do love his lunch box. Is that Power Rangers? Wow, I didn't know it was still on."

"If you don't jump, I'm going to fucking push you." Bone started towards Morton.

"Rude. Just let me finish." Morton pushed back farther towards the edge of the waterfall. "Michael let me have a peek inside. He was very keen to show me a lovely slice of chocolate brownie, his beloved mother baked just for him, you know as a very special treat for being so brave after that horrible fire."

"No!" Bone edged closer.

"He even offered a piece of it to me. That is an absolute testament to how well you've brought your lad up, or at least your wife and Jeff are these days. Anyhow, I sprinkled a little fairy dust inside, just to give them a little more *vavoom* for today."

"You've poisoned my son?" Bone growled.

"Just a smidge. The least I could do, and you are very welcome," Morton 's grin turning into an angry sneer.

"I'll kill you!" Bone screamed and lunged at him.

But before he could grab him, the farmer's son appeared from the trees and rammed sideways into Morton, driving them both over the side of the falls. Bone raced over to the edge just as the tangled pair hit the water. Three armed officers ran out from the woods.

"Down there," Bone yelled and pushed past them, running back through the woods and across the field to his car.

He got in and slammed it into first. Two police vehicles drove into the yard, one blocking Bone's way out.

"DCI Bone! Move!" Bone roared.

The officer at the wheel quickly reversed. Bone hit the gas and raced down the lane and out again onto the main road.

He checked the time. 8:03 a.m. "Fuck, fuck, fuck!" He hit the steering wheel with his fist.

When he reached Kilwinnoch, he drove back up the high street the wrong way, blasting his horn at an oncoming car, which mounted the kerb to avoid a collision. On he raced. When he finally reached Michael's school, he pulled up and dashed through the gates and into the reception.

"Where's my son?" Bone hollered at the startled school secretary.

"And which son would that be?" the secretary replied briskly.

"Michael Bone, come on!"

"Hold on," the secretary said, and she peered down at the desk in front of her.

"Come on! Come on!" Bone repeated.

"Sorry, Mr Bone. Michael is off sick today with an upset tummy, I think."

Bone ran out of the reception and back to his car.

When he reached Alice's house, he hit the brakes and leapt out.

"Alice! Open up!" he shouted and thumped the door with his fist over and over. "Alice!" he cried again. After a few moments, he ran around the side of the house and hammered on the kitchen window, but all was in darkness inside. At the back of the house, he elbowed a glass panel, and reaching through the hole, unlocked the door and ran in.

"Alice!" Bone hollered again.

Jeff appeared at the bottom of the stairs clutching what looked like his shoe. Bone pushed past him and ran up. Throwing open Michael's bedroom door, he ran over to his son's bed. But he wasn't there. Alice appeared, bleary-eyed at the bedroom door.

"Duncan, what in God's name—?" she mumbled, still half asleep.

"Where's Michael?" Bone pleaded.

Alice glanced over at Michael's empty bed, the duvet pulled back and hanging off the end.

"He's probably—" Alice began.

But Bone pushed past her and ran back downstairs, taking two or three at a time.

Bone ran into the living room. Michael sat on the floor about a foot from the TV watching early morning cartoons. Bone dashed over and knelt.

"Michael," Bone started.

"Dad!" Michael said with a smile. "Yuk, what's that?" he said, spotting the deep, dried, blood-encrusted wound on Bone's cheek.

"Where's the chocolate brownie?" Bone pleaded.

"I'm watching space aliens," Michael said, ignoring his dad's desperate question.

Bone grabbed his son.

"Your lunchbox and the brownie your mum made you this morning, where is it? He shook his son impatiently. "Have you eaten it?"

Michael's face fell.

Bone spun round. Alice was at the door.

"Where's his lunchbox?" Bone shouted.

"Lunchbox, what lunchbox?" Alice replied, confused.

"His lunchbox with the fucking... space ninja fucking things on it," Bone yelled back.

"Oops, you said a bad word, Dad," Michael chipped in.

"He has school dinners. We don't use that anymore. I think I chucked it ages ago," Alice shrugged. "Are you having some kind of relapse?"

"Aww," Michael pulled another face.

"So, no chocolate brownie?"

"What?" Alice pulled a face.

"Did you bake some brownies and give Michael one for his lunch?"

"When do you think I have time to bake bloody brownies, Duncan?"

"Brownie Brownie!" Michael thumped the carpet with his hand.

"Oh, thank God!" Bone said, and he bundled up his son, pulled him close, and squeezed him tightly.

Michael wriggled.

"I can't breathe, Dad," Michael wheezed.

After a moment longer, Bone released his grip and slumped down on the floor next to his son.

"What's going on, Duncan?" Alice asked, finally.

"So, why is he off school?" Bone quizzed.

Alice gestured for Bone to come to the door. Bone got up, and Michael resumed watching TV.

"He's been having night terrors about the fire, so thanks for that, Duncan," Alice whispered. "I just thought he could do with a couple of days off and some TLC."

"Oh God," Bone let out a long sigh.

"What the hell have you done to your face?" she asked reaching up.

Bone pressed his hand against the wound and their hands touched.

"That needs stitches," she said, clearly trying not to engage emotionally with him.

"So, no lunchbox or brownie?" Bone asked again, just to be sure.

"How many times… No!" Alice shook her head.

Bone's lips tightened. "I couldn't trouble you for a coffee, could I? It's been a long night."

"Sit down and I'll get you one," Alice said.

Bone turned, but his legs gave way. Alice caught his arm.

"Let me help you," she said and helped Bone down into the armchair next to his son.

Michael glanced back at his dad and smiled. Bone let his limbs sink deeper and deeper into the chair until the room disappeared.

EPILOGUE

Bone was later taken to A&E with mild concussion and was released the next day with half a dozen stitches and a sore head. The two jumpers were fished out alive from their long drop into the fall's pool, and Morton was arrested and taken back to Kilwinnoch station.

To the dismay of Bone and the rest of the RCU team, the procurator fiscal dismissed all charges against Robert Springsteen on the grounds of insufficient evidence. Throughout his time in custody, he denied any involvement in bird snatching and insisted that his stab wound was self-inflicted. The identity of Springsteen's alleged solicitor remained a mystery along with the whereabouts of his errant brother.

In the subsequent days and weeks that followed, John Monkland, Jr. received a community commendation for his bravery, and in respect for Jones's legacy, he defied his curmudgeon of a dad's wishes and removed the high fence from the right of way on their farm.

Oliver Morton was charged, convicted of multiple offences, and to the delight and relief of Bone and his team, as well as the whole of the Kilwinnoch community, he was sent down for a very long time and unlikely to see the light of freedom ever again.

As a tribute to the memory of Richard Jones, his environmental activism, and his contributions to the local community, Kilwinnoch Council established an annual nature photography competition in his name, and a permanent exhibition of his work went on display at Kilwinnoch Academy.

In the first year of the competition, the council offered Brandon Kinross the role of panel judge chair, and after much hair-tugging and conscience-rattling, he accepted on the condition that Jones won honorary first prize for an absentia submission of his photograph of Blood Water Falls. The image went on to win three more prestigious awards. Out of respect for his old friend and arch rival, Kinross never entered his own photographs in any competitions ever again.

And for the sake of humanity and Kilwinnoch's ageing Victorian sewerage system, Mullens finally gave up on his super-green smoothie diet. To celebrate, he treated his infuriated wife to a slap-up, all-you-can-eat-for-a fiver curry special at The Fells.

***

Campsie Fells Bird Sanctuary Director, Don Roxburgh, pulled over a step stool and helped Michael climb up to the top.

"Now, if you look through those binoculars, you'll be able to see the nest up close," Roxburgh said and held on to the excited boy's back.

Michael leaned in and peered through the viewfinder.

"I can't see," Michael said.

"Just give it a few seconds for your eyes to adjust." Roxburgh glanced over at Alice who smiled back.

"Wow!" Michael exclaimed.

"You see them?" Roxburgh asked.

"Wow!" Michael repeated, totally transfixed.

"We started with four chicks, but sadly one fell out, so now there are three chicks, or fledglings now."

"How do they stay up there?" Michael asked.

"One of nature's miracles and some expert engineering on the part of their mum and dad. Just keep watching because any second now, Mum will be back with lunch."

"Thanks so much for doing this, Mr Roxburgh," Alice said quietly.

"Please, call me Don," Roxburgh replied. "It's an absolute pleasure, but it's your husband you need to thank. He booked you in for the tour. If it wasn't for him, we wouldn't be looking at any ospreys this morning."

"Wow, wow, wow!" Michael jumped up and down on the stool.

Roxburgh grabbed his coat to prevent him from tumbling off.

"Has Mum come home?" Roxburgh asked.

Michael spun around. "She's brought a big fish. Come see, Mum."

"Have a look," Roxburgh lifted Michael down.

Alice climbed up onto the viewing platform and peered into the binoculars.

"Wow!" Alice said, replicating her son. "They are so beautiful."

"My dad saved them, didn't he?" Michael said to Roxburgh.

"Yes, he helped us protect them from bad men who wanted to steal the osprey eggs."

After a few moments, Alice stepped back down. "They are spectacular."

"They are, aren't they?" Roxburgh beamed.

"Thank you so much again, for taking time out of your busy day to show us round your wonderful sanctuary." Alice smiled. "Say thanks to Mr Roxburgh, Michael." She nudged her son.

"Thank you," Michael said. "When I grow up, I'm going to be a naturist like you," he added.

"That's great to hear, Michael. "Though you'll definitely need plenty of warm clothes up here in the wilds of winter." He turned and smiled at Alice.

On their way out, Roxburgh handed Michael a small set of binoculars in a camouflage case.

"Now that you're a proper twitcher, you're going to need the right equipment."

"Wow!" Michael repeated.

Roxburgh placed the case strap over Michael's head.

"And you'll need this book of British birds to help you identify all the birds you're going to spot."

Michael took the book and flicked through the colourful contents.

"That's too generous," Alice said.

"The least we can do," Roxburgh replied. "You know, we are always on the lookout for volunteers up here, so if you ever fancied helping us out…"

Alice looked up. "I might just take you up on that. It's an amazing place." She turned back to Michael. "Come on, we don't want to keep Mr… Don, any longer. Say bye-bye."

"Bye!"

"Bye, Michael. Bye, Alice," Roxburgh said.

And with final wave, Alice and her son headed out to the car park.

Bone was on the far side standing by his Saab.

"Daddy!" Michael called, ran over to him, and jumped into his arms.

Alice approached.

"I saw an osprey mummy feed her baby with a *huuuge* fish, and it was still alive!" Michael said, squirming around in Bone's arms.

"Fantastic. And what's this?" Bone held up the binocular case.

"Don gave me these for tweeting." Michael beamed.

"Thanks, Duncan, for arranging this," Alice said.

"No bother. I hope you don't mind, I just wanted to come and check that it went okay."

"It was a really lovely gesture, but you know it doesn't change anything," Alice tried not to frown.

"I know that." Bone put Michael down. "I am truly sorry about everything," he added.

"I know you are, and I appreciate what you did today, but you know how I feel." She turned to her son. "Go wait in the car, Michael. You can have a look at your new book."

"Bye, Dad," Michael said.

Bone knelt and hugged his son again. "See you, cheeky chops," he said.

Michael ran over to Alice's car and jumped in.

"Please don't make me choose," Bone said.

"It's up to you, Duncan. Your job or your son. Then we can talk about access again. I can't have my son's life in danger like that ever again."

"My life is in the force, Alice. It's like you're asking me to cut off my arm."

"Up to you," she repeated. "All I'm asking, is for you to put your son first."

"You know as well as I do things aren't as simple as that. I need my work, maybe more than it needs me."

"Not my problem." She shrugged. "Michael is my priority; you need to sort out yours." She set off for her car.

"Alice," Bone pleaded again.

She glanced back at him and without another word climbed in.

As Bone's past life accelerated out the car park and out of sight, he glanced down at his lanyard dangling in front of him, his pre-Peek-a-boo, pre-scarred, pre-PTSD youthful features grinning back at him. He tore it off and, opening the door, tossed it onto the back seat. He was about to climb in when he spotted a hooded figure at the farthest edge of the car park.

"Happy now?" he cried out. He got in, crunched the Saab into first, and headed back to Kilwinnoch, hoping by the time he reached town he'd know what to do next.

The End

DCI BONE RETURNS IN...
DEAD MAN'S STONE

A DCI Bone Scottish Crime Thriller

(Book 3)

Some secrets are worth killing for

When DCI Duncan Bone is contacted by a terminally ill psychiatric patient and given clues linking a thirty-year-old unsolved murder to high-profile public figures, he finds himself locked into a conspiracy at the very heart of the Scottish criminal and political establishment.

With his bosses stonewalling the investigation and his career on the line, Bone faces a race against time to hunt down a group of men who will stop at nothing to cover their murderous crime.

Read now on Amazon

Also on Kindle Unlimited

TG REID

JOIN MY DCI BONE VIP CLUB

AND RECEIVE YOUR *FREE* DCI BONE NOVEL

WHAT HIDES BENEATH

Secrets Always Surface

Scotland's hottest summer on record is already too much for DCI Duncan Bone. As if the water shortage wasn't enough, a body turning up at the bottom of Kilwinnoch's dried up reservoir sends Bone to boiling point.

With three suspects on the loose and time running out, the Rural Crime Unit needs to find the smoking gun and nail the killer before another victim is slain.

Visit tgreid.com to download for FREE.

Your monthly newsletter also includes updates, exclusives, sneak peeks, giveaways and more…

THE DCI BONE SCOTTISH CRIME SERIES

Dark is the Grave

Blood Water Falls

Dead Man's Stone

The Killing Parade

Isle of the Dead

Night Comes Falling

Burn It All Down

More thrillers by TG Reid

Agency 'O'

TG Reid

ACKNOWLEDGEMENTS

I would like to thank the following people for their on-going help, expertise, generosity, support, kindness, patience & good humour.

I would be a blubbering mess of stupidity without you.

Andrew Dobell
Emmy Ellis
Hanna Elizabeth
Diana Hopkins
Meg Jolly
Kath Middleton
Gordon Robertson
Beverly Sanford
Shakey Shakespeare
Jeni and Erin x
Steve Worsley (The voice of DCI Bone)
Also, very special thanks to my amazing *DCI Bone ARC Team*
and all the wonderful admin and crime fiction fanatics in the mighty *UK Crime Book Club* on Facebook.
You are simply the best (No, that is not a cue to start singing … Oh all right, go on then!).

Printed in Great Britain
by Amazon